*Fallen*
*Woman*

# Fallen Woman

## Ann Barker

ROBERT HALE · LONDON

ISBN 0 7090 7499 9


Robert Hale Limited
Clerkenwell House
Clerkenwell Green
London EC1R 0HT

2 4 6 8 10 9 7 5 3 1

Typeset in 12/15 Baskerville
by Derek Doyle & Associates, Liverpool.
Printed in Great Britain by
St Edmundsbury Press, Bury St Edmunds, Suffolk.
Bound by Woolnough Bookbinding Limited.

*For George and Tricia*

# Chapter One

'Goodbye! Promise you'll write!'

'Yes, of course I will,' Fay replied, smiling down from her corner seat of the stage-coach. She had been lucky to get such an advantageous place; but her friend Angela, who was even now waving to her, had made sure that they had got to the Spread Eagle in good time.

'I almost wish I was going with you,' said Angela. 'And don't forget—'

'If I don't like it, I can come back,' replied Fay, mimicking her friend affectionately. 'But I *will* like it, I feel sure.' She leaned forward, put out her hand and said, not for the first time, 'Angela, I don't know how I can ever thank you. . . .'

'Oh, pooh!' exclaimed Angela. 'Just send me plenty of letters with lots of news!'

'Time!' called the guard, and he came to shut the door. Angela stepped back. There was no chance to say any more, so Fay contented herself with simply waving until the coach swept out of the inn yard and out of sight. She leaned back in her place and closed her eyes. Dear Angela. She had been so kind and, heaven knew, she had desperately needed kindness over the past few weeks. But she was aware that she could not trespass any further upon the hospitality of Angela and her husband. She did not really fulfil any role there, other than that which the compassionate young couple had invented for her, and now with a baby on the way, their house would be quite crowded enough.

She owed Angela so much: the roof over her head, the reference for this new opportunity for employment, and even her very life. What would she have done without her? Involuntarily, she reached up to brush away a tear.

Suddenly becoming aware that she was making herself an object of curiosity for the two other people in the coach (one of whom seemed to be a farmer, and the other a lawyer, by his dress) she opened her reticule and took out the letter from her future employer.

*Dear Miss Prescott*

*After reading the reference provided for you by Mrs Hardcastle, I am pleased to offer you the post of duenna to my niece, Miss Rachel Proudfoot. Your salary will be £20 per annum, to be paid half-yearly in arrears and, provided you give satisfaction, your post will last until my niece comes to London to make her come-out in a little over twelve months' time. I will discuss your employment with you in more detail when you arrive at Old Drove House. A conveyance will be sent to meet you at the Griffin in March.*

*Yours sincerely,*

*Edwina Stratford*

The letter seemed to be amiable enough, but as far as Fay had been able to ascertain, she would not have a great deal to do with Mrs Stratford, however pleasant she might be. Apparently, the lady lived in London for most of the time, and her late husband's estate was in Hertfordshire. She was simply acting for her brother in this matter, his wife having died twelve years ago, leaving his eldest daughter Rachel and three other children motherless. At least in that respect, she would have something in common with Rachel, Fay reflected. She had not known her mother, who had died when she was born, and her father had been dead now for just over a year.

Once more feeling she was becoming maudlin, and quite determined not to succumb this time, she took her copy of *Robinson Crusoe* out of her reticule, and was soon absorbed by the exploits of the characters therein.

The journey from Cambridge was not a long one, going by the flight of the proverbial crow, but there were plenty of waterways to be circumvented, and the roads were not of the best, so it was late in the afternoon when the coach reached March and swept into the yard at the Griffin. The farmer and the lawyer, obviously arriving in their home town, were both met, the lawyer by a young man, possibly of the same profession, who shook his hand warmly and guided him to a waiting carriage; the farmer was greeted by his son, who walked with him into the inn.

Fay looked round rather forlornly and, when no one came forward to meet her, she approached the inn and stood tentatively on the threshold. She was just wondering whom she might ask about a conveyance from Old Drove House, when the voice of someone just behind her asked respectfully if she might be Miss Fay Prescott? Fay turned around, to see that she was being addressed by a young man, whom she guessed to be about twenty-seven. He was quite tall, with a pleasant, open face and hair of the shade that is sometimes called strawberry blond and, by his dress, Fay judged him to be a clergyman.

'Yes, I am Fay Prescott,' she answered. 'Are you . . . am I to understand that you have come to meet me, sir?'

He smiled at her in a kindly manner. 'Yes, I have,' he answered. 'I was bringing the gig into town today anyway, so when I learned from Mrs Stratford that you were due to arrive at the Griffin, I offered to collect you on the way home. My name is Peter Frith.'

'Are you a clergyman, sir?' Fay asked him.

'Yes, I am the vicar of the parish where Mr Proudfoot and his family reside. Shall we set off, madam, before the light goes?'

'Yes, of course,' she agreed readily. 'My box. . . ?'

'My servant will put it in the back of the gig for you, if you will tell him which one it is.' Fay did as she was asked, and in no time, she was seated next to Mr Frith with her knees covered by a rug which Mr Frith had most thoughtfully provided. March did not appear to be too busy at this time of day and quite soon, after they had negotiated the few hazards that there were, they were in the countryside, moving at a steady pace. Fay noted with approval that the vicar handled his horses well, not dragging on the reins, but controlling his pair with light hands.

'Is this your first visit to the fens, ma'am?' Frith asked her.

'Yes indeed,' she replied. 'Although I have been staying with a friend in Cambridge.'

He shook his head with a grin. 'That doesn't count, as many of our true fen tigers would say,' he said.

'Fen tigers?'

'The name given to those who are born and bred in the fens.'

'So are you a fen tiger yourself?' she asked him.

'Not really,' he answered. 'The living which is now mine was my uncle's before me, and I did live there with him, but only from the age of eleven.'

'Did your parents die, then?'

He looked solemn. 'My father died and my mother came to live with her brother, bringing with her myself and my sister Agnes.'

'And do your mother and sister still reside with you?'

'My mother died five years ago, but my sister lives with me. She has thrown herself into parish work and is an invaluable helpmeet. Please do not miss the sunset, Miss Prescott. Tell me if you have ever seen anything so fine before.' The sky was certainly painted in glorious hues of pink, purple and gold, and its colour was all the more remarkable because so much of it was visible, owing to the flatness of the land.

'I never have,' she admitted, 'and it makes me want to take up a paint brush and try to recreate what I have seen – except that knowing the standard of my skill, I should certainly fail!'

With such idle, undemanding chatter the journey passed very pleasantly and by the time they drew near to the village of Wimblington, Fay felt that she had made a congenial new acquaintance.

It was as they were just leaving the village that Mr Frith turned his horses between two stone pillars, which marked the entrance to a short drive, leading to an unremarkable but homely-looking, mellow-brick-built mansion. It was now very nearly dark and there were lights in many windows, which gave the place a welcoming appearance. The road continued around to the right, and in the gathering dusk, the tower of the church could be seen a short distance away on the right-hand side of the road.

'The vicarage is just the other side of the church,' said Frith, as they turned into the drive. 'Please do call as soon as you have had time to settle in. My sister will be very pleased to meet you.'

'And I to meet her,' replied Fay, thinking that if Miss Frith was half as agreeable as her brother, then she would make a pleasant acquaintance. 'It is delightful to think that I have begun to know people here already.'

At Mr Frith's instruction, the servant got down to ring the bell, and remove Fay's trunk from the back of the gig, whilst Mr Frith himself dismounted in order to help her down. Unsure as to whether or not to invite him in, she was relieved when he said, 'I will not come in tonight, for Agnes will be expecting me; but pray tell Mrs Stratford that I hope to see you all at church on Sunday. You can tell me then how you are settling in.'

'Yes, I will. Thank you. And thank you very much for fetching me. It was very kind of you.'

'Not at all. We had a pleasant conversation, did we not?' So saying, he bowed, and returned to the gig, whilst Fay walked towards the now open doorway. Her trunk had disappeared, so she assumed that it must have been taken up to her room already.

'Miss Prescott?' said the tall, dignified-looking butler. 'Welcome to Old Drove House. My name is Summers.' He was neatly dressed in subdued livery, but wore his own hair, which was unpowdered. Fay felt that she was entering a household of some standing but with few pretensions, and she felt somewhat reassured.

'Yes, I am Miss Prescott,' she answered, walking up the steps. 'How do you do, Summers?' Once inside, she saw that a neatly dressed maid was waiting at the bottom of the stairs.

'Holland will take you up to your room and give you any assistance that you may require,' said the butler. 'Mrs Stratford would like to see you in the library as soon as possible.' Fay followed the maid up a handsome staircase, curious to discover what kind of room might have been placed at her disposal. She was very pleased to find that the chamber allotted to her was on the principal floor, where the family must have their bedrooms. Not knowing what exact status a duenna normally occupied, she had wondered whether she might be relegated to a garret.

'Are you a fen tiger, Holland?' Fay asked, as the maid was leaving.

The girl smiled broadly. 'I am that, miss,' she replied, with a strong accent.

It only took Fay a moment or two to take off her bonnet and smooth down her hair, before going back downstairs.

'This way, miss,' said Summers, showing her into a large room with a carpet with a red background, and red brocade curtains which had been drawn against the darkness. The walls were lined with well-filled bookshelves, and Fay hoped that she would have the opportunity of taking a closer look at their contents later. A fire burned merrily in the grate, and there were plenty of candles alight, all giving the impression that whatever might be the faults of the inhabitants of this house, parsimony was not one of them.

The woman who rose from a chair close to the fire was tall and grey-haired, with a rather prominent nose and penetrating grey eyes. Her gown was an open robe of pearl grey over a petticoat of white sprigged with lilac flowers. Her coiffure was modest, as befitted country living, but her clothing was clearly the recent work of a London modiste.

'Miss Prescott,' she said, in a cultured voice, which held just the right mixture of superior assurance and hospitable welcome. 'I am Edwina Stratford. I am delighted to make your acquaintance. I do trust that your journey was not too tiresome?'

Fay acknowledged her greeting with a smile and a curtsy. 'Thank you, no, ma'am, it was quite pleasant. I am grateful to you for asking Mr Frith to meet me.' Mrs Stratford waved her hand dismissively.

'When I told him that you were arriving today, he offered to collect you, since he was going to March anyway, and as today was mild for December, I thought that you would not be too chilled in an open carriage. Please sit down by the fire. It will soon be time to change for dinner and there are a number of things I wish to say to you while there is still time.'

This last phrase struck Fay as being a trifle curious, sounding, as it did, as if Mrs Stratford perhaps had prior knowledge of the end of the world, to which other lesser souls were not privy. But she made no comment, and simply did as she was bid. Truth to tell, she was glad to sit by the fire for, despite the warm rug which Mr Frith had handed to her, the drive had been a cold one (contrary to Mrs Stratford's opinion), especially towards the end when the sun had completely gone.

Mrs Stratford must have made prior arrangements for tea to be brought just after the new employee's arrival, for no sooner had they sat down than the door opened and the butler came in with a tray which he set down on a small table next to Mrs Stratford.

'I am sure that this will be welcome,' said that lady as she poured.

'It will indeed. You are most kind. I have not had a cup of tea since breakfast-time.'

'Then you will be parched indeed.' She handed Fay her tea and there was silence for a few moments while both ladies sipped. Then Mrs Stratford put her cup down and said, 'This is an unusual household in many ways. You will remember that my sister-in-law has been dead now for twelve years, and consequently her children are motherless. My brother, I fear I must tell you, although I am embarrassed to say so, has no sense of responsibility whatsoever.' Seeing Fay look a little startled, she smiled slightly and went on, 'I am not telling you anything that I have not said to his face, and in any case you will soon find all this out for yourself. He immerses himself in his own interests, and he quite forgets that he even has children at times. There are four of them, as I believe you know. Rachel, at nearly eighteen, is the eldest. Magnus is one year younger, and the twins, Hengist and Horsa are the youngest.' Seeing Fay smile, she added 'Yes, I know the names are absurd, but I will explain later.'

'That is not why I am smiling, ma'am,' replied Fay. 'It's because I think I have guessed the nature of Mr Proudfoot's interest. Is he a Viking enthusiast by any chance?'

Mrs Stratford nodded. 'You are correct; but why he should name his children in that absurd way is beyond me. Rachel's name was my poor sister's choice, and Magnus is all very well in its way, but Hengist and Horsa! Have you ever heard anything so absurd?'

'Most of us get used to our own names,' murmured Fay. 'Probably even Hengist and Horsa would now find it strange to be called anything else.'

'Perhaps,' agreed Mrs Stratford grudgingly. 'But the fact that you have guessed the nature of my brother's interest encourages me to hope that you may be able to find a way of encouraging him to participate more in the life of the family. To move on: you have seen the remote nature of this place. Heaven knows why

14

anyone would want to build a great house here, but my grandfather did so. It's not a picturesque part of the world, as you will soon discover, if you haven't already. The consequence is that there is hardly a house of any standing within twenty miles of here, so the children have been thrown very much upon their own resources.

'I live in London, Miss Prescott. To be honest with you, I don't really care for the country at all. All my friends are in Town, and my brother and I have never really been close. But it has always been understood that when the time came, I would effect any introductions that the boys might need, and sponsor Rachel and Horsa in their debuts. But now, I am dreadfully afraid that it might all come to nothing.' She got up and started to walk restlessly about the room. Her anxiety was plain to see.

'And why is that, ma'am?' Fay asked her. The other woman looked at her for a long moment, and Fay received the distinct impression that she was measuring her words very carefully.

'Rachel has been used to having things her own way,' Mrs Stratford replied eventually. 'It is not exactly that she has had to be mother to the others; but because my brother so often withdraws from family difficulties, Rachel has become used to solving them all. Consequently, she is far more managing than any young female ever should be, and she thinks that she can organize her life in every particular.

'There is a similar problem with Magnus. He, of course, is destined to take over the running of the estate, and is indeed obliged to do much of it now, owing to my brother's inefficiency. I blame our parents. Walter was allowed to go very much his own way and bury his head in a book all the time and, sadly, Magnus will be just the same if not corrected. Well, he is not too young to change, and I am determined that he shall not be the same kind of impractical air-dreamer as his father. But forgive me; I am straying off the point. To return to Rachel: if she goes to London in this frame of mind, she will be a complete disaster.

15

And that is where you come in.'

Fay looked puzzled. 'I'm sorry, ma'am, but I'm not at all sure that I understand.'

Mrs Stratford held up her hand. 'What I am looking for in the person who is to take up your post is a lady – unquestionably a lady – older than Rachel, but not so much older as to be of a different generation. This lady would have the task of gently influencing Rachel to become more malleable and open to guidance before her debut. You, Miss Prescott, are to be the one to exert this influence. A certain amount of training I will be able to do myself at the time, but at present, she is very far from being ready – or even willing – to take her place in polite society.'

Fay's expression took on an anxious look. 'But, ma'am, how can you be sure that I will be successful?'

'There can be no doubt of it,' replied Mrs Stratford confidently. 'There is no other female of her standing in the area, apart from Agnes Frith, and she is nearly ten years older than Rachel. I have known Agnes for many years, and she has been very helpful to me at times. But Rachel needs a friend closer to her own age, and she will be glad to make one of you. Furthermore, I have been observing you closely from the moment you entered this room. You are a little shy, Miss Prescott, but you are undoubtedly a lady.'

Fay blushed and looked down at her hands, which were clasped tightly in her lap, then looked up again. 'I shall do my best,' she said honestly. 'I, too, lost my mother, and that might form a bond between us. But may I ask you something, ma'am?'

'By all means,' replied Mrs Stratford.

'Does Rachel know that I am here for this purpose?' Fay asked. 'It seems entirely possible that she may resent my attempting to curtail her normal activities, and I might then find it hard to make a friend of her.' For the first time since the beginning of the interview, Mrs Stratford looked distinctly uneasy.

'She does not know,' she said eventually. 'In fact—' She was destined not to finish her sentence, for at that moment, the door opened and a young girl came flying in, dark hair everywhere. She looked to be about fourteen years old. Without waiting for any kind of an introduction, she came hurrying up to Fay, completely ignoring the presence of her aunt.

'I knew it!' she exclaimed. 'You *are* my new governess, aren't you?'

# *Chapter Two*

Had anyone told Fay half an hour earlier that it was possible for Mrs Stratford to look nonplussed, she would have rigorously debated the idea. But now, turning to glance at that lady, she detected a look on her face which was a mixture of surprise, anxiety, confusion and supplication. The supplication was directed at Fay, and Fay found no difficulty in reading it. Clearly, to prevent Rachel from discovering the real purpose of Fay's presence, her aunt had pretended that she was there to be governess to the younger daughter. This left Fay in something of a quandary. Her own education, though thorough in some areas, had many gaps in it, conducted as it had been by her father, an elderly clergyman with more regard for Latin and English literature than for dancing and deportment. Furthermore, she had never believed that teaching was a calling of hers, and was sure that she was much more suited to be a companion than a governess.

If she did not take this position, however, then she would have to go back to her friend Angela, and she felt that she had taken enough from her already. She had learned the necessity of earning her bread in a very hard school, and did not feel justified in refusing this post, whatever it might entail. If she gave satisfaction, then Mrs Stratford, who seemed to be a woman of influence, might well put her in the way of finding other work, especially if, as now appeared, her co-operation put the older woman in a position of obligation towards her.

She looked at Mrs Stratford again, then said, 'With your permission, ma'am?' Mrs Stratford nodded, and waved her hand wearily. 'I hope to teach you something,' Fay temporized, 'but I would rather be known as a . . . a fellow student, than as a governess.' She glanced again at Mrs Stratford, and was hard put to it not to laugh. That redoubtable lady was clearly outraged at this unconventional variation on a governess's role, but was also conscious that she had her own lack of candour to blame for the present situation, and consequently could do very little about it. There was one thing that she could do, however, which was to upbraid the newcomer for her lack of courtesy.

'Horsa!' she declared. 'What must Miss Prescott be thinking of you, bursting in upon us in this way? Make your curtsy properly, if you please.' Horsa did as she was bid, proving that she had at least been taught something with regard to behaviour in company. Mrs Stratford sighed. 'Miss Prescott, may I present Horsa to you?' She went on, 'Horsa, this is your new governess, Miss Fay Prescott.'

'How do you do, Horsa?' said Fay.

'How do you do?' replied Horsa. 'I think your name is really pretty. I wish I had a pretty name instead of Horsa, which is really silly. Sometimes I think I would like to go to school, but if I did, I'm sure that I would get called stupid names like "Horsy", or something like that.'

'There's no doubt that children at school can sometimes be very unkind,' replied Fay.

'Did you go to school?' Horsa asked her. 'Did you like it? Did they make you learn mathematics? My brother, Hengist, is at school and he has to learn mathematics. I should hate it, I'm sure.'

Fay laughed. 'No, I didn't go to school, but I was taught by my father, and I still had to learn things that I didn't like at times.'

At this point, Mrs Stratford, who had gradually been regaining her composure, said 'That is quite enough now, Horsa. You have seen your new governess. I will say no more about your lack of conduct for the present. It will be for her to correct your manners in the future.' She cleared her throat, avoiding Fay's eye. 'For now, return to the schoolroom, or there will be no pudding for you tonight.' With this threat hanging over her, Horsa bobbed another quick curtsy and left the room, closing the door behind her. Moments later, she could be heard running up the stairs two at a time.

Fay looked at Mrs Stratford for a long moment. 'Is Rachel as boisterous as that, ma'am, because if she is. . . .'

Mrs Stratford threw up her hands. 'Oh good heavens, no,' she declared positively. 'And before you say anything, I am extremely sorry that I have been less than frank with you. But to tell you the truth, it was not until I had engaged you for the position that it occurred to me that Rachel might resent any interference in her life. So I must confess that I led everyone to believe that I was considering candidates as governess for Horsa, and it is true that she is in need of one, for she has been without instruction for some time. After all, you need not teach Horsa a great deal. Perhaps you could read together, or go sketching?'

'I could certainly read with her,' agreed Fay. 'As for sketching, she may do it in my company if she wishes, but I will be quite unable to correct any of her errors, I'm afraid. I never had any aptitude for drawing.' There was a short silence.

'How unfortunate,' murmured Mrs Stratford. 'But perhaps you could sew with her.'

'Yes, I can sew,' replied Fay, colourlessly.

'And perhaps she will spend some time with you and Rachel, and become more ladylike herself,' added Mrs Stratford. 'Of course, you must take all your meals with the family and associate with them at all times, so that you can set a good example to them. Needless to say, you will not be treated as a servant at all.'

Sensing Fay's uncertainty, she added 'In view of the fact that the post is not what you originally applied for, I see no reason why your salary should not be increased to, say, twenty-five pounds per annum.' Suddenly, her voice took on a note that was half eagerness, half desperation. 'Oh please say you will stay, Miss Prescott. I do not know who else we might find to come to this desolate area. And something *must* be done about Rachel.'

Fay looked at her for a long moment, then sighed. 'Very well.'

Mrs Stratford gave a gasp of delight, but Fay held up her hand. 'I must insist that you accept that anything I may do for Rachel must be done indirectly. As far as she is concerned, I am not here for her benefit at all.'

'Exactly so!' exclaimed Mrs Stratford. 'And that is what makes it all the more likely that she will make a friend of you! The more I look at this scheme, the more I like it.'

Privately thinking that she was glad that someone did, Fay excused herself and went upstairs to change for dinner. It was all very well for Mrs Stratford to smile with satisfaction as if she had thought of the whole idea; she was not the one who had been placed in an equivocal position.

When she got to her room, she found that the maid had unpacked her trunk and had laid out on the bed the gown which she clearly thought would be the most suitable. It was of a rich yellow, with a petticoat of a lighter shade, and it brought out the bronze lights in her light brown hair, soft brown eyes and creamy complexion. Fay knew that it was a good choice, but, even so, she hesitated before putting it on. The last time she had worn it had been in London, many months before, and the very sight of it brought back memories that she would much rather forget. Mentally castigating herself for cowardice, she hung the gown on one of the pegs in the cupboard, and took out one of a bronze shade, with a cream petticoat. That, too, she had worn in London, but somehow it did not bring back so many recollections.

As she brushed out her long, wavy hair, she forced herself to put London to the back of her mind, and concentrate instead upon getting herself ready. Time spent in looking after herself had accustomed Fay to managing the fastenings of her gown without assistance and, in less time than it took many a lady with the help of her maid, she had changed for dinner and made her way downstairs. She was not surprised to find that she was the first one to be ready, but no sooner had she picked up a book with which to occupy herself, than the door opened and a young woman whom she had not met before came into the room.

'Good evening,' said the newcomer. 'I suppose that you must be Miss Prescott. I am Rachel Proudfoot.' Fay eyed her with great interest and some disbelief. Miss Proudfoot was very like her younger sister in the face and, like Horsa's, her hair was thick, dark and plentiful; but there the resemblance ended. Her carriage was good, her manner poised, and her appearance neat. Her hair was becomingly dressed on the top of her head, and her dark-blue gown with the white petticoat suited her admirably. Even allowing for the fact that she was possibly on her best behaviour, Fay was at a loss to understand Mrs Stratford's anxieties. This young woman looked as though she might be ready to make her debut next week.

Fay allowed none of this to show in her face, however, and she merely said, 'Good evening, Miss Proudfoot. Yes, I am Fay Prescott. I am very pleased to meet you. I have already met your sister.'

'Then I can't frighten you with awful stories about your charge, for you must have seen the worst,' laughed Rachel. 'I must say, you do not look at all like a governess.'

'Must a governess always look like one?' replied Fay, resisting the temptation to make any comment about Horsa.

'I suppose not,' said Rachel. Then she confounded Fay by adding, 'I am very glad you have come, anyway. You will surely not need to spend all your time with Horsa and I shall be glad of your company. It can be a little lonely around here, you know.'

There was no time for further conversation, for at this point the door opened and a young gentleman of about Rachel's age came in. He was tall and slender with high cheekbones, burning dark eyes and hair that was a shade or two darker than Rachel's and a little more curly.

Rachel smiled at him. 'This is my brother, Magnus, Miss Prescott. Magnus, this is Horsa's new governess.'

'How do you do?' he said, in a voice which seemed to be far too dark and mellow for one of his age and slenderness. 'I wonder, are you conversant with ancient literature?'

'Good evening, Mr Proudfoot,' answered Fay. 'Not very conversant, I am afraid, unless you are perhaps referring to the works of Geoffrey Chaucer?'

Magnus looked disgusted. 'Chaucer? No indeed! How could you possibly think such a thing? No, I am talking about the Romans, Miss Prescott. The greatest civilization the world has ever known! And yet, how many plays have been written about them?'

'Why, I—' began Fay.

'None, Miss Prescott! None.' He waved his hand in the air in a very dramatic manner, then dropped it and added, in a tone that could not but be a bit of an anticlimax, 'Well, none to speak of, anyway. At least, not yet.'

His voice was so pregnant with meaning that Fay felt bound to ask, 'Do I understand that you plan to write one, Mr Proudfoot?'

He opened his mouth to answer her and, by the glow in his eyes, it was plain that his answer would be in the affirmative, but at that point, the door opened, Mrs Stratford came in, and Mr Proudfoot simply murmured, 'Who can say?' before wandering over to the mantelpiece to fiddle with one of the ornaments upon it.

'Miss Prescott, you have met my nephew and niece, I see,' said that lady, who was now positively regal in two shades of purple.

She was accompanied by Horsa, who looked neat, but not noticeably more subdued than earlier. 'I hope that they have been entertaining you well?' Fay happened to glance at Magnus and saw that he was looking at her a little anxiously.

'They have been most courteous,' she said simply, and was conscious that the young man relaxed visibly on hearing her reply. She remembered what Mrs Stratford had said earlier about her brother's air-dreaming, and felt sure that she must disapprove strongly of Magnus's play-writing activities. It also seemed likely from Magnus's behaviour that he was aware of his aunt's disapproval.

Fay had been told that they were to dine at six o'clock, an hour later than usual in order to accommodate her arrival, but the hour came, then five minutes past, then ten and still the elder Mr Proudfoot had not appeared. Eventually, Mrs Stratford walked to the bell pull with a sigh, and gave it a vigorous tug.

'Summers, for goodness' sake have someone see where Mr Proudfoot is before we all die of hunger,' she said impatiently.

'At once, madam.'

'We will go in now,' she went on, standing up. 'Walter can have his dinner cold if he wishes, but I do not see why the rest of us should do so.' Mrs Stratford took her nephew's arm and led the way, with Fay, Rachel and Horsa following behind. They entered a handsome dining-room, where the table, laid at present for six, was plenty big enough for twenty. Mrs Stratford took the foot, with Magnus on her right and Rachel on her left. Fay was placed on Magnus's other side, and Horsa sat next to her older sister. They were just taking their places when there was the sound of hurried activity outside the door, and a rather untidy looking man in evening dress came in. His features unmistakably proclaimed him to be Magnus's father, but he was shorter and stouter than his son and whereas Magnus had looked intense earlier, the older man simply looked harassed.

24

'I suppose it was necessary to disturb me?' he said, addressing no one in particular.

'Most certainly it was,' replied Mrs Stratford. 'Dinner is ready, and here is Miss Prescott, wondering why you have not made it your business to meet her before sitting at table.'

Mr Proudfoot looked around at those seated at the table as if he failed at first to recognize any of them. Eventually, his gaze rested on Fay, and he bestowed upon her a smile of unexpected sweetness, which revealed another likeness to his son. 'You must be Miss Prescott,' he said. 'How do you do? Are you a friend of Rachel's?'

'Well, I——' began Fay.

'Really, Walter!' exclaimed Mrs Stratford. 'I sometimes wonder whether you inhabit the same world as the rest of us! Miss Prescott is Horsa's governess.'

'You must forgive my lateness,' Mr Stratford went on, sitting in his place at the head of the table. 'I have reached a critical point in my work, and am finding it very difficult to leave it; but if you are a governess, you will appreciate the importance of learning.'

'Your work, sir. . . ?' ventured Fay.

'The Vikings, Miss Prescott, the Vikings,' he said impatiently, as if she had asked a question which she could have answered herself quite easily with just a little thought. 'I am attempting to make a thorough survey of all English place-names, showing which come from the Viking, and then establish which of these places were substantial Viking settlements.'

'It sounds fascinating,' said Fay politely.

'And so it is, so it is,' he responded enthusiastically. 'You may spend some of your time with me, helping me in my work, if you wish.' She murmured something non-committal, then Mrs Stratford rescued her by changing the subject.

The meal was well chosen and also well cooked and presented, and Fay wondered who was normally responsible for giving orders to the cook. It could be that it was Mrs Stratford on this occasion, but she was clearly only staying for a short period of time. Quite plainly, it could not be Mr Proudfoot, whose contact with the real world was obviously minimal. Fay noticed that it was Rachel who spoke quietly to the butler just before the order was given to clear away the first course. Perhaps it was Rachel who had the running of the household?

By the time she retired to bed, Fay decided that she had a great deal to think about. The evidence of her eyes and ears told a very different tale from what Mrs Stratford had led her to believe. That lady's account had left her with the impression that Rachel was some kind of unmanageable hoyden. Her own observations, however, seemed to indicate that Rachel was possibly the most civilized of the whole family. Was this some kind of elaborate act put on, perhaps for her, Fay's, benefit? Or did Rachel's rebellion lie in some other direction? Mrs Stratford had clearly been about to say more when Horsa had come in earlier and interrupted her flow. Perhaps, she had thought, she would find the opportunity to say more the next day.

After dinner, however, when the ladies retired to the saloon, where there was a good fire burning, Fay had made an unsettling discovery.

'At what hour tomorrow do you plan to leave us, Aunt?' Rachel said, conversationally.

Mrs Stratford had looked sideways at Fay, whose expression betrayed her surprise, and then looked away quickly. 'Quite early in the morning,' she said. 'After breakfast, in fact. I would like to get as far as Cambridge in the light.' Rachel got up and wandered over to the piano, where she stood picking out a tune, and Horsa had followed her. Whilst her back was turned, Mrs Stratford had leaned towards Fay and whispered, 'I will come to your room tonight and explain the rest.'

Magnus had entered soon after this, explaining that his father had returned to his work, and soon afterwards, the whole company retired, with Mrs Stratford saying to Fay, 'You have had a long journey today, and I have one tomorrow, so we must both get our sleep.'

Fay had gone to her room and begun to prepare for bed. It was not long before there was a soft tap on the door and Mrs Stratford came in, glancing to the left and the right, in the manner of some kind of spy. A fire had been lit in Fay's bedchamber against the winter chill, and now the two ladies sat in chairs either side of it.

'I was interrupted earlier, just as I was about to reach the most important part of my story,' said Mrs Stratford. 'And you must hear what I have to say, otherwise you will not be able to fulfil your task.' She was already speaking in hushed tones. Now, she dropped her voice even further and, leaning towards Fay, she said, 'I am afraid that Rachel has developed a most unsuitable attachment.'

'An unsuitable attachment?' queried Fay in her normal voice.

'Ssshhh!' hissed Mrs Stratford imperatively. Then she went on, 'I have it on the most reliable authority that she has become entangled with one of my brother's tenants; a farmer's son, would you believe? My fear is that with her managing disposition, she will decide to marry him! Well, it will not do. She is to have a season next year, and already I have made a list of suitable men whom she is to meet. What is more, if she does not marry well, who is to introduce Horsa when it is time for her to make her debut? No, this must be scotched, and you are the one to do it.'

'Me?' exclaimed Fay ungrammatically.

'Yes, you. I gather that you have spent some time in London. You can talk to her; make a friend of her. Interest her with stories of how fascinating life can be in a big town or city. Lure her away from the farmer's boy. It's only a childish attachment, of course, fostered because there is no one else of her age around here. It would never have flourished had my sister been alive, or had my brother had but half an eye to his responsibilities.' She looked away, fidgeting with the fringe of her shawl. 'Of course I realize that I am to blame as well. Perhaps I should have been here more myself to keep an eye on things. But I love the town, Miss Prescott, and I fear that I have sometimes made excuses not to come here because I find it too solitary. What's done is done, however. I shall return in a few weeks' time for Christmas, and I shall bring a party with me. By the time I arrive, you will have whetted her appetite for a livelier existence. The guests I bring will complete the plan. Well, what do you think?'

'I suppose it might work,' murmured Fay cautiously. 'But—'

'Of course it will,' interrupted Mrs Stratford. 'And now I shall bid you goodnight.'

Fay sat by the fire for quite a long time after she had gone. So Mrs Stratford wanted her to entertain Rachel with stories of London life! If only she knew, she might be a trifle more cautious in what she asked, and of whom she asked it. Sighing, she got up from her seat by the dying fire, paused by the chest of drawers in order to pick up her monogrammed hairbrush and trace the letters gently, then she laid it down, extinguished her candle and got into bed.

# *Chapter Three*

The following day, Mrs Stratford left just after breakfast as promised, and to honour the occasion, the whole family made an appearance at the table. There was no opportunity for her to say more to Fay about her employment, only to remark in a general way that she hoped that she would be happy with the Proudfoots.

'I look forward to seeing you again at Christmas, and discovering how you are getting on,' she concluded. Fay merely smiled and thanked her politely for her kindness; but she could not help wondering if she might find herself out on her ear if the attachment had not been broken by then. The original conception of her employment as straightforward chaperonage of a young girl was rather far off the mark.

After Mrs Stratford's carriage had left, Mr Proudfoot rubbed his hands together, declaring 'To work! To work!' and disappeared into his study. Magnus also excused himself, and Fay was left with Rachel and Horsa.

'You don't want to start lessons today, do you?' Horsa said pleadingly.

Repressing the urge to say 'I don't want to start lessons at all', Fay merely shook her head, and said, 'I would like to see a little more of the house and gardens, first.'

Horsa brightened visibly and Rachel said, 'Yes of course, there was no time yesterday to show you everything, was there?'

It was not a very large house, nor was it very old or very grand.

'Magnus would have liked it if there were priests' holes or hidden passages, and so would Hengist, but there aren't any,' said Horsa regretfully when they had finished their tour, having been careful to disturb neither Magnus nor Mr Proudfoot.

'You sound as if you would have liked it too,' smiled Fay.

'Well, only because Hengist and I have always done everything together, and we have only been apart since he started school last year. And Hengist and Magnus would have liked them for different reasons. Magnus would have written about them, but Hengist and I would have gone down them.'

The day was a cold one, and no one wanted to spend very long in the grounds, which, truth to tell, were neither extensive, nor very inviting.

'When the wind blows from the north, Joe says that it feels as if it comes straight from Russia,' said Rachel to Fay, as they were hurrying indoors. Horsa had already gone ahead of them.

'I would be far from disagreeing with that,' laughed Fay, thankful for her thick cloak. 'Who is Joe, by the way?'

'Oh, just someone I know,' replied Rachel. 'Oh, look at that cloud, Miss Prescott. It looks just like a . . . a sheep.' Fay looked dutifully, but failed to notice any similarity. It did occur to her that Rachel's colour was rather high, but that might just have been caused by the strong wind.

Once inside, they went upstairs to put away their cloaks and bonnets. They had just reached the top of the stairs when the bell clanged in the hall. Rachel paused to discover who the arrival might be and, on hearing the voices below, her face took on an arrested look.

'It's Peter Frith and his sister,' she said. 'You go down as soon as you're ready. I'll try and come later, but I . . . I've got rather a lot to do.'

Fay looked at her. According to Mrs Stratford, Rachel was

officially her charge. She was nearly eighteen, and she should give these guests the courtesy of an appearance. But she did not know that Fay was her duenna, and Fay felt that she would have little chance of earning her trust if she insisted that she should come downstairs now, so early in their acquaintance. Fay therefore contented herself with saying merely, 'Please come, if only for my sake! I've only met Peter Frith once, and I've never met his sister at all.'

Rachel smiled. 'I'll try,' she said. Fay took off her bonnet and smoothed down her hair, then hurried down to the saloon where Peter Frith and his sister were waiting. Mr Frith looked every bit as pleasant and friendly as he had the day before.

'I hope you have not been waiting long,' Fay said. 'We have been walking in the garden this morning. Rachel hopes to join us in a little while, if she can.' Peter Frith bowed politely, then begged leave to introduce his sister.

Miss Frith was tall and slender, like her brother, but her hair, instead of being strawberry blonde, was simply a mousy brown, and was neatly braided beneath her simple bonnet. Her gown and cloak were both of a sober brown hue, and altogether she presented an image of neat and dull propriety. None of the extremes of fashion for Miss Frith, evidently! Her smile was polite rather than warm, but Fay decided that might be because she was shy, rather than because she was unfriendly. She greeted the visitors, invited them to be seated, and assented to the butler's suggestion that they might all like tea.

'I trust that you have recovered from the rigours of the journey, Miss Prescott,' said Mr Frith, when they were all seated.

'Completely, thank you,' replied Fay. 'This is a new part of the world to me, so I found the journey very interesting.'

'It is not a region that appeals to everyone by any means,' commented Miss Frith. 'Many people like to see a type of country-side that is a little more rolling.'

'I can understand that,' agreed Fay. 'But your brother drew

my attention to the wonderful sunset, and that was certainly a compensation.' It was at this point that the butler brought in the tray and placed it on a table at Fay's elbow.

'Whereabouts do you come from, Miss Prescott?' the vicar asked her, as she started to pour.

Fay coloured a little at the question, but went on with her task, and answered calmly enough, 'Not so very far away. I am from Bedfordshire and, like your uncle, my father was a clergyman.'

'Indeed?' exclaimed Mr Frith with pleasure. His sister, too, relaxed noticeably. 'I believe that you said your father was no longer with us?'

'That is correct,' agreed Fay. 'He died about a year ago.' For the first time, Agnes Frith's expression looked warmly sympathetic.

'I am very sorry indeed,' she said kindly. 'It is very hard to lose one's natural protector. Have you been having to find employment ever since?'

Fay coloured again. 'I lived with a friend in Cambridge for a time,' she said. 'And I was . . . in London for a little while.'

'And did you—' began Agnes.

'Agnes, my dear,' Peter Frith interrupted, with a concerned look at Fay. 'This style of questioning is distressing Miss Prescott, I can see. Shall we talk of something else, instead?' The conversation turned to the difficulty of shopping locally, and what facilities could be found in March. While Miss Frith was explaining how Fay might find the library, the very respectable librarian of which only stocked literature of a seemly nature, Rachel slipped in quietly.

The vicar rose courteously to his feet. 'Miss Proudfoot, you are looking very well this morning,' he said with a bow. 'Did you have an agreeable walk?'

'Yes, thank you,' she replied with a curtsy. 'It was rather cold, though. How kind of you to call on us on such a chilly day.'

'We wanted to make sure that Miss Prescott was settling in

well,' said Mr Frith. 'And I wanted to introduce my sister to her.'

'It must be very agreeable for you to have a congenial companion, Miss Proudfoot,' said Agnes.

'Of course,' replied Rachel; but although her comment was appropriate, if a little brief, her smile did not reach her eyes.

'I will have to spend much of my time with Horsa, but it is always pleasant to make new friends,' said Fay. Then, before the subject of governesses or companions could be explored – for she could not remember what she had said to Mr Frith the previous evening concerning her position – she went on quickly 'Is that tea hot enough, Miss Proudfoot? Shall we send for some more?'

Not long after this, the Friths took their leave.

'You must come to visit us in the vicarage some afternoon, Miss Prescott,' said Agnes. 'Or whenever your duties permit. And do bring Miss Proudfoot with you. We should be so pleased.' Fay thanked her and promised that they would go soon.

'No doubt we shall meet at church tomorrow, anyway,' concluded Mr Frith, as they left.

After they had gone, Fay said to Rachel, 'I might be mistaken, but just now I received the distinct impression that you do not care for Miss Frith very much.'

Rachel looked scornful. 'Well, if you gathered that, I wonder why you committed me to visiting her with you,' she declared forthrightly. 'She's an interfering busybody who can't keep her nose out of other people's affairs.'

'In what way has she interfered with your affairs?' Fay asked mildly. Rachel coloured and looked at her as if she was already regretting her brief outburst. She shrugged carelessly.

'Oh, not in anything in particular. It's just a feeling that I have about her.'

'Might I venture to suggest that any tendency on her part to be over-interested in your affairs will scarcely be reduced if you refuse to visit her as politeness demands,' said Fay diffidently.

Rachel stared at her for a moment. 'Oh, all right then, I'll go,' she said, a little ungraciously. Then, after a short silence, she added, 'I'm sorry if I was rude, but she does annoy me dreadfully.' Fay allowed the subject to drop, but she could not help wondering whether Miss Frith's interfering ways and Mrs Stratford's employment of herself had anything to do with one another. Mrs Stratford, by her own admission, seldom came to the fens. She had let slip the fact that she knew about Rachel's unsuitable romance from a reliable source, and she had also said that Miss Frith had been helpful to her. It therefore seemed entirely possible to Fay that the vicar's sister might be Mrs Stratford's local informant. There was nothing wrong in this, of course, but Fay resolved not to tell Miss Frith anything that she did not want Mrs Stratford to know.

That evening, Fay sat down to write to Angela, as she had promised. Since her friend had provided her with a reference, it seemed only fair to tell her how things were going. As well as telling her about the Proudfoots, she gave an account of her meetings with Peter and Agnes Frith. She smiled as she did so, wondering what Angela would make of her description of the young country vicar. Pausing in her task, she sat brushing the quill against her lips. Already he seemed favourably disposed to her, and if his attitude continued, who knew what might happen? If she ended up living in the village permanently, then she would not be too far away from Angela.

Pulling herself together before her imagination went completely out of control, she ended her letter by promising to write again. Angela's interest would surely be aroused by all the detail with which Fay would fill her correspondence, in preference to confiding in the possibly indiscreet Miss Frith.

The following day, the whole family attended church. Fay was a little surprised to see Mr Proudfoot among the company, for she had half suspected that the lure of the Vikings might prove to be too strong, but he appeared, albeit only just in the nick of time, to escort his family. There was about him a faint air of dishevelment, which Fay had begun to think was probably characteristic of him.

The day was bright and sunny, although very cold, and the decision was made to walk, rather than use the carriage. Nobody complained at this, which made Fay realize that the family had probably been brought up to enjoy healthy pursuits. Remembering how readily London inhabitants ordered their carriages for journeys of only a few yards, she could not help wondering whether Mrs Stratford would have walked as readily as the rest of them, had she been present.

It was not quite as cold inside the church as it was outside, for a small stove had been lit. Much of the heat went straight up into the roof, however, and it seemed probable that the combined heat of bodies – for the church was full – would do more than the stove to warm those present.

The Proudfoots were the most important family present, and Fay noticed that their pew was the closest to the stove. Before the service began, another family of some standing came in, and sat almost level with them on the other side of the aisle. Looking across at them, Fay concluded that they were probably a mother, with her son and daughter, or possibly daughter-in-law, and one other daughter.

The service was conducted by Peter Frith, who looked very imposing in his crisp and spotless vestments. Fay, remembering the ironing that she had had to do for her father, wondered whether this fell to Agnes's lot. The young clergyman preached sensibly, if unexcitingly, on the story of the lost sheep, and he seemed to hold the attention of most of the congregation.

For her part, though, Fay found her attention wandering during the service. The ancient words of the prayers and the responses struck a welcome note of familiarity amid all the changes that had taken place in her life recently. In her mind, she was transported back to the days when she would sit alone in the pew set aside for the vicar's family, and take part in services conducted by her father. She felt as if she were coming home and, at the end of the service, it was almost a surprise to look up and see not her father but Peter Frith standing at the front, pronouncing the blessing.

After the service was over, the Proudfoots left first, followed by the family that Fay had noticed earlier on. As they gathered together outside the church, she could see from their likeness to each other that the two eldest of the young people were brother and sister.

Rachel led Fay to where they were all standing. 'Miss Prescott, allow me to introduce Mrs Fairburn to you. Her husband was my father's tenant until his death, but now his son Joe has taken over the tenancy. This is Miss Prescott, who is Horsa's governess.' Mrs Fairburn acknowledged the introduction very simply and naturally. She was clearly an ordinary country-woman, but her manner indicated a degree of education, and she was well, if not fashionably, dressed.

'I'm very pleased to meet you, Miss Prescott,' said Mrs Fairburn. 'Miss Rachel'll be pleased to have some company too, I reckon. It'll save her from coming to the farm so often, espe-cially when the weather's bad.'

Fay noticed a look of dismay cross Rachel's face, before she said, 'You know I love coming to the farm, Mrs Fairburn.' Then, turning to the young people she said, 'And this is Matty, who is my age, and Joe, who is older, and Jenny their sister who is the same age as Horsa.' Fay found herself obliged to look up at Joe Fairburn, who was much taller than his mother, and when he took her hand and bowed courteously over it, she could feel the latent strength in his.

He was a handsome young man of about her own age, with broad shoulders and fair wavy hair. Like his mother, he was dressed neatly if not fashionably in clothes made from material of the finest quality. As he looked down at her, he smiled a smile of such sweetness that she felt her heart skip a beat. This, she thought, is the kind of young man I might have loved and even have married, had not fate intervened. She remembered how Rachel had quoted something that someone called Joe had said the previous day, and she began to suspect that this was the 'undesirable attachment' from which Mrs Stratford wanted to remove her niece. After all, she had been told that the young man was a farmer's son.

It was far too cold to be standing about outside, so after a little more conversation, during which Rachel prettily asked if she might bring Miss Prescott to visit the farm, and was given permission to do so, they set off for their homes.

Later, Fay thought again about the encounter. On the surface, it had been impossible to tell for certain whether there was indeed an attachment between the two young people. Rachel had performed the introduction just as she should, and if she had had any desire to monopolize the young farmer, or take him on one side, she had certainly made no attempt to carry out her plans.

For his part, Joe had behaved just as well, not putting himself forward in any way. It would clearly be necessary to observe them further in order to discover whether any kind of attachment existed between them. After that, she would do what she could, but if Mrs Stratford expected her to part them by main force, then she would find herself sadly disappointed. Anything of that nature could only be carried out by a member of the family and, from what Fay had already observed of Mr Proudfoot, probably by Mrs Stratford herself. One thing was certain: with no other young man living in the immediate neighbourhood, Rachel was almost bound to fall in love with someone like Joe Fairburn; and those of her family who wished to prevent such a thing from happening should have intervened much earlier than this.

# Chapter Four

After church, Agnes Frith had repeated her invitation to pay a visit to the vicarage. It occurred to Fay that there were very few ladies of Agnes's age in the vicinity. She recalled her own solitary youth as the only daughter of a clergyman, and she wondered whether Agnes, like Rachel, might be a little lonely, however busy she might be. When Fay stated her intention of visiting the vicar's sister, Rachel refused, pulling a face, and Fay did not insist that she accompany her. For one thing, it had become clear that Rachel did in fact have the ordering of the household, and she certainly had duties to perform which could not be neglected. For another, Fay could not forget that Rachel had described Agnes as a busybody. Without Rachel present, Agnes might be drawn into talking more freely about rumours concerning any possible attachment between Rachel and Joe, and might even disclose whether she was Mrs Stratford's informant. Thinking guiltily that Horsa's lessons could well be put off for a little longer, Fay set out for the vicarage.

Miss Frith was delighted to receive her, and welcomed her into the cosy parlour at the back of the house where there was a good fire burning. Fay eyed it with appreciation, for fires had been considered an extravagance in the home of her childhood and, for the most part, had only been lit in the evening.

'I am so pleased that you have come,' Miss Frith assured her, as soon as they were sitting down. 'You cannot think how delightful it is to have another young lady in the neighbourhood. Peter and I are close, but it is not the same as having a friend of one's own sex.'

Fay thought about her own past life and smiled a little wistfully. 'I never had a brother or a sister, but I am sure you must be right,' she said. The maid brought in tea, and soon they were sitting enjoying the warming brew.

After a little while, Agnes said, 'I'm sorry if I appeared to pry when we came to see you. I didn't intend to, but Peter tells me that I should beg your pardon for being vulgarly intrusive.'

'Oh no,' exclaimed Fay. 'There is no need for that.'

'You see, I am very interested in people's lives,' Agnes went on.

'Surely that is a most appropriate attitude for a clergyman's female relative,' put in Fay, with a smile.

'Yes, perhaps, but if I am not careful, I ask more questions than I should. I realize now that my probing reminded you of the difficulties of your situation and the keenness of your loss.'

Fay coloured. 'It is true that I would rather not discuss my life, but I never thought you vulgarly intrusive,' she said. Even as she spoke, however, there was a feeling of uneasiness at the back of her mind, as she recalled her suspicion that Miss Frith was Mrs Stratford's informant.

'Thank you. You are very good. Now tell me instead how you are getting on. Are you finding your situation congenial?'

'Certainly,' replied Fay. 'Rachel and Horsa are both delightful girls, and Magnus seems a pleasant young man. Hengist I have yet to meet, but I believe that he is due home from school in a day or two.'

'I am glad for their sakes that you have come,' confessed Agnes. 'I know that they have felt the lack of a mother's care. At times, I have tried to supply that lack, but my efforts have not always been received in the spirit in which I intended them.' Ah, thought Fay, that might partly explain Rachel's antipathy.

Out loud, she said, 'I understand that there has been no governess there for some time.'

'That is right. Not many people want to come to this part of the country, especially when they learn that the family never removes to London. It is so bleak here, you see; or at any rate, it can be.'

'Do you think that Rachel finds it lonely here?' Fay asked, hoping with this oblique question to discover exactly how well informed the vicar's sister might be.

'She and Horsa get on well, and I know that she enjoys the company of the Fairburn girls, and especially of Matty, who is her age. She does not seem to be the kind of giddy girl who wants excitement all the time, and this is to her credit. Whether constant association with the inhabitants of Fir Tree Farm is entirely a good thing is not my place to say, but I often see her going there, sometimes alone.'

'The quietness of her life now will make the contrast all the more stark when she comes to make her debut in London,' responded Fay, choosing not to respond to the last part of Miss Frith's speech.

'I am sure that Mrs Stratford will do all that she can to make the visit enjoyable,' replied Agnes. It was only later that it occurred to Fay that Miss Frith had shown no sign of surprise upon hearing that Rachel was to go to London, even though she herself had said only moments ago that the family never went there. Could it be that there had indeed been correspondence between Mrs Stratford and Agnes? The thought that Miss Frith might be telling tales about Rachel in order to enable her aunt to plot against her was rather distasteful. After a little more conversation, Fay got up to leave. She was just securing her bonnet strings when Peter Frith came in.

'Never say that I have just missed you,' he exclaimed in dismay. 'Pray, Miss Prescott, take off your bonnet and stay for a little longer.'

Fay smiled. 'I think I must go, Mr Frith,' she replied. 'I cannot justify being absent from Rachel and Horsa for longer.'

'Then I shall put my coat back on and walk with you,' he announced. Fay protested, but not very hard. Mr Frith, if not precisely handsome, was young and well made, and it would be agreeable to have such an escort. She bade farewell to Agnes, and assured her of a welcome at Old Drove House, should she call again.

'The more Rachel can experience company, the less intimidating London will seem to her when she makes her come-out,' she said, privately reflecting that in London, Rachel would certainly have to get used to receiving visits from people she didn't much care for. It was also true that if the vicar's sister was given the opportunity of observing Rachel at close quarters in her own home, she might be less likely to spy on her on other occasions.

It was while she was walking back towards Old Drove House, the vicar politely keeping step with her, that an idea suddenly occurred to her. She began impulsively. 'I wonder whether . . . but I don't want to impose.'

'I'm sure that nothing you could ask would ever be an imposition,' Peter Frith assured her with a smile. 'In what way may I serve you?'

'It cannot be denied that the life which the Proudfoot family lead is a somewhat isolated and restricted one,' she replied. 'Rachel will find herself very ill-prepared for her London debut if she does not travel beyond the confines of this parish. I was wondering whether, if you are ever going to March, you might be prepared to take us – myself, Rachel and Horsa – with you? It would at least broaden their horizons a little.'

'By all means,' he responded enthusiastically. 'There is nothing I should like more. In fact, Agnes was only saying recently that she would like to go to March to buy some Christmas gifts. We could all go together and have lunch at the Griffin.'

It had not occurred to Fay that it would be strange for a party to go to March under the vicar's protection without the vicar's sister, and she hoped that her presence would not put Rachel off going. After all, she reflected, an outing was an outing, and in the town there would be plenty of opportunity for the party to split up.

'Thank you,' said Fay. 'That sounds delightful. Pray let us know when you decide to go, and I will make sure that we are free.'

Fay knew that she was not a born teacher, but she decided that to put off the moment for starting her work as a governess would be foolish and cowardly. As soon as she got back to the house, therefore, she announced that the following morning, they would commence lessons. When Horsa looked a little mutinous, Fay said, with great aplomb, 'I have a very modern attitude to education. I believe that more is learned if a pupil is allowed a large amount of choice in what they study. I also believe that learning can take place in any situation, and that the student needs time for reflection upon what has been learned. I therefore propose that we spend the morning in reading. As to what we read, I shall leave the choice to you, Horsa.'

Horsa looked amazed. 'You mean, we can read *anything*?'

'Anything,' Fay reiterated firmly, hoping that the young girl would not come up with something indecent.

'Then . . . can we read *Roderick Random*?' Horsa asked. 'Miss Frayne hit my hands with a ruler when she found me reading it, because it is a novel.' She put her hands behind her back as she spoke, almost as though she expected to be struck again.

'By all means,' said Fay cordially. 'It is well written, and will be a good model for your own writing. Let us begin at once.' Over the next few days, the reading proved to be very popular. First of all, Rachel joined them, and listened whilst she was sewing. Then Magnus came in as well, and his presence proved to be a real gain, for he had a very good voice for reading, and was quite

42

happy to read a chapter or two, whilst the others got on with their sewing. Horsa, who declared herself to be no lover of needlework, and who was bored by the embroidered chair seats which absorbed Rachel, began almost despite herself, to take an interest in Fay's neat white work, and soon she was busily copying it.

This gave Fay an idea, and when Rachel suggested that they pay the promised visit to the Fairburns' farm, she decided to put the idea to the farmer's wife as soon as an opportunity occurred. On the day when they visited the farm, it happened that Joe was working in one of the more distant fields, so there was no opportunity of a meeting between Joe and Rachel, had either of the two desired it.

Mrs Fairburn welcomed them all warmly, and although she was clearly very busy, she put aside her tasks for the day, took off her apron, and showed them into the best parlour.

'Well, this is lovely and no mistake,' she said, beaming. 'And here was I, thinking that you would not have time to come with all your studying. Ruth,' she went on, turning to a maidservant, 'bring some fruit cake into the parlour, and some of my elderflower wine.'

Rachel, Fay and Horsa all went with her into the parlour, and they were soon joined by Matty and Jenny. When a break in the conversation occurred, Jenny said politely, with a soft country burr, 'May Horsa come and see the kittens, please?'

'I've no objection, if Miss Prescott is quite happy,' said Mrs Fairburn. Fay nodded smilingly, and when Matty asked if she and Rachel might go too, she assented, guessing that they wanted to talk secrets. At the same time, Fay decided to take this opportunity of talking to Mrs Fairburn. She was unsure as to how to proceed, however, so she was glad when the farmer's wife broke the silence by asking her how she was settling in.

'Very well indeed, thank you,' replied Fay warmly. 'They are a lovely family.'

'They certainly are,' agreed Mrs Fairburn. 'And I know them all far better than you might expect. Mrs Proudfoot died twelve years ago, and the children were left to be cared for by their nurse. That was all very well for a time, but when, four years later, the nurse died as well, the housekeeper discovered that she was expected to see to their needs, and she, being at the end of her tether as you might say, applied to me for help. So there was a time when the children spent nearly as much time here as they did at home.'

'I see,' replied Fay, feeling that this explained a lot.

There was a brief period of silence, and then Mrs Fairburn took a deep breath and said, 'We must make the most of this time, Miss Prescott, for I do not know how long we may have, and there are things that should be said, and I'll be bound you know what I'm talking about, for you look shrewd enough to me.'

Fay smiled slightly. 'I believe I may have a suspicion,' she admitted, reluctant to commit herself. Mrs Fairburn sighed. 'It's natural enough, I suppose,' she went on. 'I'm not one to criticize my betters, and never was, but it seems to me that it would have been as well for Miss Rachel not to have spent so much time here. But it's so lonely hereabouts, you see. There're no other quality families about at all, and even had she not come here so much out of necessity, she would probably have been drawn here anyway, to make a friend of Matty. But of course, there was always Joe.'

'Mrs Fairburn—' began Fay, but the other lady interrupted her.

'I don't want you to think that I've been encouraging anything between them,' she said earnestly. 'Nor that they've met clandestinely, from what I can tell, for Miss Rachel and my Matty are very close, and Matty tells me everything and would be sure to have let it slip if there'd been secret meetings. But while Miss Rachel comes here for company, they're bound to meet from time to time.' Fay smiled, and the anxious look on the farmer's wife's face began to recede.

'Mrs Fairburn, I don't want you to think that I blame you in any way,' she said. 'And I think that it is much better that they should meet here under your eye, than be sneaking off some-where.'

'Exactly so,' put in Mrs Fairburn, looking relieved. 'And it's my belief that it's the sneaking off that makes it all exciting and romantic.'

Fay nodded. 'I am sure that you are right,' she agreed. 'Tell me, ma'am, do you think that there is any local gossip going around about Joe and Rachel?'

'Not that I've heard – but then, people wouldn't be likely to repeat it to me,' answered Mrs Fairburn. 'And I've not said anything about it myself, because gossip is one thing I can't abide.' That dealt with the tiny anxiety that Fay had had that Mrs Fairburn might be the source of Mrs Stratford's informa-tion.

'Well maybe the whole thing will die a natural death,' said Fay. 'In the meantime, I have an idea that I think might help, if you will only consent. I have started reading with the young people every morning, from ten until twelve, and they are enjoying it very much. I was wondering whether you might allow Matty and Jenny to join us sometimes? I know that they must help on the farm, but if they came to us, Rachel would not have so much reason to come here, and the attachment might start to fade a little.'

Mrs Fairburn beamed. 'I think that that sounds a very good idea,' she said. 'The girls are always up early, and they can each do an hour for me before they go out. And I know they'll love it.' Not long after this, the four girls came back in, and the news was broken to them of the forthcoming reading sessions. They all looked very pleased, but Fay thought that Rachel looked a little thoughtful as well. Clearly, she could see the implications of this new scheme.

On their return to Old Drove House, they took their outdoor garments upstairs in order to put them away. As she hung her cloak in the cupboard in her room, Fay thought about Fir Tree Farm, and about the family who lived there. It was obvious why Rachel was attracted to its members, quite apart from the looks of the young farmer, of whose charms Fay herself was certainly aware. The farmhouse had a welcoming atmosphere, because of the loving care shown to the family by Mrs Fairburn. The Proudfoot children had all needed a mother figure. Mrs Stratford, though clearly a loving aunt in her way, was not the right person to fill that role, even had she been present to do so. Having for a father a slightly eccentric historian whose driving interest was the Viking conquest, Rachel was quite understandably drawn to the motherly farmer's widow.

Fay sighed, as it occurred to her that the only person in the house at present who might be a mother to Rachel was herself – and she, being only Rachel's senior by four years, was hardly qualified. She would just have to hope that the new stratagem conceived by herself and Mrs Fairburn would be successful. The less that either she or Rachel saw of the handsome young farmer the better!

Matty and Jenny came to join them for reading the next day. Rachel had been looking out for them from the window and, when she ran down to meet them, Fay was not surprised to observe that they were escorted by their older brother. He might have passed anywhere for a country gentleman, and he was far from the bucolic figure that Mrs Stratford had led her to expect. As she hurried down as well, ostensibly to meet them also, Fay wondered whether Mrs Fairburn was aware that Joe had come, and suspected that she was not. Matty engaged her in animated conversation, but not before she suspected that she saw a note being passed from Joe to Rachel.

'Good day, Mr Fairburn,' she said politely. 'There is no need for you to return later. I will make sure that the girls are brought safely home.' Joe touched his hat and left, but neither he nor Rachel seemed noticeably dashed by her pronouncement. Inwardly cursing Mrs Stratford, Fay led her charges upstairs. If only she were officially Rachel's duenna, then she could make some rules with regard to Rachel's conduct and see that they were adhered to. As it was, Rachel did not have to acknowledge her authority, and she was having to try to fulfil the requirements of her employment by subterfuge and cunning.

The reading session was a great success. Both Matty and Jenny had learned to read fluently ('Mother taught us', said Jenny) and they knew how to listen attentively. They had also been taught to sew – an essential skill for a farmer's daughter or wife – and were very ready to accept further instruction from Fay.

After the session was over, the girls shared a light lunch with them before going home with Magnus as their escort. The two Fairburn girls treated Magnus with casual friendliness, thus setting to rest a tiny fear that had passed through Fay's mind. It would be too bad if Rachel were to be detached from Joe, even whilst Matty was busy falling in love with Magnus.

Rachel disappeared for a short time, and before Matty left, Fay noticed another note being exchanged. It was something that she would have to watch very carefully. Rachel might not perceive Fay as having any authority over her, but a clandestine correspondence was not something that she could allow to pass, whatever her perceived position in the household.

Before any more reading sessions could take place, however, Mr Frith came to the house with an invitation for Fay, Rachel and Horsa.

'I am obliged to go to March tomorrow to collect some books that I have ordered, and my sister has decided to go as well. I wondered whether you would like to accompany us?' Rachel was present when the invitation was issued, and Fay was glad that Mr Frith did not mention the discussion that they had had concerning the scheme. The last thing that Fay wanted was for Rachel to feel herself the victim of a conspiracy. She looked questioningly at the other girl, who nodded at her, smiling.

'Thank you,' Fay said. 'We should like to go very much. How do you intend to convey us?'

'I shall send a message to bespeak a chaise from the Griffin,' he replied. 'That is what I generally do, if Agnes wishes to travel in the winter months.'

'I am sure that Papa would let us use our chaise,' said Rachel. 'I will go and ask him straight away.' Mr Frith protested a little, but he was clearly glad to be spared the cost of hiring a conveyance for his party. When Rachel returned with the news that the chaise could indeed be used, he willingly agreed to bring his sister to Old Drove House the following morning at ten o'clock, so that they could set off in good time.

After he had gone, Fay ventured to say to Rachel, 'I wasn't sure whether you would want to go with Miss Frith.'

Rachel shrugged. 'An outing to March is always welcome,' she said, 'and there are one or two purchases that I want to make.'

The next day dawned bright and clear, although cold, and Fay, Rachel and Horsa were all ready in good time, warmly dressed and facing the day with pleasurable anticipation. When Peter and Agnes Frith arrived, the carriage was waiting at the door. Horsa and Fay insisted that the Friths should enjoy the luxury of facing forwards, and this they agreed to after a short protest, and only after insisting that they should all exchange places with one another on the way back.

The last time that Fay had travelled this road, it had been almost dark, and she was interested to see what it would be like in the daylight. The countryside proved to be every bit as flat as it had seemed before, and without the glowing colours of the evening sky, there was a bleakness about it that could easily sap the spirits.

'How are the lessons going?' Agnes enquired, breaking into her reverie.

'We have only just started,' admitted Fay, 'but things are going quite well, I think.'

'We are reading together a lot, and sewing while we listen,' put in Horsa. 'And Matty and Jenny are to join us sometimes.'

'And what are you reading?' asked Agnes, posing the question that Fay had dreaded.

'*Roderick Random*,' answered Horsa. 'We are enjoying it very much, and Magnus reads so well, doesn't he?'

A look of disapproval crept over Miss Frith's face whilst Horsa was speaking. 'A novel!' she exclaimed. 'Miss Prescott, are you sure that this is wise?'

'I think that young people learn best when they are enjoying what they are reading,' she replied, weighing her words carefully.

'Ah, but what are they learning?' responded Miss Frith.

'My dear, you are not being fair,' said Peter Frith mildly. 'You cannot criticize the reading matter without suggesting something else in its place.'

'Well, perhaps some passages from the Bible,' Agnes said thoughtfully. 'Or maybe something else of an elevating nature? I have a copy of Fordyce's Sermons, if you would care to borrow it.'

Both Rachel and Horsa looked utterly aghast, and to prevent them from saying anything rude, Fay said quickly, 'How kind of you, Miss Frith. I will certainly consider using them. But in the meantime, I have had a wonderful idea! We could read some scenes from Shakespeare. One or two could read the parts whilst the others listened.'

Miss Frith looked doubtful. 'I have never been entirely convinced of the propriety of some of Shakespeare's work,' she said primly. 'But if carefully selected, I suppose it might not do any harm.'

The day in March proved to be a very enjoyable one. Both Rachel and Horsa had come with the intention of buying Christmas gifts for members of their family, and much amuse-ment was derived from picking up, comparing and discarding various items, and elaborately concealing the presents which each had bought for the other. Looking at the two of them made Fay realize, with a little stab of envy, that she could hardly remember what it was like to be so carefree. It also reminded her that there was very little in age between Rachel and Horsa. Apart from the desirability or otherwise of a match with Joe Fairburn, Rachel seemed to be much too young to be thinking of marriage just yet.

They enjoyed a light luncheon at the Griffin where they met Mr Frith after his business was concluded and, as all their purchases were made, they set off for home soon afterwards. Fay had had very little money to spare, but she had bought presents for all the family, including Mrs Stratford. She had purchased a number of plain handkerchiefs on which she planned to embroider initials for Rachel, Horsa and their aunt, and after some thought she decided to do the same for Agnes Frith. She had not bought a present for the vicar. She did not know what construction he might place on such a gift from a comparatively new female acquaintance, and she had no wish to appear fast.

A few days later, Agnes came to visit her with a copy of the works of Shakespeare, which she offered rather diffidently. 'We have more than one at home, and it occurred to me that if you plan to read it together, you might be glad of another copy.' She paused for a moment, then went on tentatively, 'I do hope you did not think me too critical when we were talking together in the carriage. I know that Shakespeare is very fine, but surely there can be no doubt that there are parts that are not at all suitable for young ears – or even for any ears at all.'

Fay found it quite impossible to agree to the whole of this, for her father's scholarship had been such that all learning had been welcomed, so she merely murmured, 'You may be sure that I will select the passages very carefully.'

'I'm sure you will,' said Agnes, laying a hand on her arm. 'You cannot think how relieved I am that you said you would be reading the plays rather than acting them.'

'You do not approve of acting, then,' said Fay, colouring a little.

'I disapprove of anything to do with the theatre,' replied Agnes, also flushing. 'It is full of painted women with loose morals, and unscrupulous coxcombs, ready to profit by other people's *naïveté*. I think that the entire theatrical profession is a disgrace to humanity.' There was a thump as the book which Miss Frith had passed to Fay slipped out of her hands and fell to the floor.

'Oh, I beg your pardon! How clumsy of me!' exclaimed Fay, as she bent to pick it up. 'There's no harm done. Does your brother also disapprove of the theatre?'

'Not so strongly, perhaps,' replied Agnes. 'But gentlemen, even men of the cloth, do not have such fine feelings as we do.'

Fay smiled slightly, then changed the subject by asking whether the Friths were expecting guests for Christmas. Soon afterwards, Agnes Frith left, expressing the wish that Fay would call at the vicarage again soon. After she had gone, Fay put the book down; it was only then that she realized that her hands were shaking.

# Chapter Five

The experiment with reading Shakespeare proved to be very successful. Fay chose *Julius Caesar* knowing that it would capture Magnus's interest and thus, she hoped, guarantee his presence. She had also been careful to avoid anything even remotely suggestive of star-crossed lovers. She did not want to give Rachel any ideas.

To her surprise, Peter Frith joined them on one occasion and he and Magnus gave a spirited rendition of one of the interchanges between Mark Antony and Brutus. When they had finished, Magnus exclaimed, 'Bravo, sir! You should have gone on the stage!'

Immediately a look of distaste crossed the vicar's features. 'By no means,' he replied. 'I have no high opinion of the theatre or of those who take part in it. But I do not see that a rational man cannot learn a good deal from reading well-written drama such as this.'

Fay said nothing, and kept her eyes on her sewing, but it was a moment or two before she felt she that she could trust herself to set another stitch.

Soon afterwards, it was time for the lesson to end, and Matty and Jenny returned home, accompanied by Magnus. Peter Frith lingered, clearly wanting to speak to Fay, and when Rachel and Horsa asked if they might go with Magnus she agreed, rather than become involved in an argument in front of the clergyman.

'We both very much enjoyed the visit to March,' he said, when they had gone. 'My sister has said so, more than once. It was a happy day for us that brought you here.'

'You are very kind,' replied Fay, tidying away the sewing things and the books. 'But I think that I am the gainer as much as your sister.'

'I am not just speaking on my sister's account,' answered Mr Frith earnestly. Fay was so surprised that for a moment she could not speak. 'I have startled you, I can see,' said Mr Frith. 'I know that I am speaking too soon, so I shall say no more for the present. But may I come and join your reading sessions again?'

Fay found herself blushing. 'I thought that you did not quite approve of my choice of material,' she murmured.

'Not at all,' he replied. 'I can see no harm in the reading of drama. It is the performing of it that brings about so much evil. But you have not answered my question: may I come again?'

'Yes . . . yes, of course,' she replied, self-consciously.

'Then I shall bid you good day,' he said, kissing her hand politely before leaving.

Feeling a sudden need for fresh air, she went to her room, put on her bonnet and cloak, and walked down the stairs and into the garden, in order to clear her head. She strolled about in the garden, a prey to several different emotions. It was very agreeable to have a presentable young man take an interest in her – for there was no doubt that that was exactly what Mr Frith was doing. She had woven a fantasy about this very possibility as she had written her first letter to Angela, but to dream about it was very different from encouraging it to happen. In other circumstances, she could well imagine that she might be ready to allow his courtship to progress further. Unfortunately, however, there was that in her past which was an insuperable barrier to any relationship, and of that past she found herself quite unable to speak.

\*

The five young people walked to Fir Tree Farm chatting companionably, Rachel giving no hint that she had anything on her mind apart from the present conversation. When they arrived at the farm, however, she hung back a little and grasping Matty's arm, she whispered, 'Take the others inside, will you? I want to speak to Joe.'

Matty, although naturally enough quite unable to see what possible attraction her brother might have for any woman, said 'All right then, but don't be too long or Mother will be suspicious.' She dropped her voice. 'I think that Joe will probably be in the barn. There was some timber he wanted to replace, and I doubt if he'll be finished yet.' Rachel smiled her thanks, gave her friend's hand a little squeeze, and hurried away from the house to the barn which Matty had indicated. On approaching it, she heard a sound of hammering and, as she stood in the doorway, she could see Joe fastening a new wooden panel into the side of the barn. He was wearing a long, leather waistcoat, and his shirt sleeves were rolled up to his elbows, and Rachel took pleasure in watching the play of the muscles in his forearms.

Suddenly becoming conscious that he was observed, he looked up and seeing that it was Rachel, he put down his hammer and came hurrying over to her. She took a step or two inside the barn and he picked her up as if she were a feather, swinging her round in his arms before putting her down.

'How do you manage to look lovelier every time I see you?' he asked her, smiling.

'In the same way as you manage to look more handsome every time *I* see *you!*' she replied, reaching up to kiss him. When at last he let go of her, she wandered over to where he had been working.

'What are you doing?' she asked him.

'Meg kicked one of the panels out last week, so I'm repairing it,' he said. 'The wood must have been a bit rotten anyway.'

She took hold of one of his hands. 'How clever you are,' she murmured.

He smiled at her, but his expression held a hint of anxiety. 'Rachel, you shouldn't be here,' he said.

She squeezed the hand that she was still holding with both of hers. 'It's perfectly proper,' she replied, smiling up at him. 'I've come with Magnus and Horsa to bring Matty and Jenny back. And anyway, Miss Prescott said that I might.'

'I'll warrant she didn't say that you could come round to the barn and see me on your own,' he replied.

Her smile faded. 'No, but if I waited until someone said that I could see you, then I'd never see you at all, would I?'

He turned away from her then. 'Perhaps it would be as well if you didn't,' he said, in subdued tones.

'Joe,' she faltered uncertainly. 'You can't really mean that. We pledged ourselves to each other two years ago. I meant every word of the promise I made then. Did you?'

'Yes, of course I did,' he replied wretchedly. 'But we should never have done it. *I* should never have done it. I didn't have the right. You're only eighteen now, and I'm twenty-four. I should have known better.' He looked down at her sadly. 'You're out of my reach, Rachel.'

She looked aghast. 'I'm not,' she declared. 'Who says so?'

'Almost anyone you could name would say so – your aunt would, for example.'

'My aunt!' she declared scornfully. 'She leaves me alone here for most of my life, with a father who buries himself among the Vikings, and only comes out for meals. She allows your mother to help to bring me up and to care for me and the others when it suits her, and then again, consulting nothing except her own convenience, she comes here interfering in my life, and bringing with her people from London for me to entertain. No, Joe, my aunt has no right to say anything about what I may do with my life – or about whom I marry!'

'She only wants the best for you,' put in Joe. 'And after all, to have you to stay in London when the time comes will put her about quite a good deal.'

'My presence will only give her another reason for doing what she enjoys doing most – going about in society,' retorted Rachel. 'And in any case, if she really wants the best for me, then she ought to be able to see that *you* are the best.' He took hold of her hand in his large rough one, and raised it to his lips. 'If only she could understand that I'm not interested in society, or fancy clothes, or big occasions of any kind, or in making what she thinks is a good match. It's not even as if I'm a son, or the only heir.' They were both silent for a few moments.

'You should forget me and marry someone of your own station,' Joe said painfully.

'Why?' demanded Rachel. 'It makes me so angry that if I wanted to marry some titled wastrel without a penny, no one would mind, but I want to marry a hard-working farmer with almost enough money saved to buy his own property! Besides, I notice that you do not make the same suggestion for yourself.'

He turned his head away. 'You know that there'll never be anyone for me except you,' he said.

She took hold of his hand. 'Yes, I do,' she answered. 'So why don't you realize that I feel just the same way?' There was another silence then Rachel spoke again. 'Joe?'

'Yes?'

'How close are you to having enough to buy the farm from my father?'

He shrugged his shoulders. 'Close enough. But would your father ever be prepared to sell this farm to me? And if not, where else would I be able to buy property? And what about Mother and the girls?'

Rachel looked thoughtful for a time. 'Something will come to me,' she said at last. Reaching on tiptoe she kissed him gently.

They walked together to the barn door. 'But I'm not giving up. They're not going to make me marry anyone except you – whatever they do.' She ran back to the farmhouse. Joe stood watching until she had turned the corner, then with a sigh, he went back to his work.

The following day, after the morning's reading session, Magnus lingered in the schoolroom after everyone else had gone. 'If you have nothing else to do, I was wondering whether I might talk to you about my play?' he asked, over casually. 'I have had one or two ideas, but I am not at all sure how some of the scenes will work out.'

'Yes, of course,' said Fay with a smile. 'Do you want to talk here, or shall we go to the library so you can tell me about it?'

Magnus smiled gratefully. 'Let's go to the library,' he said. 'You're very kind,' he went on as they descended the stairs. 'Nobody else takes any kind of interest in my work. In fact,' he went on confidingly, 'my aunt thinks that it is a waste of time.'

'But your father is interested in history,' replied Fay. 'Surely he. . . ?'

Magnus shook his head. 'Anything that isn't to do with the Vikings bores him, and he doesn't think it worth the trouble,' he replied. 'But we can't all be Viking enthusiasts, can we?'

'No indeed,' agreed Fay sincerely.

'Besides,' went on Magnus, 'Father wants me to learn to administer the estate.' He sounded very despondent.

'I take it that this is not to your taste?' Fay speculated.

'Of course it isn't,' declared Magnus scornfully. 'I'm a *poet*. Father ought to understand that if he's a historian, shouldn't he?' Luckily, their arrival at the library meant that Fay was not obliged to answer this question.

The next half-hour was spent in listening to Magnus explaining the plot of his play so far. As the work appeared to embrace the whole of Julius Caesar's life, beginning with his birth, and ending with his assassination at the hands of Brutus and the other conspirators, she judged that it would be quite a lengthy piece when finished.

'I am not at all sure how the actual arrival in Britain is to be shown,' he said thoughtfully. 'I should like to have a scene on board the boat, with the standard bearer leaping into the sea and the others following him, but I am uncertain as to how to achieve it. Might it have to be an outdoor performance, incorporating a lake, perhaps? Or do you think that that would make it difficult for everyone to hear what was being said?' Fay agreed that this might be a problem.

'There is another difficulty, of course, which is that we do not happen to have a lake here. Do you think that Father might create one, if I dropped a subtle hint that he might be able to use it for Viking re-enactments?' At this point, Fay appeared to choke, but beyond asking briefly if she was all right, Magnus took very little notice. 'Of course, there are plenty of dykes around here, so perhaps one of those would do, and it might act as a kind of echo chamber.' Having mastered her difficulty, Fay agreed that this might be possible.

Taking advantage of the momentary cessation of the flow, she asked him if he intended drawing on any of the ideas expressed in Shakespeare's play. He drew himself up very straight. 'I do not intend to copy anyone else's work,' he said grandly. 'Of course, I have enjoyed looking at what he has done,' he conceded, 'and he has some skill in writing speeches; but I intend to improve upon it.' It seemed as if nothing would prevent Fay's having another choking fit, when fortunately, Magnus was suddenly struck by an idea. 'I say, do you think it might be better if I did the whole thing in Latin? If you will excuse me, I will go and look into it immediately.'

Fay managed to hold back her laughter until he was well out of hearing distance. Once he was gone, however, she chuckled heartily at the picture which came into her mind, namely that of a boatload of Romans struggling to hold their craft steady in one of the long cuts which criss-crossed the fens, whilst declaiming in Latin to a bemused populace gathered on the bank. She was just wishing for someone with whom to share this exquisitely humorous picture, when the door opened, and the butler announced Mr Frith.

'In a good hour,' said Fay, her eyes still full of laughter. 'I have something very diverting to share, and no one to share it with.'

'Then I have indeed come at a fortunate moment,' replied the vicar, thinking how very pretty Fay looked when she was smiling. They sat down, and Fay began to tell him what had happened. His attentive demeanour was of one waiting to hear what the humorous incident might be, and although he smiled, he did not laugh as she had hoped, but waited in the same attentive way after her tale was done.

'Of course it is very difficult to explain something amusing to someone who was not present,' Fay concluded, feeling a little disappointed.

Mr Frith nodded. 'Your amusement must also be tempered by concern, I am sure,' he said.

'Concern?'

'At the fact that Magnus is pursuing an interest which does not meet with his aunt's approval. She is quite right, of course. Contact with the theatre can lead to all kinds of excesses. But I have said this before. And it is clearly Magnus's duty to administer the estate, if his father requires it.' Fay opened her mouth to say that it was surely Mr Proudfoot's duty rather than his son's, when she recalled the impropriety of criticizing her employer so openly, and instead offered the vicar some refreshment. 'No, I thank you,' he replied. 'I have simply come to bring you my newspaper. I have one delivered from London every week, but had not previously thought to bring it here after I have finished with it. Mr Proudfoot is not really interested in current affairs. But since you lived in London for a time, I thought that perhaps you might like to have a look at it.'

Fay coloured. 'That is most kind of you,' she said. 'I would not have you go to any trouble on my account.'

'Not at all,' he replied. 'I count it a privilege.' He left soon afterwards. Fay sat with the paper in her hand for quite some time, before giving herself a little shake and opening it, almost tentatively, as if afraid of what she might read. She scanned the announcements, but none of the names was familiar to her, and with a sigh she put it down.

Not long after this, Rachel came looking for her with a letter in her hand. 'It is from my aunt,' she said. 'She sends details of the guests who are to be staying here over Christmas. They will be arriving in a week, so I suppose we had better set about making preparations.' She handed the letter to Fay, then wandered over to the window.

'You don't sound very excited,' remarked Fay. 'I should have thought that living in an isolated place such as this, you would have been pleased at the prospect of more varied company.'

Rachel turned around. 'Yes, of course, it can be very dull here in the winter, but there are always things to do. And besides, I know what my aunt is about. She wants to convince me that I will enjoy London, when I go there for my debut, but I won't. I don't want fashionable parties and balls. I just want. . . .' She coloured.

'Yes?' prompted Fay gently.

'A quiet life,' concluded Rachel rather lamely. Then she went on quickly, 'Remind me of what my aunt says about the numbers of guests. I didn't take it in.'

'Two single gentlemen, a married couple with a son and a daughter, and a widow and her daughter.'

'Two single gentlemen, and a family with a son! I can see exactly what she is about! She wants to marry me off to one of them,' declared Rachel cynically.

'My dear, your aunt is going to the very great expense and

trouble of giving you a London season,' said Fay patiently. 'I doubt very much whether she wants to see you married to anyone just yet. I'm sure that her purpose in inviting these people here is simply to enable you to feel a little easier in fashionable company.'

'Just so,' answered Rachel, her eyes narrowing a little. 'Miss Prescott, you are either very perceptive, or very well informed. Are you quite sure that you came here just to be Horsa's governess?' Their eyes met, then Fay took a deep breath.

'The one thing I *am* sure of is that there is a great deal to do in just a week. Shall we send for the housekeeper, the cook and the butler, and have a council of war?'

There was certainly a good deal to be done and Fay, Rachel and Horsa all did their share in preparing the rooms. Horsa, who seemed to be much more enthusiastic about the coming guests than Rachel, confided that there had not been visitors to Old Drove House in such numbers for some considerable time.

'Not since I was very little and Mama was alive,' she told Fay, as they carefully inspected the bed linen and put on one side the items that needed to be repaired. 'I think that I just remember it, but it might be that I have been told about it since. Of course, I was too young to play any part in it then. Do you suppose that I might be allowed to go to some of the things? Oh please, Miss Prescott, say that I may! After all, I am allowed to dine with the family now that I am fourteen. And Christmas is a family occasion. It wouldn't be fair to send me to the schoolroom over Christmas, would it?'

Horsa's enthusiasm was so refreshing after Rachel's decidedly lack-lustre approach to the whole business that Fay was sorely tempted to agree that she might attend every possible event. But erring on the side of caution, she said instead, 'You will have to ask your aunt when she arrives. It will be her decision. Oh mercy!' she exclaimed, having been struck by a sudden thought. 'We have forgotten to put a room aside for your aunt!' Horsa giggled at the thought of the dignified Mrs Stratford being informed that there was nowhere for her to sleep, ('She'll have to sleep in the stable, just like Mary and Joseph,' said Horsa.) In the discussion about which room she should occupy, the question of Horsa's attendance at any of the entertainments was forgotten.

There was one awkward moment, and it came after Matty and her sister had gone home one day. The reading sessions had continued even during the busy time of preparation, but those who were sewing confined themselves to the mending of any items of linen that would be needed while the guests were staying at the house. On this occasion, Joe collected his sisters in the gig. He and Rachel exchanged a few words, and Rachel came in looking a little flushed. But soon afterwards, she said to Fay, 'I don't suppose Matty and Jenny, or . . . or Joe will be invited to anything, will they?'

'Well. . . .' began Fay, 'your aunt—'

'You don't have to tell me,' replied Rachel, her chin up. 'It's all right for them to come here and help, like servants, but it won't be all right for them to come as guests because they aren't quality.'

'We have been working too, and we haven't asked them to do anything that we haven't done ourselves,' pointed out Fay, quietly. 'And as for coming as guests, Jenny is far too young anyway. But I promise that I will ask if Matty might come, although I doubt whether Mrs Fairburn will allow it.' She did not mention Joe's name, but it hung in the air between them.

'It doesn't matter,' replied Rachel. 'I know what my aunt will say.' Fay rather thought that she did too, but she did not say so. Rachel then surprised her considerably by saying, 'Thank you for being ready to try. I am glad you've come.' After that, the subject of invitations to Fir Tree Farm was not discussed any further.

The preparations, which continued apace, were not helped very much by any of the menfolk of the house. Hengist returned from school and managed to dirty a room which had just been cleaned by allowing his dog into the house after it had swum across the dyke and rolled in the mud. Magnus had now decided to write the whole play in Latin, and since he had discovered that Fay had learned classics with her father, he was for ever coming to check verbs and declensions when she was absorbed with other things. Mr Proudfoot kept out of the way for the most part, but occasionally put his head around the door to demand an opinion on the Norse gods, Viking placenames, or burial rites.

At last, however, the day came when everything had been done, apart from actually bringing in the greenery to decorate the house. Fay stood in the hall, looking round with satisfaction at her work – and much of it *had* been her work. The house had been without a mistress for too long, and although the house-keeper did what she could, and Rachel held the reins of the household in a way in which someone of her age should never have been expected to do, the place lacked the touches which only a mistress could bring.

'Today, we shall gather the greenery,' she said to Hengist, Horsa and Rachel. 'And you can help as well,' she added to Magnus. 'You are tall and will be able to reach better than us. The holly at the end of the long walk has berries on some of the high branches, and we won't be able to reach them.'

Magnus looked aghast. 'But what about my writer's hands?' he asked anxiously.

'Put some gloves on,' she answered him tartly. 'Now come on, let's get this done while it's sunny. The first visitors arrive tomorrow.'

They all put on warm clothes – not their best ones – and Fay was very amused at the size and thickness of the gloves that Magnus had managed to find.

'Do you suppose that you will know any of the people who are coming?' Hengist asked her, as they walked down the path. He was a cheerful boy, who had soon attached himself to Fay with the utmost friendliness, and without a hint of shyness. 'You were in London, weren't you?' he went on.

For a moment, Fay's heart went right down into her boots at the very idea, but then she said, 'I don't suppose so. I wasn't there for very long, and I lived very . . . very retired.' Which was true enough in its way, she reflected.

Once Magnus had forgotten about the possible danger to his 'writer's hands', he joined in with a will, and they piled the gathered greenery into a wheelbarrow, which one of the gardeners pushed for them. At last, the work was done, and they went back into the house by a side door, the gardener being allowed to push the wheelbarrow just into the passage where an old sheet had been spread on the floor to keep it clean.

'Can we start straight away?' Horsa asked eagerly.

'Yes, by all means,' replied Fay. 'Let's just take off our outdoor things.'

Hengist, who always seemed to be two steps ahead, hurried before them, but came back to say, 'My aunt's here, with one of the guests, I think.'

'I'm sure she said that they would be arriving tomorrow,' murmured Fay, wrinkling her brow. They walked into the hall where Mrs Stratford was talking to her brother, whilst behind her, a gentleman was handing his hat and coat to the butler.

'Ah, there you are,' said Mrs Stratford, in high good humour. 'I have acquired an escort, and so am here a little early as you see.' The young people came forward politely to greet their aunt, and Fay, moving to stand behind them, found that as the gentleman came away from where he had been exchanging a word or two with the butler, she was looking straight at him, and he at her. 'This is one of our guests, Sir Jackson Hooper,' Mrs Stratford said. Fay, finding herself for the first time in nearly a year looking into the eyes of the man who had ruined her, fainted dead away.

# Chapter Six

She was vaguely aware of someone carrying her upstairs, and placing her on her bed, and from a long way away she seemed to hear someone saying, 'It was the warmth, after coming in from the cold, no doubt.'

A harsh voice that she appeared to recognize, said, 'She'll soon recover. She just needs some peace and quiet.' Then mercifully she was left alone. For a time she lay still, half-way between sleeping and waking, going over in her mind the things that had happened to her, which had culminated in her becoming Sir Jackson Hooper's mistress.

She had always been an only child. Her father was the vicar of a country parish, and her mother was the daughter of another. Her mother had died when she was born, and she only had a picture in a locket to give her any idea of what her mother was like. Her father was not an influential clergyman with many livings to his name, and all that he earned was needed in order to run the home, feed and clothe the two of them, and pay the wages of one indoor and one outdoor servant. A nurse, Mary Frost by name, had also been employed to look after Fay in her infancy, but once Fay reached the age of ten, the nurse was dismissed, her wages being deemed an unnecessary expense. Fay had been very upset when Mary had left, especially since she married soon afterwards and went to live in Cambridge. To comfort the child, the woman had promised to write, and from then on, a correspondence had taken place between them.

Her father had taught her himself, and so, not surprisingly, the curriculum had tended to include the subjects that he himself enjoyed, namely Latin, Greek, mathematics, and literature, in particular the works of the great dramatists. Sewing, she had learned of necessity. A lady who had lived in the village for a time had taught her a great deal in that respect, and she soon discovered that she had an aptitude for the needle. It had been a quiet and, in many respects, a lonely childhood, but she and her father always enjoyed one another's company.

Then, just over a year ago, her father had died suddenly. It was not an eventuality that she had ever considered, although afterwards she acknowledged that she had been extremely foolish not to realize that almost inevitably, he would predecease her. After his death, it was discovered that there was virtually nothing for her. The incoming vicar needed the house and, by great good fortune, he also wanted to buy the furniture. The sum raised came to enough for her to be able to afford a ticket on the stagecoach to go to Cambridge, where her old nurse lived. She had written to her, telling her of the death of The Revd Henry Prescott, but had had no reply. In the circumstances, though, she had nowhere else to go.

But when she arrived at the address to which she had been writing, a terrible shock awaited her, for the house had burned to the ground. A neighbour, seeing her distressed state, had taken her in, and informed her that all those who had lived in it were safe, but she could not tell her where they had gone, only that she thought they had taken refuge with Mary's sister, who lived in the north somewhere.

Alone, with nowhere to go, and hardly any money, Fay tried to find work, but without success. Her accent was too refined for her attempts to get work as a maid-servant to be treated with anything but suspicion, but no position of greater responsibility was available to her without a reference.

At last, becoming tired and desperate, she went back to the inn at which she had arrived in Cambridge earlier in the day, intending to ask for work as a serving maid. She met with no better success there however, and she was just trying to decide whether to leave Cambridge and look for a barn where she might shelter for the night, when she heard the last part of a conversation between the innkeeper and a stout, self-possessed man, rather loudly dressed, with a resonant voice.

'Half our profits, my good man? You must be demented! We are the finest company that ever set foot in Cambridge.'

'I dare say – but I still want to have my share,' protested the innkeeper.

'And so you shall, my man,' answered the other in the tones of a monarch conferring favour upon a suppliant minion. 'Remember that the presence of my company will draw many to this charming inn of yours. And all of them will buy food and drink. Of course, if you prefer, I could go to the Spread Eagle instead,' he added, casually.

'No, no, wait,' said the innkeeper quickly. 'Maybe half was a bit too much. What say I take a quarter?'

'I say, let us shake hands,' said the other. 'You have a bargain with Augustus Llewellyn! Three performances, as we agreed, beginning on Thursday.'

Twenty-four hours ago, Fay would never have dreamed of approaching such a man, but since then, she had received more rejections than she could count, and she was becoming desperate. She stepped forward quickly, before she lost her courage.

'Mr Llewellyn,' she said earnestly, and thereby immediately gained herself a hearing, for two reasons. The first was that she knew his name, and the one thing that a director of a theatrical company wants is that his name should be known. The second reason was that her voice was low and melodious, and Mr Llewellyn's sensitive ear was caught.

'Yes, my dear young lady, in what way may I be of service?'

She coloured painfully. 'I am looking for work,' she said. Seeing his face becoming grave, she went on quickly, 'Oh please, sir, I have trudged over this whole town and asked in so many places, and I have no money and nowhere to go. . . .' Her voice shook and she took out her handkerchief.

Accustomed to seeing such actions performed as 'business' on stage, Llewellyn was strangely touched at seeing it done in good and earnest and, much to his surprise, he found himself asking this young woman if she had eaten that day? Fay had not had anything since breakfast, and it was only now that she realized how hungry she was. But determinedly she straightened her spine, and said, 'There is no need, sir. I do not wish for charity.' This response did her no disservice in the theatrical manager's eyes. He waved his hand dismissively.

'I was about to eat in any case,' he lied, 'and they will be bound to bring far more than I can consume. Pray join me, and tell me something of your story. That, if you wish, can be your payment, for I am curious as to why a young lady such as your-self should be destitute like this.' Fay allowed herself to be persuaded, and soon, she was hungrily tucking into a portion of meat pie with potatoes.

While they were waiting for their food, she told him her story, and Mr Llewellyn was very interested when she informed him that she was acquainted with the works of the great dramatists.

'Ah, Shakespeare!' he sighed. 'We are to perform Shakespeare here this week. You must come and see it.'

'Which play is it to be?' Fay asked him.

'*King Lear*,' he replied. 'I myself am to take the title role.'

'I should like to see it,' she replied quietly, not at all sure what might have become of her by Thursday. 'But I have to admit that it is not my favourite Shakespeare play. It is so very dark.'

'Indeed, and that is its great weakness,' he replied authoritatively. 'But you will be pleased to hear that I have rectified that weakness.'

'Rectified?' Fay ventured tentatively. 'You have rectified Shakespeare?'

'Certainly,' he declared. 'My dear, none of us is perfect, and even the bard made mistakes. In my version, the good are rewarded and the evil punished. You will find it much improved.' When she had finished her meal and thanked him, he said, 'Now, my dear Miss Prescott' – for she had disclosed her name, not judging it right to withhold it from someone who was buying her meal – 'to your dilemma. I have thought about this, and I cannot see how I can help you. We are all performers you see, and I have a full complement at present. Virtually all other tasks we do for ourselves, sharing them out amongst us. All cooking, all tidying, everything.' Fay's face fell. Anxiously, she fidgeted and pulled at the handkerchief in her hands. Llewellyn, always interested in anything that might be of use on stage, said, 'Don't rip up that handkerchief – such fine lace!'

Fay smiled wryly. 'I can always make another,' she said.

An arrested look crept across his face. 'You *made* it?' he asked, amazed.

'Yes. Needlecraft is one of my few useful skills.'

He smiled slowly. 'Then – strictly temporarily, I'm afraid – I am able to offer you a position with my company.'

Fay's face was suddenly suffused with happiness and relief, and had the table not been between them, she might have hugged him. 'Really? Oh thank you, thank you!' she cried.

'You don't even know what it is, yet,' he reminded her.

'I don't care what it is,' she replied frankly.

'Well, I will tell you. But remember, I did say that it must only be temporary. Our wardrobe mistress has had to attend the sickbed of an elderly relative, and she will be away for some weeks. While she is away, we have been managing without anyone, but it is not a very satisfactory state of affairs. Some of my performers are very careless, you know, and things get torn very frequently and need mending quickly, and with skill. Then, when we start preparing for our new play, some items of costume will have to be made entirely. I cannot afford to pay very much, but you will have food and shelter all in.

'We are to spend nearly a week here in Cambridge, then we will make our way towards London by degrees, where our wardrobe mistress will rejoin us. And there in London, my dear, there will be many more opportunities for employment, and I am sure that you will find something to suit you.' Fay happily agreed to his terms. At least her immediate future was settled; for the rest, something would probably turn up: it would have to.

She found the other members of the theatrical company to be very friendly, once they had discovered that she was a quick and accurate worker. No one ever had to go on stage with his costume half-completed because she had been too slow; no one ever had to complain that she could not be found because she was flirting with members of the audience around the front of the theatre. Truth to tell, she enjoyed the work, and the excitement created by the need to have everything ready on time.

The new version of *Lear* – which she did manage to see, despite her work – was a revelation, incorporating as it did a happy ending in which Lear was restored to his throne. The final scene was the wedding of Cordelia, at which her two wicked sisters begged pardon and were forgiven. Although Fay could not help but deplore – albeit secretly – such drastic alterations to the text, she could not deny that they certainly made the play a much more cheerful spectacle.

Lodgings had been procured for all the company, and Fay found herself sharing a tiny room with a character actress called Angela. Angela was not pretty in a conventional sense, but her face was full of animation, and her figure was excellent. She always seemed to have quite as many men pursuing her as Elsie Dunn, the attractive blonde girl who took the leading roles. Fay had never shared a room with anyone else before, and she found it an agreeable novelty to chat with someone while getting ready for bed, especially with someone of her own age who, nevertheless, seemed to have quite a store of worldly wisdom.

'Be very careful,' Angela told Fay, early on in their acquaintance. 'There are plenty of men ready to get the wrong idea, just because you have anything to do with the theatre.' She was dispensing her advice as they were preparing for bed after their last performance in Cambridge. 'They only want one thing, because they think that all actresses are fast.'

'One thing?' asked Fay naïvely. Angela gave her a long look, and Fay blushed and looked down.

'One thing,' repeated Angela, brushing her hair vigorously. 'And now that you are tainted with the theatre, some of them will think the same about you. It won't make any difference to them that you aren't an actress.'

'But surely some. . . ?' protested Fay, sitting up in bed with her arms clasped around her knees while Angela finished braiding her hair for bed.

'Oh yes, some are different. In fact, don't tell anyone, but I rather think I might have met one here – in Cambridge.'

'Really?'

'Yes. He's a doctor, and he's asked me to write to him, and I think I will.' She tied her braid, and came over to get into bed beside Fay.

'Oh Angela, I do hope that everything comes right for you,' said Fay sincerely.

'So do I,' replied the other girl as she blew out the light.

Fay remembered what Angela had said, and tried, for the most part, to keep out of the way of any men who might come backstage to whatever area might have become the Green Room in search of girls. Most of the time she managed to efface herself very successfully. The majority of those who came backstage wanted to see Elsie, or Angela, or one of the others whom they had seen in the performance.

After her lonely childhood, she enjoyed the camaraderie of the theatre company, and especially the friendship of Angela, but all the time, she kept telling herself not to become too attached to any of them. She kept warning herself that the position was only temporary and that she would have to find work somewhere else; and the closer they came to London, the nearer drew the time when her employment would come to an end. About one thing she was quite determined: she would not beg Mr Llewellyn for help. He had been kind enough already.

One day, after they had reached Islington, Fay was unpacking in the room which had been allotted for the costumes. She was just sorting out which items needed ironing, when a sharp-featured young woman approached her and said, 'You've kept my costumes nice, I'll say that for you.' Fay looked up, her heart sinking within her, and she knew that her despondency was written all over her face. 'You were told that I'd be back, weren't you? I hope you aren't going to put upon old Gus, 'cause he isn't as well off as you might think, and he can't afford to keep any extra people.'

Fay's pride came to her aid, and she squared her shoulders. 'No, of course not,' she said. 'In fact, I've made other plans already.'

The woman's face relaxed. 'Well you don't mind my speaking plain, I hope. We're here for four performances this week. You can stay on for those, if you like. There's lots of costumes to see to, so I could do with some help.' Fay agreed. Despondently, she decided to look around during the day to see if there was any employment to be had locally.

This time, her problem was a different one. In some strange way, those whom she approached knew that she was connected with the theatre company, and she was therefore suspected of being immoral at best and dishonest at worst. When the first night of the performance arrived, she still had no idea of what she was going to do when the company moved on.

Out of all the girls in the company, Miss Elsie Dunn was the prettiest by far. Wherever they went, she had her admirers, but, as they drew closer to London, the quality of those admirers increased. Sometimes, they hardly seemed to be interested in the performance at all, but spent most of their time in whatever passed as the Green Room, chatting with the performers, and paying Elsie and Angela and the others extravagant compliments.

On the first night, three gentlemen came into the room which The Angel had set on one side for the performers and began to talk with Elsie as usual. Fay had a great deal to do in a short period of time, since Angela had ripped her hem and something had to be done about it before she went on stage in ten minutes.

'Got some real quality in tonight,' whispered Angela, as Fay pinned away. 'One of them is Lord Hadleigh; another is Mr Moorford or Monksford or something. Anyway, he's related to a duke; and the third one is Sir Jackson Hooper.' The strangeness of the name made Fay look up involuntarily. She glanced across and saw a tall, dark-haired man looking at her and, in an instant, she dropped the pin box, and the pins spilled all over the floor.

'Oh no!' she exclaimed. As if she had time to do anything else at this stage! She began to pick up the pins, but suddenly became aware that one of the gentlemen had crossed the room, and was standing next to her. Looking up, she saw that it was the dark-haired man.

'Allow me,' he said, going down on one knee. 'I think I startled you.' So saying, he began to pick up the pins and put them in her box.

'Thank you, sir,' she said, in a low voice, being careful not to look at him, for she felt strangely aware of his closeness. By the time he had retrieved them all, she had finished Angela's hem. They both stood up together, and she discovered him to be quite as tall as she had thought when she was crouched on the floor, probably about six feet, and considerably taller than she was herself. His hair was not so much dark as jet black and very straight and silky-looking, and it was caught back with a black velvet bow. His eyes and brows were dark too, and the deep lines riven from his straight nose to his rather thin-lipped mouth made his expression look sardonic. 'Thank you, sir,' she said again. 'I was in haste, and you saved me some time.'

'Jackson Hooper at your service,' he replied, with a slight inclination of his head, and with that, he went to rejoin his friends. 'Who is the little waif with the pins?' he asked Elsie.

Elsie, whose other two admirers were being very attentive, did not begrudge giving the information. 'Oh, that's Fay,' she replied carelessly. 'She's been our wardrobe mistress for a little while, but she's leaving us at the end of this run.'

'Fay,' murmured the baronet. 'Strangely appropriate.'

Her presence with the company intrigued him. Her voice and her manner proclaimed her to be a lady, but if she was gently-bred, what was she doing with a theatre company? His idle speculation lasted until he and his friends were about halfway back to town, by which time his mind had turned to other pursuits.

Fay was far too busy to think about the dark, sardonic gentleman, and in any case, the incident had been far too trivial to absorb her thoughts for long. The following evening, however, he was there again. She had spent the day looking unsuccessfully for work. Now, as he watched her going about the many tasks that had to be done for the evening performance, he thought that she looked tired.

'You still have plenty to do, I see,' he remarked when, to her surprise, he wandered over to speak to her.

'There is *always* plenty to do,' she replied, carrying on with her ironing whilst she was speaking to him. For some reason, she did not want to look into his eyes.

'Don't you ever wish that you could tread the boards yourself, rather than serve the needs of those who do?' he asked her, picking up a collar which she had just ironed and examining it idly.

She did look up at him then, smiling at the very idea. 'Good gracious no, I should be far too shy,' she answered frankly. His eyes narrowed. The smile which lit up her face revealed her to be a very pretty girl.

'And yet you are not too shy to speak to me,' he murmured. Immediately, she blushed and looked down at her work. Then one of his friends called him over, and there was no more conversation between them.

The following day, Fay went out yet again to look for work with no better fortune than before. There was only one more day to go before the company was to move on, and she was becoming very frightened. The security that she had enjoyed over the past few weeks made the prospect of its cessation seem doubly hard to bear. It seemed as if there would be nothing for it but to throw herself onto Mr Llewellyn's mercy, at least for a short time, little though she wanted to do so. She had made up her mind to do that very thing, and she went to the parlour which had been set aside for his own use, in order to broach that very subject. The door was not quite closed, and before she could knock on the door, she heard her name mentioned.

'You know we will have to let Fay go,' his wife was saying. Mrs Llewellyn had been reluctant to accept her at first, but as soon as she realized that her husband's newest recruit was not some kind of adventuress, she had become quite cordial.

'I very much regret the necessity,' Llewellyn replied. 'She is a good worker and Maisie could do with the help.'

'But we cannot afford to keep her,' insisted his wife. 'Look at the books. Our profits are not at all good at the moment. We cannot afford to feed a single extra mouth.' Fay walked away without bothering to knock. It would be unfair to embarrass the Llewellyns by asking for any more help when they clearly could not afford to give her any. She had a small sum of money from the wages that Mr Llewellyn had paid her and with that she would go in to London. Surely, in such a large place, it would be possible to find employment?

That night, the last one that the company would be spending at The Angel, Fay prepared the costumes with a heavy heart. If I concentrate very hard on what I am doing, I might be able to stop myself from crying, she told herself. It was as if from a long distance, therefore, that she heard her name spoken as she was working and, looking up, she saw Sir Jackson Hooper.

'You look unhappy,' he remarked, surprising her with his perception. 'What is it?'

'It's just that the company is moving on tomorrow,' she replied, trying to sound unconcerned. 'I shall miss all my friends.'

'You enjoy being part of the company,' he observed.

'Yes, very much. Everyone is so friendly.'

'And what will you do when they are gone?' he asked her.

'I have a . . . a relative in London to whom I am going,' she improvized. He smiled ruefully, took a step or two forward so that he was standing immediately in front of her and, before she could guess what he was going to do, he took hold of her chin in his long fingers, bent and kissed her lightly on the mouth.

'And so we are to part,' he murmured. 'Ah well, what might have been!' Fay did not comprehend his meaning, and had no idea how to respond to his caress, so she was not sorry to see him go. She found him rather unsettling.

The next morning, she waved goodbye to the company with a determinedly cheerful face, but with a sinking heart. Only when Angela hugged her did she nearly give way to tears.

'I'm sure we'll meet again,' Angela said reassuringly. 'I've never had a friend quite like you before.'

When the wagon containing the costumes and properties had disappeared from sight, she stood for a time, feeling lonelier than she had ever felt in her life before.

The landlord of The Angel – who had regretfully refused to give her a job, for he had plenty of people to work for him – told her when the stage-coach would be coming through. The Angel was the last staging post on the Great North Road before London itself, and within a very short space of time, she was alighting at The Bull and Mouth in St Martin's-le-Grand.

Everyone else with whom she had travelled on that short journey seemed to have somewhere to go. They either went into the inn, or were met, or set off purposefully into the bustling streets. It had seemed to be a good idea to come to London; now, in the capital city for the first time in her life, she was seized by panic, not knowing where to turn.

In the midst of her anxiety, she heard a well-bred voice saying, 'You look lost, my dear. May I be of any assistance?' Fay turned to see a well-dressed woman of about forty smiling at her pleasantly.

Fay smiled back gratefully, her relief at being spoken to so kindly over-riding her natural caution. 'You are very kind,' she replied. 'I am come from . . . from the country, and need to find some occupation, but I have no idea how to go about it. I don't suppose. . . ?'

'Well, of course,I will help you,' said the lady. 'My name is Lavinia Bellham, and I have for some time been concerned about the plight of girls like yourself who are from the country and have nowhere to go. I have a house set aside for the very purpose of caring for such girls, and you may stay there for a short time until you have found work.'

'You are very kind, ma'am,' Fay repeated, 'but I do not want to take charity from you.'

Mrs Bellham laughed charmingly. 'Do not think any more about it,' she said. 'My husband left me very well to pass, and this venture is part of what I see as my Christian duty. And besides, when I have helped you to a useful occupation, you can pay me back out of your wages, if you wish.' There seemed to be no more to be said, so Fay readily agreed, and went willingly with her new friend to obtain a hackney. 'My house is rather too far away for us to walk to it,' confided Mrs Bellham.

They travelled through the crowded streets and, as they went Mrs Bellham obligingly pointed out some of the sights. On her journey into London, Fay had been far too anxious to notice the passing scenery. Now, she felt able to look about her with interest, and asked her companion to tell her about some of the things that she saw.

As they drew nearer to the house, Fay thought that the streets began to look a little less smart, but as soon as that idea came into her mind, she chided herself inwardly. No doubt keeping a house especially for charitable purposes was expensive. She should just be grateful for having found this obliging new friend, and try to be a little less critical.

They got out of the hackney carriage, and Mrs Bellham paid the driver.

'Got another one then, mother,' he called to her, as he drove off. Fay looked at Mrs Bellham questioningly.

'Some of these drivers are so droll,' she commented, with a light laugh. 'Now come inside and we'll have a cup of tea.'

They were just going up the steps, when a voice that Fay recognized spoke from the pavement. 'If it isn't Mother Bellham and one of her nuns!' The two women turned to see Sir Jackson Hooper looking up at them. When he saw Fay, his expression changed from one of cynical amusement to one of astonishment. 'Fay Prescott! What the deuce are you doing in such company?' Fay looked from him to Mrs Bellham in some surprise. On Mrs Bellham's face was an expression of unmistakable chagrin.

'It's none of your business,' she replied, her accent almost imperceptibly a little less refined than before. 'She's with me willingly.'

'No doubt; but does she know for what purpose?' asked the

baronet, setting his foot on the bottom step.

'Pray, what is this about?' Fay asked, feeling it was time she took a role in this scene. 'Mrs Bellham has been kind enough to offer me lodging—'

Hooper gave a crack of laughter. 'I'll wager she has,' he replied. 'Has she told you what you have to do in order to pay for your lodging?' Fay looked uncertainly at her benefactress, and then at the baronet, who held out his hand imperatively and said 'Come.'

Mrs Bellham caught hold of her arm, none too gently, and said again, 'She came with me willingly.'

Hooper drew closer. 'Do you let her come with me now, or do I shout out here and now at the top of my voice exactly what you do and what you are?'

Mrs Bellham released Fay so suddenly, that she almost fell. 'Take her, then,' she said, her refined accent almost completely gone. 'But mark my words, you're no better than I am in what you intend by her.' Fay was so bemused by this interchange, that she allowed Sir Jackson to steer her into a hackney before she said anything.

Once they were sitting down, she took a deep breath and said, 'Who is that woman, if you please?'

Hooper settled himself in the opposite corner of the carriage and stretched out his long legs in front of him. 'She's a bawd, my dear. She runs a brothel, and obtains new girls by meeting the stages that come into London, and pretending to come to the aid of country girls who know no better. I'm surprised that someone who has lived and worked with a theatrical company should be so naïve.'

Fay turned a little pale at this, but said in a low voice, 'It's the first time I have been to London. I had no idea what to expect.'

'You told me that you had somewhere to go. I take it that was a fabrication?' Fay nodded, looking down at her hands. There was a long silence. Eventually, he said, 'I can offer you two choices: I can take you back to whichever inn you've come from and I'll pay for a night's lodging for you. That will give you more time to look for honest work. Or you can come with me.'

'Come with you?' she echoed in a small voice.

He laughed cynically. 'Oh come, my dear, you've been part of a theatrical company. There's no need for you to play the complete innocent with me. I'll treat you well, and you'll want for nothing. If we suit each other, then the arrangement may continue for some time. When we part, if you've been careful with your money, you should have saved enough to make a new start somewhere. What do you say?' He put out his hand to her as he concluded his speech.

Fay thought about the weary fruitless hours spent trudging the streets, the fear, the hunger, the panic that she had faced before, and the peril that she had only just escaped. Suddenly it seemed as if she could not face it all again. Silently, she put her hand in his.

# Chapter Seven

A knock on her bedroom door roused Fay with a start from the reverie into which she had fallen. Her heart was in her mouth, as she imagined for a brief moment that it might be Sir Jackson, but then common sense reasserted itself. He would hardly come up to her room in broad daylight, in a house to which he was a visitor.

Sitting up and smoothing her gown, she called, 'Come in.' The door opened and Rachel entered, followed by Horsa, carefully carrying a cup of tea. They both looked anxious.

'Are you feeling better?' Rachel asked her. 'We were so worried when you fainted like that.'

'I feel perfectly all right now, thank you,' Fay assured her, standing up. 'I don't usually faint.' Then, recalling what she had heard someone say, she added, 'Perhaps it was the effect of the warmth of the house, after coming in from the cold.'

'I thought that a cup of tea might make you feel better,' said Horsa.

'Thank you, I feel well now, but a cup of tea is just what I need.' It was only when she took a sip that she realized how thirsty she was. She drank the beverage gratefully and did indeed find that she felt much refreshed.

'Aunt was not sure whether you would want to dine in your room, or whether you would feel well enough to come downstairs for dinner,' Rachel said. For the first time, Fay began to wonder what Sir Jackson might have been disclosing about her past life in her absence. In many ways, she would have liked to have played the coward's part and remain in her room, but she decided that she would rather find out straight away what was being said about her, than discover it later.

'I will come downstairs. A change of scene will do me good.' The two girls were about to leave when Fay said, 'Wait a minute. Who carried me upstairs?' She did not really need to hear Horsa's answer.

'Why, Sir Jackson Hooper. He looked ever so concerned.'

When Rachel and Horsa had left her, she changed for dinner. She had taken very few clothes with her when she had left Sir Jackson's protection, and her two evening gowns, both of which she had worn at Old Drove House, had been bought for her by him. Normally she wore them on alternate evenings, and tonight it should have been the turn of her yellow evening gown. The yellow one had been Sir Jackson's favourite, however, and she did not want him to think that she was dressing to please him, so she took out the bronze one instead.

Once changed, and conscious of looking her best, she felt a little more confident. It had occurred to her that if the baronet had disclosed the scandalous details of her past to her employers, then someone, probably Mrs Stratford, would have appeared upstairs by now in order to dismiss her forthwith. Nevertheless, the danger had certainly not passed, for it remained to be seen what use Sir Jackson would make of the information that he had.

She had hoped to be one of the first downstairs in order to speak to him as soon as possible, but perhaps the faint had affected her more than she thought, for even the simplest of tasks seemed to take her longer. When eventually she arrived downstairs, she was almost the last with, unsurprisingly, only Mr Proudfoot to come.

As she entered the room, her eyes were drawn instantly to the man whose mistress she had been. He was dressed in coat and breeches in a matching shade of pewter, with a black and silver striped waistcoat. He looked much as she remembered him, except that if anything, he had lost a little weight, and there was a touch of grey at his temples. At her entrance, he smiled and walked straight over to her, and for a moment she almost shrank back, unsure as to his intentions.

'My dear cousin,' he exclaimed, shocking her rigid. 'I'm very glad to see that you are recovered.' He took her hand and kissed it, and it took all the will-power of which she was capable to resist snatching it away from him. Of all the eventualities that she had anticipated, that he should claim a family relationship had never occurred to her. 'If only I could be sure that it was not my sudden and unexpected advent that caused your temporary *malaise*,' he went on, grinning impishly.

'It . . . it was the heat,' Fay stammered.

'Sir Jackson,' exclaimed Mrs Stratford, coming over to them. 'I did not know that you were related to Miss Prescott.'

He smiled disarmingly. 'Only very distantly,' he replied. 'But we did meet on several occasions in London, and I try to have a care of her.' He smiled again at Fay as he spoke, but she moved away from him as soon as possible and, indeed, did her best to avoid him for the rest of the evening. Others present – notably Mrs Stratford – seemed to be impressed at her elevation to the aristocracy. Fay herself could only feel alarmed and deeply mistrustful of his motives, and she retired to bed with no great feeling of optimism with regard to her ability to sleep that night.

So unsettled was she that after the rest of the household had settled down for the night, it was almost a relief when there was a soft tap on her door. With a fast beating heart, she opened it cautiously, to find Sir Jackson standing on the threshold.

'What do you want?' she asked him in a furious whisper.

'What do you think you are doing here? Do you want to compromise me completely?'

'Let me in then, or that's exactly what I *will* do if I'm discovered standing here.' She looked at him doubtfully, then seeing the sense of what he said, stepped back in order to allow him to enter. He stood there in her room, clad in a long, blue brocade dressing-gown, his hair hanging straight to his shoulders, and the sight of him thus was suddenly so familiar that for a moment or two, she almost felt herself transported back in time.

Then pulling herself together, she said sharply, 'Why are you here? Or perhaps I might be able to guess.'

'I should imagine you might,' he answered casually. 'I'm here quite simply because I was invited. I'm a friend of Hervey Bragg who's also coming, and so Mrs Stratford invited me. One has to go *somewhere* for Christmas, you know, and there's no reason why I should not be here as a guest. The question that does need to be asked, though, is what the deuce are you doing here as a governess, or duenna, or whatever it is that you are?'

'I have to earn my bread honourably, Jackson. Perhaps you thought I couldn't do that.'

He flushed. 'That was unworthy, Fay,' he said quietly.

'What of your wife?' she asked him, also flushing. 'Does not she have to go somewhere for Christmas?'

'I am still unmarried,' he replied shortly.

'Your betrothed, then.'

'My engagement is over.'

Fay smiled cynically. 'What a lucky escape – for her,' she remarked.

'Don't be a bitch, Fay,' he said calmly. 'It don't suit you.'

Fay stared at him for a moment in silence, before saying, 'When I asked you why you were here, what I meant was, why are you here in my bed chamber?'

He shrugged. 'You've been avoiding me all evening, and I've had no chance to speak to you. There are one or two things that

I want to say to you for which I don't want an audience.'

'And if I don't want to hear them?' she asked, her chin high.

'Oh, for God's sake, Fay!' he exclaimed, running his hand through his hair. He sighed, then went on, 'I want to ask you one question, and to give you one assurance, that's all. By your leave?' he finished in an ironic tone. She shrugged. 'Why did you run off without telling me where you were going and why?' he asked her.

'I was free to come and go as I chose,' she responded. 'You weren't my—' she stopped abruptly.

'Your keeper?' he finished, raising one eyebrow. 'Well, yes, as a matter of fact I was, but let that pass. Of course you were free to choose. You always were, you know. But obviously you're not going to tell me any more, so the only other thing I wanted to say was that I won't give you away. No one will learn about our relationship from me.' He took a step closer to her, and took hold of her chin in one hand. 'Fairy Fay,' he added. It had been his pet name for her.

Fay smiled cynically. 'Perhaps I can guess the price of your silence,' she said.

He stared at her for a moment, then let go of her, turned, and walked to the door. 'I don't suppose you can,' he answered, his hand on the door-knob. 'But rest assured, the price isn't re-admission into your bed. You obviously won't tell me why you ran away from me, but clearly you decided you had had enough of me, and I don't force myself on to unwilling women. Goodnight.'

He was about to leave, when she said, 'Wait.'

He turned back to her and grinned wolfishly. 'My dear Fay,' he purred.

She held up her hand. 'Why, if you don't want to thrust any unwanted intimacy on to me, have you claimed me as your cousin?'

He took a step or two back into the room. 'Simple,' he said.

'You and I know one another rather well. We had a shared life in London. It would be so easy for one of us to forget; to use the other's Christian name, for example, or to make one of those 'do you remember?' sort of remarks, and then there would be all kind of gossip and speculation. Oh, don't worry. I shan't presume! I'll be the most proper cousin you ever saw, and by establishing a distant relationship, we kill any gossip stone dead before it's even begun.'

'And of course, you have always been so sensitive about gossip,' said Fay sarcastically.

'Use your brains, girl,' he retorted impatiently. 'Any gossip about the two of us would hurt you rather than me. What did I do, after all? I went to bed with a girl from a theatre company.'

'I wasn't what you thought me,' she said hotly.

He took a step or two towards her. 'Quite the little actress altogether, aren't you?' he said nastily. 'And what particular lie did you tell to get this position?'

'No lie,' she replied. 'I simply expunged you from my history, and I wish to God that I really could.' Hooper lost a little of his colour, stared at her for a moment or two, then left the room, closing the door behind him rather more loudly than Fay would have liked. She was left feeling relieved, on the whole, but also very perplexed. At least it seemed that he would not betray her to this household, which was a great cause of thankfulness. In the short time since she had arrived at Old Drove House, she had become fond of the family, and especially of Rachel and Horsa, and she did not want to leave. She had so much hoped that this position would be a new start for her. It would be too bad if one mistake came back to destroy what she had achieved.

The majority of the guests were due the following day, and Fay was very relieved when Mrs Stratford gave her wholehearted approval to the arrangements that she and Rachel had made over the past few days. They met at the breakfast-table, where they, together with Rachel and Horsa, were the only ones present.

'I could not have done better myself,' said that lady sincerely. 'But why did you not tell me that Sir Jackson Hooper was your cousin?'

Fay coloured slightly, but she had prepared herself for this question, and said simply, 'I did not want to presume on the relationship, ma'am, which truth to tell is a very distant one. And besides, I did not know that he was to be one of the guests. Anyway, I did not think that it would make any difference.'

'My dear Fay,' exclaimed Mrs Stratford, '– you do not mind if I call you Fay, I hope? – all the difference in the world!'

'I don't see that it makes any difference,' said Horsa, in matter-of-fact tones. 'She's just as nice as she was before. Miss Prescott, can we all call you Fay, if my aunt does so?'

Fay smiled. 'I have no objection, but it is for your aunt to say.'

'Well, perhaps Rachel may, as she is older. But I think that you, Horsa, should continue to address your governess as Miss Prescott.' Horsa looked mutinous, but knew better than to say anything.

After breakfast, the only thing that still remained to be done to prepare the house for guests was to put up the greenery which had been collected the previous day. It had been steeped in water overnight to keep it fresh. After they had finished breakfast, Rachel, Fay and Horsa set to with a will, ably assisted by one of the footmen who, following careful instructions, went up the ladder in order to fasten up the higher branches.

It was as they were almost finished that Sir Jackson and Magnus returned from their ride. As they entered, Fay overheard Magnus saying, 'So if I can read some of it to you later, sir. . . .' She turned to look at him, and saw that his handsome young face looked flushed and eager, and bore an expression that was very like hero-worship. He had clearly been telling the baronet about his play, surprising in itself when Fay considered how anxious the young man was to keep his writing secret from his aunt. She could not imagine the older man being the slightest bit interested in such a project, or even tolerant of hearing about it, so she was surprised at his answer.

'By all means – although I think you'll find my Latin is a little rusty.'

'I say, that looks splendid,' said Magnus, looking at the results of the morning's work. 'And Cliffe has been up the ladder for you. I am glad! I was afraid that that might fall to my lot, after yesterday.'

'And what do *you* think of our efforts, sir?' Rachel asked Sir Jackson.

'You have achieved as artistic a result as I would have expected from ladies of such excellent taste,' he replied with aplomb. 'But there is one tiny omission, which I was wondering whether it would be possible to repair.'

'Oh really,' said Fay. 'In what way have we fallen short?'

'There appears to be no mistletoe for the kissing bunch,' he replied innocently, but with a twinkle in his eye.

'Surely that is not necessary,' Fay said coldly.

Here, unexpectedly, Rachel came to the baronet's support. 'Oh no, there must be mistletoe,' she declared positively. Then, colouring slightly, she went on, 'I think that they have some at Fir Tree Farm. I will go and get some, if you like. Do you want to come with me, Horsa?' Her younger sister agreed eagerly.

'Very well then,' murmured Fay. 'If it is essential, then let us all go together. We have been inside all morning, and the exercise will do us good.'

'Be careful of the sudden changes of temperature, Cousin,' warned Sir Jackson. 'I should hate to see you faint again.'

'I assure you, that is not at all likely,' replied Fay frostily. 'Come, girls, let us go while the day is still bright.'

As they were walking to Fir Tree Farm, Horsa said, 'Don't you like your cousin, Miss Prescott?'

Not comprehending her meaning at first, Fay said blankly, 'My cousin?'

'Yes; Sir Jackson Hooper. Don't you like him?'

Fay coloured, and hoped that Horsa would put it down to the exertion of the walk. 'Oh. Yes . . . yes of course, I . . . I like him very well. Why do you ask?'

'Well, you do not call him 'cousin' although he does you, and you don't smile when you speak to him.'

Fay thought rapidly. The last thing she wanted was for her behaviour towards him to draw attention to herself and arouse the least suspicion. 'I don't want to presume,' she said at last. 'After all, he is a man of rank, and I am a . . . a kind of servant. And I don't really know him very well.'

'Well, I think that it would be a good idea to cultivate his acquaintance,' said Horsa, slashing at some nettles with a stick that she had picked up. 'He might be able to recommend you to a good situation.'

Fay did not know how to reply to this, so she was very relieved when Rachel exclaimed, 'Don't do that, Horsa. Just look at the state of your glove!' In the ensuing argument, the subject of Sir Jackson Hooper was dropped.

They arrived at the farm just as Joe was crossing the yard, dressed in his working clothes. He looked tanned and healthy, and Fay could easily understand why Rachel should flush and look flustered at the sight of him. For her own part, she found that on this occasion, she could look at him without the slightest flutter, and she was glad of it.

'Good morning, ladies,' he said, in what could be described as an educated country accent. 'You have had a cold day for your walk.'

'Good morning, Mr Fairburn,' replied Fay. 'Cold, perhaps, but at least it was bright and crisp.'

'Joe, we haven't any mistletoe at the house; do you think we can have some of yours?' burst in Rachel impulsively, impatient at this polite interchange.

'Rachel!' exclaimed Fay, in shocked tones. Then she went on, 'Rachel has expressed our need, if not as courteously as one would wish.'

He smiled. 'Christmas makes us all excited, I reckon, from the greatest to the least,' he replied. 'We have plenty of mistletoe this year, and I'll be glad to get you some. Why don't you go inside and have something to eat or drink with Mother, and I'll gather you a bunch?'

Rachel opened her mouth to protest, but before she could say anything, Fay said, 'Thank you Mr Fairburn. Come, Rachel; Horsa.' Rachel looked reluctant, even a little sulky, but she did as she was bid, and soon the three visitors were being warmly welcomed by Mrs Fairburn. 'I expect you must be very busy, with Christmas nearly here,' remarked Fay, when they were all settled comfortably with tea and cake.

'I am indeed,' replied Mrs Fairburn, 'and like you folk up at the big house, we have guests coming to stay. My niece married a lawyer who works in March, and they are to come for a few days.'

'You must be looking forward to that very much,' said Fay.

'I certainly am, and all the more so because they have a new baby that none of us has seen yet.'

'May we come and see you at Christmas?' Rachel asked.

Mrs Fairburn smiled. 'By all means, if you've the time, but I expect you'll be very busy with your own visitors.'

'I could never be too busy to see you,' Rachel responded, returning her smile.

It did not take Joe long to gather the mistletoe, and soon he was putting his head round the door, letting them know that it was ready. 'I'll come back with you and carry it for you if you like,' he said. Rachel looked at Fay pleadingly, and it was quite beyond her to be so hard-hearted as to say 'no'.

'Thank you,' she answered him. 'You are very kind.' Although

Fay made sure that there was no opportunity for private conversation between Rachel and Joe, she could not help thinking that this was rather a poor sop to offer her conscience when she considered how disloyal she was being to Mrs Stratford. After they had walked a little way, she said to him, 'For how long has your family farmed this land?'

'For about as long as there's been a big house here, I reckon,' he answered. 'Fairburns have always been tenants here.'

'So you have followed your father,' Fay said.

'That's right,' he replied. 'I'd like to farm for myself one day, and be no man's tenant, but that'll take some saving for.'

'Is the land good around here?' she asked him.

'Yes, very good. But I'm not always convinced that we get the best out of it.' As they walked along, he went on to describe some of his ideas on land management, and she allowed her attention to be taken by Rachel's expression and reactions. Joe was talking about something which should logically have been of no interest to a girl of her age and situation, but her expression was one of keen interest, and the questions which she put from time to time, and the comments that she made, showed that she had some understanding of the issues involved. Fay could not help wondering whether in fact she would make a good farmer's wife, and if it was a kindness to take her to London at all. She certainly did not appear to look forward to the opportunity, unlike Horsa who clearly could not wait for her chance to go. The younger girl was taking no interest in the conversation about farming, and looked as if she might be ready to resume her earlier occupation of destroying nettles with a stick.

When they reached the house, Joe offered to come in and tie up the mistletoe wherever it needed to go. Fay was about to say that this was not necessary, when she encountered another pleading look from Rachel, and said instead, 'That would be most kind, Mr Fairburn.' It would do no harm to allow the young man to perform that service for them, and it would save taking the footmen from necessary tasks at this busy time.

She conducted him to the hall where the kissing bunch was to be hung. The ladder had been left out, and all that was necessary was for someone to hold the bottom of it whilst Joe climbed up with the completed garland. She was about to offer to do this herself, when one of the doors leading into the hall opened, and Sir Jackson appeared. He was dressed for riding in a coat of green cloth, buckskin breeches and top boots. Before this Christmas visit, Fay had always seen him in town dress, and she was interested to see how well country clothes suited him, and how comfortable and at ease he seemed to be in them.

'So you have collected the mistletoe,' he said. Then, turning to Joe and putting out his hand, he said, 'Good morning. I don't believe we've met. I'm Jackson Hooper.' Fay was surprised to hear him address Joe as an equal. She had not expected him to be so much at ease with his fellow men.

Joe grasped the hand that was held out to him. 'Joe Fairburn,' the farmer replied, showing not the least sense of self-conscious-ness. 'I'm one of Mr Proudfoot's tenants, as was my father before me.'

The baronet grinned. 'I dare say,' he replied. 'What is your fighting weight?'

Now Joe did look embarrassed. 'Fifteen stone, but I don't get to fight these days. There's too much to do on the farm.'

'Let me know if ever you are in London,' said Hooper, reaching inside his coat and handing Joe one of his cards. 'There's someone I would like to introduce you to. Now, shall we get these decorations hung?' Joe mounted the ladder whilst Sir Jackson held the bottom and Rachel stood with the finished kissing bunch in her hand, ready to pass it to Joe when he gave the word. Fay and Horsa stood watching, Fay thinking of the way in which the floor had been polished that week, and praying that the ladder would not slip, as Joe was so big.

'I should hate to climb a ladder, wouldn't you?' Horsa asked her fervently, and Fay agreed. Taking her eyes off Joe, her gaze met that of the baronet, and she was surprised to see a cynical expression on his face.

Once the bunch was safely attached, Joe came down the ladder carefully. 'Are there other places where the mistletoe needs to be hung?' he asked.

'Yes, I'll show you,' said Rachel eagerly. She led the way and Joe followed with the ladder, with Horsa bringing up the rear, carrying the remaining mistletoe. Fay turned to go with them, but Sir Jackson caught hold of her arm.

'The farmer isn't for you,' he said.

She shook him off. 'And what if I say that he is?' she demanded, chin up, glaring at him. He caught hold of her again, this time by both arms, and pulled her against him. He looked upwards and, following his gaze, she saw that they were standing immediately below the kissing bunch. He bent towards her, but just as he was about to kiss her mouth, the bell pealed and the butler entered the hall. As he opened the door, Peter Frith, who was standing on the threshold, was treated to the sight of Sir Jackson Hooper bestowing a chaste kiss upon Miss Prescott's cheek. The young clergyman looked healthy and vigorous from his walk, and he looked expectantly at the couple standing under the kissing bunch.

'Happy Christmas, Cousin,' said the baronet.

At this, Fay could do no other than reply, 'And the same to you – Cousin.' She then stepped forward and said, 'Good morning, Mr Frith. How good of you to call! You must allow me to present you to my . . . my cousin. This is The Revd Peter Frith, who is the vicar of this parish. Mr Frith, this is my distant cousin, Sir Jackson Hooper.' The two men bowed to one another and, when the greetings were all made, the butler opened the door for them to go into the saloon.

'Did you know that your cousin was living here, sir, or was it just a lucky chance?' Mr Frith asked rather stiffly once they were inside the room.

'It was a complete surprise to us both,' said Sir Jackson, smiling at Fay. 'In fact, my cousin was so surprised to see me that she fainted dead away.'

Mr Frith looked shocked. 'My dear Miss Prescott!' he exclaimed. 'Had I known that you were unwell, I should have visited you!'

Fay shook her head. 'Mr Frith, you make too much of it,' she said. 'And so does my cousin. It was the sudden warmth of the house after an excursion into the cold air that made me faint. In any case, I made a very quick recovery.'

'I am glad to hear it,' he answered, still looking concerned. 'But I must say that I myself am surprised to hear that you have a cousin, and such a distinguished one at that. I had formed the impression that you were all alone in the world.'

Fay could not think how to answer this, so was glad when the baronet interposed smoothly, 'Fay is a very independent young woman, but I help her when I can.'

Peter Frith looked approving. 'It is all very well for a young lady to be independent,' he said, 'but there are times when the guidance of a gentleman is needed.'

Fay ground her teeth silently.

'You are quite right,' agreed Sir Jackson, nodding sagely. 'But may I, on my host's behalf, offer you some refreshment?'

'Thank you, no' replied the vicar regretfully. 'I know that guests are expected, so I will get out of your way. I merely came to bring Agnes's reply to the very kind invitation to join the party for dinner on Christmas Day. We shall be happy to do so.'

'I shall pass on your acceptance and your thanks,' said Sir Jackson.

'Thank you.' The vicar cleared his throat, and went on 'I am also given to understand that there may be dancing on that occasion and, if so, I would like to apply for Miss Prescott's hand for one of the dances, if you, sir, will permit it, of course.'

'Certainly,' declared Sir Jackson, in his most avuncular of

accents. Fay looked aghast, unsure which of them to hit first, the vicar for applying to her 'relative' rather than to her, or the baronet for accepting the privilege which having the status of a male relative conferred.

'One moment, gentlemen,' she said, after taking a deep breath. 'Sir Jackson, I am of age and can speak for myself. Mr Frith, I thank you for your invitation, but as I may be needed to chaperon the ladies, I cannot say with any certainty that I will be able to dance with you.'

Mr Frith looked a little disappointed, but said cheerfully enough, 'Oh, well, time will tell. I must be on my way. Pray give my regards to everyone.'

'How dare you!' exclaimed Fay, as soon as the door had closed behind him.

'How dare I what?' asked Sir Jackson, his hands casually in his breeches pockets.

'Assume responsibility for my life – my decisions! It is none of your business with whom I may or may not dance!'

'I know that,' he replied. 'When I said certainly, I wasn't saying that he may dance with you. I was simply saying that he might ask you. Though if I were you, unless I was very interested in him, I should find another partner. He looks a bit too stiff to me to make a good dancer.'

'But you had no business to say "certainly"!' she stormed. 'You had no business to say anything at all!'

'But I had to say *something*,' he answered reasonably. 'If I'd just stood there looking at him, he'd have thought me either devilish rude or deaf!'

Fay tried again. 'This would never have happened if you hadn't insisted upon saying that we were related,' she said wretchedly.

'No, and what would he have thought about my kissing you under the mistletoe, *then*?' he demanded. At that point, Horsa came hurrying in demanding that they both come and see how the mistletoe looked in the other places where they had hung it, and so Fay was relieved of the necessity of answering this question.

# Chapter Eight

It was not until after luncheon that the rest of the guests began to arrive. The first to appear were Mr and Mrs Napier, with their son and daughter. Mr Roger Napier, a stocky, sandy-haired young man of twenty-two, took after his father in appearance and, like his father, also appeared to be a quiet, steady sort of man. Miss Chloe Napier, at eighteen, was slim and dark and whilst lively enough, showed at times a gentle restfulness that was very engaging. She and Rachel seemed to hit it off immediately, and soon looked as if they were talking secrets. Observing them with their heads together, Fay decided that a friend like Chloe, with experience of the London season and all the excitement that entailed, but who had clearly not allowed it to go to her head, would do more to take Rachel's mind off Joe Fairburn than anything else.

Lord Bragg was the next to arrive. He was of a similar age to Sir Jackson, and of much the same height and build, but with light-brown hair, and heavier features. He looked to be a good-humoured man, the kind who would cheer everyone up after a day or two's boredom, when bad weather kept the company inside. He and the baronet greeted one another as good friends and, for a moment or two, Fay held her breath until she heard that Lord Bragg had been abroad with the diplomatic service until very recently. There was no chance that he could have seen her in Jackson's company.

Unexpectedly, Bragg had brought with him his younger brother, the Honourable Toby Bragg, who was like his brother in appearance, but with an extra touch of mischief in his eye. He and Magnus soon made friends, and it was not long before Magnus was taking him off to the stables in order to look at his horse.

After they had gone, Fay was surprised to see a look of relief on Sir Jackson's face. He turned to her and said under his breath, 'Perhaps, now that Magnus has other company, I shall be able to avoid dredging up my very rusty Latin.'

Fay could not help laughing. 'Has he definitely decided to have his *whole* play in Latin?' she asked him. 'He had only just hit upon the idea when last he spoke to me about it.'

'Oh had he? Well, all I can say is that he is a very quick worker, and he knows whole chunks of it off by heart,' replied Sir Jackson. 'And the worst of it is, I can't even drift off elsewhere because he keeps asking me questions about what he has just told me.'

'Is he going for the dyke or the lake?' Fay asked him. He raised his brows quizzically, and Fay told him what Magnus had said before about his anxieties with regard to staging his play.

Unlike Peter Frith, the baronet immediately appreciated the humour of the situation, and let out such a loud laugh that the other occupants of the room stared at them, and Fay was forced to say that they were enjoying an old family joke, of no interest to anyone else. As Sir Jackson stopped laughing, he looked down at her, his eyes still alight with amusement, and suddenly Fay noticed, as if for the first time, how handsome he was. At the same moment, she was conscious of the stirring of some emotion within her to which she shrank from giving a name.

Last to arrive were Mrs Fleetwood and her daughter Lucilla. Mrs Fleetwood was a handsome woman with regular features and a fine head of chestnut hair. Her daughter was similarly well-looking, but she had developed an air of precocious self-consequence which was rather disturbing in one of only seventeen. Since Rachel and Chloe had struck up a friendship so quickly, Fay hoped that they would have the good manners not to exclude Lucilla.

The guests were welcomed with hot punch on their arrival and, obedient to Mrs Stratford's wishes, Fay was standing by, ready to help serve it. Most of the guests took their punch with a smile and a thank you, but Mrs Fleetwood took hers without a word, and wandered over to speak to Sir Jackson.

'My dear Jackson, of all the delightful things,' she exclaimed, laying her hand on his sleeve. 'Why did you not tell me that you were going to be here? We could have shared transport.' The expression in her eyes seemed to suggest that there might have been other things that they could have shared as well!

'My dear Deborah, until a short time ago, I had no idea that I would be coming here myself,' he answered, in a similarly bantering tone.

'I'm sure you do not really expect me to believe that,' she murmured.

He laughed gently. 'I am sure that I have no right to expect you to believe anything,' he replied blandly. She looked at him with a completely nonplussed expression, clearly having no idea as to his meaning, or even whether he was being serious or not.

Eventually, she gave a little laugh and said, 'It doesn't matter after all. We can enjoy Christmas together, and that is all that counts.'

'You flatter me, ma'am,' replied the baronet. 'But come, you must allow me to introduce my cousin to you.' Mrs Fleetwood looked around at the assembled guests, expecting to be introduced to one of them, or perhaps to one of the Proudfoot family, and the expression on her face when she found herself meeting the young woman who was handing out the glasses was quite ludicrous to behold.

'Miss Prescott,' she drawled, her brows raised. 'I had no idea that you were Jackson's cousin.'

'Our relationship is a distant one,' said Fay.

'Not so distant that I do not keep a watchful eye on her,' put in the baronet.

'How chivalrous,' said Mrs Fleetwood, turning away from Fay. 'And talking of your family, tell me Jackson, how is your mother these days?' They wandered away towards the window. Fay watched them go and, as she saw his dark head bent to hear something that Mrs Fleetwood was saying, wondered whether he had introduced the two of them deliberately in order to humiliate her. Mrs Fleetwood's manner towards him certainly indicated that they knew one another very well indeed, and Fay could not help wondering whether perhaps they were, or had been, lovers. After all, it had been some months since she had left his protection, and he was a man who liked the company of women. She could not help feeling surprised and a little disappointed, however, that he should be drawn to such an artificial kind of female.

Be that as it may, although she watched the couple as carefully and as unobtrusively as she could both then and later, during dinner and afterwards, she could detect no sign of any kind which indicated any special relationship between them. In fact, if anything, Hooper seemed to be paying more attention to Rachel and she, responding to his interest, became more animated than Fay had ever seen her in company before. This alerted her to a previously unforeseen danger, and she resolved to speak frankly to the baronet on this subject as soon as possible, and also to put Rachel on her guard against the wiles of an experienced man-about-town.

An opportunity to do this occurred the very next day. The gentlemen all chose to ride after breaking their fast early, whereas the ladies who were visiting decided to breakfast in their rooms. Fay, Rachel and Horsa therefore had the table to themselves – a normal state of affairs prior to the visitors' arrival, but given that the house was now so full of visitors, rather unexpected. Fay was not sorry. Most of the guests seemed perfectly amiable, but she had caught Mrs Fleetwood eyeing her with a measuring look, which she had found quite unnerving.

'What should we do, Miss Prescott?' Horsa asked. 'Should we wait for everyone to get up, or do we just do what we normally do?'

'I don't see why we should change our plans at all,' said Rachel, a hint of belligerence in her tone. 'After all, we didn't invite them, did we?'

Fay could not help smiling at this, but she said, 'That would not be a very courteous attitude, would it? After all, it's quite possible that at least some of the guests, the young people for example, have no more chosen to be here than you have chosen to have them stay; and I know that you, Rachel, get on very well with Miss Napier in particular. I think though, in response to your question, Horsa, that we do not need to change all our plans. In fact, some of the younger guests might like to join in with our reading.'

'Can Matty and Jenny still come to read with us?' Rachel asked, in the same challenging tone.

'By all means,' replied Fay. 'As long as their mother does not need them at home.'

'May we all walk over to the farm and tell them after breakfast?' asked Horsa, as she took another piece of toast. 'Nobody else is up to read with us yet.'

'Yes, very well,' Fay answered. 'It would be a good opportunity to say thank you again for the mistletoe. But we must not linger, in case any of the guests *does* get up.'

The visit to Fir Tree Farm was soon made. There was no sign of Joe on the premises, so Rachel had to be content with seeing his sisters and his mother. Fay watched her carefully, but was relieved to find that no notes were passed on this occasion. Mrs Fairburn was pleased to see them, and equally gratified to hear that Matty and Jenny were still welcome at the house, but she did say anxiously, 'Are you sure, Miss Prescott? I know that the house is full of people of quality, and I don't want my girls to intrude where they don't belong.'

Privately thinking that the behaviour of the two Fairburn girls was certainly better than that of Mrs Fleetwood and her daughter to name but two, Fay said out loud, 'Matty and Jenny have excellent manners. In fact, sometimes I think that they are better behaved than Rachel and Horsa.' The Proudfoot girls grinned at each other. 'I do know, however, that you are expecting visitors yourself,' Fay went on, 'and I am sure that there may be times when you will need Matty and Jenny here. Shall we agree that if either of us feels that things are getting too busy, that we shall cancel the arrangement as a temporary measure until after the Christmas season?' Mrs Fairburn readily agreed with this sensible suggestion and they parted on as good terms as ever.

From Fir Tree Farm, it was possible to enter the grounds of Old Drove House in two ways. To get to the main entrance, any kind of horse-drawn conveyance would need to take the road that swept round to the left where the boundary wall was reached, and follow the course of that wall to the posts that marked the entrance to the drive, first passing the church and the vicarage on the left. The main entrance was also the one that would be taken if a visit to the village of Wimblington was intended. Anyone on foot or on horseback, however, could continue straight ahead down a narrow lane that led to a side gate. This gate opened immediately into the gardens, and those who used it would find themselves able to walk through the trees and across the lawns, reaching the house in a matter of minutes.

Fay and the girls went through the side gate, and Fay gave Horsa permission to run on ahead. This gave her the opportunity to say to Rachel, 'I am glad of the chance to speak privately with you. Something happened last night which concerned me a little, and I thought that it would be sensible to speak to you about it.' Rachel said nothing. When Fay had started to talk to her, she had been very afraid that she might say something about Joe. Since the incident that was worrying Fay had clearly taken place the previous evening, that could not be the case, and Rachel was so relieved that she felt she could hear whatever it was that Fay wanted to say without the slightest concern.

Fay went on, 'I noticed that Sir Jackson Hooper—'

'Your cousin,' put in Rachel.

'Yes, my . . . my cousin, was paying you some attention last night.'

Rachel smiled. 'Yes, he was very amusing. He made me laugh,' she replied.

Fay pressed her lips together before saying, 'You will forgive me if I tell you that you are not the first young lady who has found him amusing. He is a practised man-about-town, and being attentive to young ladies is his stock-in-trade. I should hate you to think that he was being serious.'

Rachel laughed. It had suddenly occurred to her that to pretend an interest in Sir Jackson Hooper might effectively throw those in authority over her off the scent of her real romance with Joe. 'I had no idea of his being serious,' she replied. 'I never thought that he was doing anything other than flirting agreeably. Not but what even the most confirmed flirt usually settles down eventually if he finds the right woman,' she added, with a sideways look at her companion.

'That is not always true,' Fay replied in subdued tones. 'Believe me, I know.'

'Fay, he is your relative,' Rachel said impulsively. 'You said before that you didn't dislike him, but you don't sound as though you approve of him very much.' They were now coming to the corner of the house, around which they would go in order to approach it from the back and enter by the door that opened on to the terrace.

'I don't approve of his way of life,' Fay admitted, anxious not to make Rachel think that there was anything unusual in their relationship. 'But I assure you that I like my kinsman very well.' At that moment, Sir Jackson came round the corner and met them from the opposite direction.

'You relieve me exceedingly, Cousin,' he said grinning impishly. 'Good morning, ladies. Have you had an agreeable walk?'

'Yes, thank you, Sir Jackson,' replied Rachel, with a curtsy. 'We have been to Fir Tree Farm to say thank you for the mistletoe. Did you have an agreeable ride?'

'It depends what you mean by agreeable,' he replied. 'Sadly, I have proved to be such an appreciative audience that Magnus has chosen my company in preference to Roger Napier's.' He gave a little sigh. 'Paying close attention to Latin poetry on horseback has never been one of my skills, but I believe my ability is increasing.'

'Poetry?' exclaimed Fay involuntarily. 'Has he abandoned his play, then?'

'By no means. It is simply that Magnus has decided that it should be in verse. I am now having to brush up on my knowledge of Latin words that rhyme!'

'*Non omnia possumus omnes,*' Fay murmured.

Sir Jackson turned towards her with an arrested look. 'I didn't realize that you knew Latin,' he said.

'You never asked,' she replied.

'What does that mean, if you please?' Rachel asked.

'It means, my dear, that we are not all capable of everything, which is undoubtedly true, but sadly, my cousin's use of that particular tag at this time shows her low opinion of my Latin scholarship. But I do not repine! I take comfort in the fact that I will surely improve with practice. And, furthermore, Magnus's Latin drama provided a welcome diversion. The countryside around here, I am afraid to say, is deuced flat.'

'It's in the nature of the fens to be so,' retorted Fay, already

regretting the previous friendly interchange. 'I wonder you both-
ered to come, if you don't like it.'

The baronet smiled wryly at Rachel. 'You see, we breed
termagants in the family,' he said to her. Then, turning to Fay, he
went on, 'My dear cousin, how will Miss Rachel ever learn how
to go on in society, when you set her such a bad example?'

Fay turned a fulminating glance upon him, but she made no
reply to this inflammatory comment. Instead, she turned to
Rachel and said, 'Will you please make sure that Horsa has put
away her outdoor things properly? I will be upstairs shortly, but
I wish to have a few words with my cousin in private first.'
Rachel sketched another curtsy, then disappeared into the house.
'A word with you, *Cousin*,' she said to Sir Jackson as soon as the
younger woman had gone inside.

He raised his brows. 'So you accept our relationship,' he
exclaimed. 'How gratifying!'

'You may not be so gratified when you hear what I have to say
to you,' she replied. 'Shall we walk about beneath the trees?'

'By all means,' he agreed, walking with her to the place she
had indicated. 'Unless, of course, you would like to hit me, in
which case I would prefer a little more privacy.'

'Why? So you can hit me back?'

He caught hold of her arm then, causing her to stop in her
tracks. 'Have I ever hit you?' he demanded. 'Answer me!' She
noticed that his face was a little pale.

'No,' she replied honestly. 'You never have. I'm sorry. That
was unfair of me.'

'You always did have the ability to disarm me,' he said ruefully,
releasing her. As he did so, she breathed a silent sigh of relief. His
closeness was beginning to affect her strangely.

'Beneath the trees will do very well,' she said quickly. 'I shan't
hit you.' When they had reached the appointed place and were
walking beneath a group of beech trees – all of which were now
bare, but which would undoubtedly look magnificent newly

leaved in spring, or dressed in gold in the autumn, and which even now had a certain austere majesty – she said, 'I observed last night that you were paying marked attention to Rachel.'

'Rachel is a charming girl,' he replied, in what Fay considered to be the most brazen way.

'She is not for you,' she said firmly. 'You must be twice her age.'

'I would think, almost exactly,' he agreed, not noticeably dashed. 'It may surprise you, but I find that she brings out the paternal instinct in me. I think I should have made rather a good father.' Fay stumbled over a clump of grass, and the baronet caught hold of her arm. He looked into her face, but apart from looking a little paler than usual, she seemed to be perfectly all right.

'Take care you do not mislead her as to the seriousness of your intentions,' she warned him. 'Girls of that age are very impressionable, and Rachel is far more vulnerable than many, because of her sheltered upbringing. She has no idea how to distinguish between a confirmed rake and an honest man.'

'Which leaves me in no doubt into which category you place me,' he remarked. 'Did you actually say that I was a rake?'

'I said that you were a practised man-about-town,' replied Fay, feeling embarrassed without knowing why.

'That sounds like much the same thing, only wrapped up in clean linen,' he observed. 'Has it occurred to you, my dear, that by describing me to her in that way, you have probably made me even more fascinating than before?'

'What do you mean?' she asked him.

'It appears to me that quite a number of girls toy with the idea of reforming a rake – or rather *trans*forming him – by the love of a good woman, you know.'

She stared at him for a long moment. Then she declared, 'Impossible – as I know from experience. But hurt Rachel, and you will have me to reckon with.' So saying, she turned to walk back across the grass to the house, but before she had got very far, he had caught hold of her arm to detain her.

'I wouldn't dream of hurting Rachel,' he said to her. 'But tell me, Fay: when did we develop this strange ability to hurt one another?' She stared at him for a long moment; this time when she walked away, he made no attempt to hold her back, but stood watching her, his face thoughtful.

Fay hurried inside and went to her room, her mind fully occupied with the conversation that had just taken place, and especially with the last words that the baronet had spoken. For so long, she had assumed that she had been the one who had been hurt during the course of their relationship. Now, for the first time, it occurred to her that *she* might have hurt *him*. The thought gave her surprisingly little satisfaction.

# Chapter Nine

Christmas Day dawned bright and clear and Fay woke early, the morning sunlight piercing between her curtains, which she had not closed properly the night before, and shining directly on to her face. She got out of bed, pulled on her dressing gown, slid her feet into her slippers, and went over to the window to observe the effect of the bright rays upon the frosty cobwebs on the hedges and shrubs below her window. The beauty of the scene was as striking as she had expected it to be, but she had hardly been admiring it for more than a few seconds, when she caught sight of a cloaked female figure hurrying across the lawn in the direction of the back gate. Rachel, she thought to herself, but before she had pulled herself together sufficiently in order to call out to the girl, she had gone almost completely out of sight. If she shouted now, she would risk rousing the whole household, and then everyone would see that Rachel was keeping a rendezvous with a tenant farmer — for Fay was convinced that was where she was going.

She sighed and turned away from the window. Whatever else Joe Fairburn might be, she was convinced that he was honourable. There was no chance that Rachel would find herself in the kind of predicament that she, Fay, had been involved in. She got back into bed and allowed her mind to go back twelve months to Christmas the previous year, when she had still been living with Sir Jackson Hooper.

At that time, she had been his mistress for nearly four months. He had been generous, as he had said he would be, and he had also been kind in his way. He had been very surprised to discover that he was the first man to share her bed, and in all justice, she could not blame him for believing that she must have had lovers before. Angela herself had warned her that men would make assumptions about her, simply because she was part of a theatrical company, and she had observed for herself with what enthusiasm Elsie Dunn and others in Mr Llewellyn's company had dispensed their favours. Almost any man of his station would have thought the same.

Once she had settled in with him, she had gone out and about with him a little, but she did not care for the parties to which the other men had brought their mistresses, and where everyone flirted outrageously with everyone else.

'You should have been called Violet, rather than Fay, so shy and retiring as you are,' he had teased her once. She often stayed behind in the house that he had rented for them, going neither to the rowdy occasions, where she would have been welcome, nor to the more refined ton parties, at which she no longer had a place. The baronet often encouraged her to go out with him, but never put any pressure upon her, for which she was grateful. The outings she enjoyed the most were the ones when they simply went out driving in the countryside, away from curious eyes.

It was almost exactly twelve months ago when she became convinced that she was pregnant. Her first involuntary reaction was one of delight at the thought of having someone to call her very own. Then, when she thought of Sir Jackson's possible reaction to the news of this child for which he had not planned, and which he would almost certainly not want, she began to be afraid. When she was a girl, one of the maids at the big house near the next village had become pregnant, and had been turned out of the house. She had come to the vicarage, and Fay's father had taken her in. But the girl had not been well, and before the baby was born, a fever had carried her off. Fay did not think that Sir Jackson was the kind of man to do that to his own child, but she could not be sure.

Then, just after Christmas, he had come home with some news. He had wandered into the bedroom, where she was brushing her hair with the monogrammed brush which he had given her, and which she still used. He stood watching her for a few moments, then said, 'Fay, my dear, I have taken a decision that is bound to affect you in the future, so I thought it only fair to tell you now, before you find out from any other source. Today, I have become engaged to be married. The wedding between myself and Miss Edith Pargeter will probably take place in the summer.'

For a moment, Fay felt as if she had been dealt a blow to the stomach. She was glad that she had just laid the brush down, otherwise she might easily have dropped it with the shock of his disclosure. Never had he given even the slightest hint that he was thinking of marriage. 'I see,' was all she had felt capable of saying.

'No congratulations?' he asked. 'It is customary, you know.'

'Even from someone in my situation?' she asked.

He chuckled ruefully. 'Your point is taken,' he agreed. 'But I confess you have surprised me. Not one woman in a thousand would have taken that news without recrimination. Perhaps that is because you really don't care for me very much.'

Fay turned her face away. In truth, she had no idea how to answer him. Her feelings for him were very confused. He bent and kissed the side of her neck. 'But my change in circumstances need not affect us for some little time yet,' he said.

It was then that she decided she could not tell him about the baby. Three days later, the baronet's friend, Tony Nantwich, came round for a few companionable games of picquet. Fay sat in a corner sewing unobtrusively. After the third rubber – from which the baronet had risen a modest winner – they stopped for a glass of wine and a chat.

'Have you heard about Brixworth?' Tony asked, lounging back in one of the straw-coloured Chippendale chairs which stood either side of the fireplace.

'What about him?' enquired the baronet, pouring a glass of Madeira for the two of them, after offering one to Fay, which she refused.

'It seems his mistress and his wife are both with child. The bet is all over White's as to which one will pup first.'

The baronet grunted. 'No doubt with two daughters already, he's hoping for an heir this time,' he said.

Tony took a sip of wine. 'Ah, but what do you wager on the chance that there'll be a sister for the two Brixworth girls, while the little bastard turns out to be a boy?'

Hooper laughed shortly. 'Nothing more likely,' he replied. 'Brixworth always did have rotten luck.' Neither of the two men noticed when Fay got up and quietly left the room. Had she not done so, then she would have found it hard not to voice the question, '*What about my "little bastard"?*'

The following day, she went out to buy some lace. Hooper paid her a generous allowance, but she did not spend anything like all of it. At first, he was inclined to be exasperated with her determination to 'make do and mend', but was somewhat mollified when she explained to him that she enjoyed the challenge of it.

'I like sewing – that was what I was doing when you first saw me,' she reminded him.

He laughed incredulously. 'My last mistress wanted a barouche and a team of cream horses to go with it. You want a length of lace and a packet of pins!'

One of her bonnets needed some trimming, and it was to Bond Street that she went in order to find some lace at one of the haberdasheries there. Fay soon found the kind that she was looking for. While she was hesitating between three slightly different designs, she heard two ladies talking just behind her. It had not been her intention to eavesdrop, but when one lady called the other Edith, she immediately recalled that that was the name of the baronet's fiancée, and she could not then do anything but listen. The other woman had been asking when the wedding was to be.

'Probably at the end of the season,' replied the lady called Edith. 'There is a great deal to do, of course. Mama says we need to think about my bride clothes straight away.'

'Where will you live when you are married?' asked the other.

'Oh, in London most of the time, I expect,' said Edith carelessly. 'Jackson has a house in Bedford Square, and he says I can have it decorated as I please. I expect we will spend part of the year on his Berkshire estate. He has promised to take me to visit it soon.' At this point, Edith's companion glanced around, then whispered something in her friend's ear. 'Oh, I know all about it,' replied Edith carelessly. 'But never fear, I shall put a stop to that. From now on, he will be so busy attending to me, that he won't have time for some little nobody! Oh look, Jane, some ribbons of the very colour I was looking for!'

Fay automatically made her purchase, picking one of the three kinds of lace quite at random, and blindly made her way home. To do him justice, Jackson had made it plain that their association would end with his marriage. Now, it seemed that his fiancée would expect it to cease forthwith.

Fay was conscious of a pain somewhere in the region of her heart, and she decided that it must be fear with regard to her fate, and that of her unborn child, for she had two to consider now. She had found it hard enough to find work before. How much more difficult would it be now, especially when the child began to grow?

As the days went on, she thought more and more about escape, as it gradually became more likely that her condition would become plain to Jackson. Daily, she expected him to declare an end to their association; indeed, he was out more, and seemed more abstracted when he was at home. Anxiety about her fate made her nervous and jumpy with him, and he lost his temper with her on one or two occasions. But however angry he was, he never became violent, nor did she ever think that he might. She might be afraid of what would happen when he abandoned her, but never was she actually afraid of the man himself.

Some of his friends were quite sympathetic. Tony Nantwich, in particular, treated her kindly, and she wondered sometimes whether he knew what was afoot, for she noticed him eyeing her speculatively.

Then, one evening when Tony was visiting Jackson, she decided to retire to bed early. She had only just reached the bedroom door, when she realized that she had left her shawl downstairs. She had almost reached the door of the drawing-room, when she heard Jackson saying, 'I wish to God the whole thing was over.'

'Does she know about. . . ?' asked Tony.

'Oh yes. I blame myself entirely. I should never have allowed things to go so far. Now, I don't know how to be rid of her.'

'I'll take her off your hands, if you like,' said Tony.

Then Jackson said the fatal words. 'My dear fellow, if you could do that, you would earn my eternal gratitude.' Fay's heart sank to the very toes of her slippers. No wonder Tony had been eyeing her speculatively! He was hoping to take Jackson's leavings! But the humiliation of that was as nothing when set next to the fact that Jackson saw her as an unwanted encumbrance. She left the following morning, the few belongings that she had decided to take with her packed in a canvas bag.

The call of a robin in the winter garden brought Fay back to the present, and she drew her head inside, suddenly aware of how cold it was. She would have to speak to Rachel later.

Conscience dictated that she should speak to Mrs Stratford about the matter as well, but she couldn't do it. It would feel like a betrayal.

By hook or by crook, Mrs Stratford somehow managed to make sure that the entire household was assembled downstairs, ready to go to the morning service. Rachel, her errand accomplished, appeared with everyone else, looking demure, but very happy. Either she had eaten breakfast at the Fairburns, or she was living on love, Fay reflected cynically.

Sir Jackson Hooper was there amongst the others, looking very distinguished in a dark greatcoat and shiny boots. Fay's hands trembled a little inside her warm velvet muff. It had been one of his Christmas presents to her the previous year and it had seemed foolish not to keep it when it was so warm. She looked up and saw his eyes upon it, and knew that he remembered as well.

Mrs Fleetwood glided forward to take the baronet's arm as they set off for church. Her blue cloak and bonnet were of the latest fashion, but her muff was not the equal of Fay's, and she eyed the latter with narrowed eyes, before saying to her chosen escort, 'Such a fine morning, Sir Jackson, is it not? Just the day for walking to a Christmas morning service.'

He smiled down at her. 'No other day would be quite so suitable for such a purpose,' he murmured. Fay had to choke back a giggle and, as she did so, she caught the glint in his eye; no one else seemed to have grasped the humour of his remark.

Rachel walked with Chloe Napier and, as the two soon had their heads together, Fay wondered whether Rachel might be telling Chloe about her meeting with Joe. Lucilla did not appear to be at all put out, since Magnus had offered her his arm. She was soon chattering to him very happily about the London season that she had enjoyed that year, and the success that she had had, quite unaware that he was not listening to a word that she said. He was in fact planning the next scene of his Roman drama, and calculating when he would have an opportunity of writing it down.

Mr Proudfoot had been persuaded to come, and he appeared to be enjoying an earnest conversation with the older Mr Napier. Fay found this very surprising, until she overheard part of it and realized that Mr Napier was very well informed with regard to the early history of his own locality.

When they arrived, they discovered that the church was already quite full. The Fairburns were there, occupying their usual place, and Fay noticed a smile pass between Rachel and Joe.

Peter Frith looked as healthy and vigorous as usual, and preached rather better than he sometimes did, on a text in keeping with the season. Agnes sat alone in the pew set aside for the vicar's family, and although she did not do anything so vulgar as to turn around to look when the Proudfoots arrived, she had a warm smile and a greeting for Fay at the church door after the service was over.

The Proudfoots and their guests did not linger for, although sunny, the day was very cold. Peter Frith had his duty to do by his parishioners, but he urged Agnes to walk back to Old Drove House with Fay, promising that he would join them as soon as all the congregation had gone and the church was locked up.

'Has the advent of the visitors made your life less busy or more so?' Agnes asked, as soon as they had left the church behind them.

'A little of both,' Fay admitted. 'Lessons are more spasmodic, but there always seems to be something else to demand our attention.'

'Are the young people enjoying having visitors from London? I know that it is the first time that so many guests have been invited here, so it must be a very exciting experience for them.'

'Yes, it is, but they are enjoying it I believe,' smiled Fay, nodding towards Chloe and Rachel, who were once more exchanging confidences. 'It will be particularly good for Rachel I think.'

'I happened to see Rachel this morning,' said Miss Frith after a slight pause. 'I was at my bedroom window when I saw her hurrying in the direction of Fir Tree Farm.'

Fay felt her heart skip a beat, but she merely said, in calm tones, 'Yes, she had a present for Matty which she did not want to bring to church.' She decided that associating with the theatrical profession had made her into more of an actress than she had supposed. Looking sideways at Agnes's face, it seemed to her that the vicar's sister almost looked disappointed at these tidings, and she found herself torn in two. Loyalty to Mrs Stratford obviously meant that she should inform her employer of any developments in the romance between Rachel and Joe. On the other hand, since she had arrived at Old Drove House, she had built up a relationship with Rachel which meant that she felt a degree of loyalty towards her as well. Her misleading account of Rachel's reasons for leaving the house might have deterred Agnes from telling Mrs Stratford about what she had seen that morning, had such been her intention. There was no guarantee, however, that the vicar's sister would not speak to Rachel's aunt about the matter at some point. Little though she relished the necessity, Fay decided that she would have to talk to Rachel about Joe. But then she brought her attention hurriedly back to the present, for Agnes was speaking again.

'Peter was telling me that one of the guests is a cousin of yours. How agreeable it must have been to discover that quite by chance, a relative was to stay here over Christmas!'

Deciding that to say that it wasn't agreeable at all would occasion too much remark, Fay simply answered, 'Yes, very agreeable.'

'He looks quite the London smart,' went on Agnes, looking at Sir Jackson, who was now strolling beside Magnus, listening indulgently to his animated chatter. The baronet's caped greatcoat swung about his ankles, and he looked easily the most styl-ish man of the company.

'Yes, he is,' she replied shortly. At that point, Horsa, who had been walking with Rachel, went skipping up to the baronet, and tucked her hand in his arm, as confidently as if she had known him all her life. He looked down at her, smiled, and patted her hand indulgently, before turning back to Magnus.

Noting this episode, Miss Frith went on, 'He is obviously good-natured too.'

'Yes, very good-natured,' responded Fay, aware that her replies had been tediously similar, and wishing that Agnes would change the subject.

'Is he staying very long?' the vicar's sister asked her. Fay's heart sank. O heavens, she thought, Agnes Frith is taken with Jackson Hooper, and there isn't a thing I can do to warn her off.

'His plans are uncertain, I believe,' she said eventually. To her relief they had by now arrived at Old Drove House and, in all the business of taking off coats and hats, the subject of Sir Jackson Hooper was dropped. But Fay could not dismiss him from her mind so easily. Agnes might be older than Rachel, and her firm principles would no doubt arm her well against any rakish assault, but, like Rachel, she was a country-bred female, with no conception of how dangerous a man-of-the-town such as Sir Jackson could be. It clearly behoved Fay to observe the pair of them very carefully, and if Agnes seemed really taken with the wretch, or he seemed to inclined to flirt, then it would be neces-sary for her to speak, certainly to him, and possibly to them both. Agnes might be Mrs Stratford's informant, but she still did not deserve to be left with a broken heart.

They sat down eighteen to the table for Christmas dinner, with Mr Proudfoot at the head, and looking, if anything, rather surprised to be there, and Mrs Stratford at the foot. Hengist and Horsa were among the company at table as usual, but Mrs Stratford had taken the wise precaution of seating Hengist next to Fay and Horsa next to Magnus. Hengist was an intelligent lad, who talked amusingly about some of his experiences at Eton, and as Peter Frith was on Fay's other side, she was assured of pleasant conversation. Sir Jackson was seated on Mrs Stratford's left, with Lucilla on his other side, but as they were on the same side of the table as Fay, she was unable to see whether or not they seemed pleased with one another as dinner companions.

The Proudfoots' cook, if truth were told, sometimes became disheartened with a household in which the two eldest males occasionally forgot to eat, if in the midst of intellectual pursuits. Having the novelty of a houseful of guests to feed, therefore, she had excelled herself in honour of the occasion. As well as a goose, which the Honourable Toby Bragg carved, Mr Proudfoot being quite unequal to the task, there was a joint of beef and one of ham, a beef pie with oysters, a pigeon pie and a fricassee of vegetables. Everyone ate with great enjoyment, and when the dishes were returned to the kitchen, much lighter than when they had emerged from it, the cook had the satisfaction of seeing that all her work had been well and truly sampled.

The second course saw the advent of the Christmas pudding, together with a trifle, a blancmange, some small tarts, and macaroni. It might have been supposed that this course would have gone back barely tasted after the inroads that had been made into the first, but somehow everyone found some space, although very few of the tarts went, and the macaroni was not touched. After this, the covers were removed and the diners were invited to partake of nuts, apples and little cakes. By this time, however, most of them were replete.

'As excellent a Christmas dinner as any I have had,' remarked Peter Frith, as he cracked a walnut for himself, Fay having refused one.

'Yes indeed,' agreed Fay. 'And in such pleasant company.' She had been thinking of the quiet Christmases that had been her experience throughout most of her life, with her father often going out afterwards to visit a parishioner, and she had not intended the remark to be flirtatious in any way. She coloured, half expecting that he might take it so, but to her relief, he merely nodded understandingly.

'You have lived a solitary life, so large gatherings must be quite unusual for you,' he said.

'Yes they are,' she agreed, reflecting that even during her time with Sir Jackson, she had not mixed a great deal in company, chiefly from her own choice. She thought of last Christmas, when she and the baronet had dined together, just the two of them. After the meal, he had gone out to meet with friends, and she had retired early.

Almost as though her thoughts had conjured up the man's name, Mr Frith said, 'It must be especially agreeable for you to have a member of your own family here. Agnes and I were saying to each other only this morning before the service, you must be particularly thankful to have him with you at Christmas – the time when all families should be together.' His words reminded her of how completely alone in the world she really was. As she looked round at the assembled company, realizing that she belonged with none of them, she suddenly felt tears spring to her eyes, and she was glad that Mrs Stratford rose at that moment to lead the ladies from the room. So anxious was she to escape, that she did not notice Mr Frith's concerned look, or the eyes of Sir Jackson upon her as she left.

It had been agreed that gifts should be exchanged after the meal was over, and Fay went upstairs to collect her parcels. In the end, she had embroidered handkerchiefs for Rachel, Horsa, Agnes Frith and Mrs Stratford. For Mr Proudfoot and Magnus, she had bought books on the Vikings and the Romans respectively, devoutly hoping that they did not already have them. For Hengist, she had bought a miniature frame, in which she thought that he might like to put a picture of his home, or a member of his family, to take with him when he went back to school. But Horsa, wiser than Fay to the ways of her brother, declared that what he would like best would be a picture of his dog. Being an artist of some promise, she drew a picture of Rufus herself, and when she suggested that it be put in the frame, and that the gift could then be from both of them, Fay readily agreed.

After much heart-searching, she had decided that she must buy a present for Sir Jackson. Since everyone believed them to be cousins, it might be considered strange if she had not got him anything. Mrs Stratford had gone to March a few days before, and she had begged leave to accompany her, saying, quite truthfully, that as she had not known her kinsman was coming, she had failed to buy a gift for him, and was anxious to repair the omission. Mrs Stratford had readily agreed, and had even had some ideas to contribute as to what Fay might give her noble relative. In the end, she had chosen to buy some more handkerchiefs, this time large ones in finest white lawn, and embroider his monogram on them, also in white. She did not have time to do more in addition than crotchet some simple lace around the edge; but she hoped that it would be sufficient to convince everyone that she held him in high esteem. If only they knew!

The gentlemen did not linger for long over their wine, and those who had presents to give went to their rooms to collect them before coming back to the drawing-room.

Naturally, the Proudfoots, as hosts, received a flattering number of presents, and Fay was surprised and touched by those that she was given as well. Horsa had carefully drawn the view from Fay's bedroom window, and Hengist had made a wooden frame for it.

'I hope you don't mind,' said Horsa, 'but when you got the frame for Hengist, and I drew the picture to put in it, it gave me the idea for your present.'

'I don't mind at all,' Fay assured her. 'I think it's delightful. You have both worked so hard.'

Rachel's gift was a new lace collar, and Mrs Stratford presented her with a new reticule. Magnus apologized for not having very much money to spare, and he rather sheepishly handed her a parcel which contained a selection of ribbons.

'But,' he assured her, 'when my play is published, I intend to dedicate it to you, among others.' Fay declared herself to be extremely gratified at the idea of having an artistic work dedicated to her, and she assured him that the ribbons were exactly what she needed. Fay and Agnes had to laugh, for they had each bought handkerchiefs for the other, but Agnes declared that Fay's hand-embroidered ones were much better than the ones that she had given.

Her own gifts were very well received. Mrs Stratford was delighted with her handkerchiefs, as were Rachel and Horsa. Magnus was very pleased with his book, but Fay suspected that he was far more delighted with the stylish waistcoat which his aunt had brought him from London.

Rachel said nothing about any present that she might have received from Joe; but Fay caught a glimpse of gold around her neck, which she had not seen on previous occasions. Horsa received the gift of a puppy from the Fairburn family, and the little creature threatened to wreak considerable havoc in the drawing-room before it was removed by Magnus. Toby Bragg offered to help her train it, but Lord Bragg advised against it.

'His dogs are the worst trained ever,' he said frankly. 'You'd do much better to ask Hooper for his help, my dear.' Horsa did so very prettily, and the baronet agreed with a smile.

All the time that she had been unwrapping her presents, Fay had been watching Sir Jackson out of the corner of her eye. She had not yet given him her gift, and was waiting for the right moment to do so. When all her presents were unwrapped, she looked up and noticed that at that moment, he was unwrapping something whilst Mrs Fleetwood looked on, a satisfied expression on her face. It seemed to give the lie to her assertion that she had not known that he was coming to Old Drove House.

While she was watching this scene, she did not notice that Horsa had picked up her parcel destined for the baronet. Before Fay had chance to say anything, Horsa was crossing the room with it, saying, 'Sir Jackson, Miss Prescott has a gift for you.'

Wishing that she could just clamp a hand over the girl's mouth, and silence her, Fay followed her, saying, 'It's just a trifle.'

Sir Jackson's eyes widened. 'You are too good, Cousin,' he murmured, taking the parcel and undoing it. He took the hand-kerchiefs out and examined them.

'Oh, handkerchiefs,' said Mrs Fleetwood, in a tone that was only just the right side of contempt. Her gift to the baronet had been an enamel snuff-box.

'Miss Prescott embroidered them herself,' said Horsa help-fully. 'She worked long into the night to get them finished.'

'Horsa!' exclaimed Fay, blushing.

Sir Jackson looked up from contemplation of the handker-chiefs, and smiled at Fay. 'Something that none of us can do without,' he said. 'My dear Fay, you have lost none of your skill in embroidery. These are quite exquisite. Thank you for your thoughtfulness.' Fay smiled back at him, feeling absurdly pleased. 'You will be thinking that I have forgotten to give you a present,' he went on. 'But my gift to you would not be easy to bring downstairs. It has been placed in your bedroom, and I hope that you will find it to your liking.'

Horsa and Rachel could not wait to hurry her out of the drawing-room and up the stairs, in order to find out what Sir Jackson's gift to her might be.

'I think that it is a parrot in a cage,' said Horsa, as they walked along the passage.'

'No, it is a bonnet,' declared Rachel.

'In that case, why not bring it downstairs, silly?' asked Horsa. 'Anyway, just imagine Sir Jackson buying a bonnet!' Fay, who had been present when the baronet had bought a bonnet for her on more then one occasion, kept her peace. By this time, they had reached Fay's bedroom, and Horsa opened the door. Lying on the bed were three bolts of cloth, one gold, one of rich blue brocade, and one of warm red broadcloth.

'Oh, how beautiful,' exclaimed Rachel, fingering the broadcloth.

Horsa pulled out some of the gold fabric, and held it against Fay. 'This will suit you perfectly,' she said in a very adult way. 'Will you make an evening gown out of it? May I help?'

'I . . . I don't know,' murmured Fay, rather faintly.

'Sir Jackson must know you very well, to give you such a suitable present,' said Rachel.

Fay laughed, and her laughter had a cynical ring that made the girls look at her curiously. 'Oh yes,' she answered, 'he knows me very well indeed.'

# Chapter Ten

Fay knew that she had to decide very soon what to do about Sir Jackson's gift. Her first instinct was to demand that he take it back immediately. When she had seen those fabrics across the bed, for a moment she had been transported back to the days when she had been his mistress, and garments had been delivered to the house which she had shared with him – garments which he had paid for. The memory had so affected her, that she had almost felt physically sick. It was all that she could do to answer Rachel and Horsa civilly, and to encourage them to go and join the company, pretending that she wanted to stay behind and examine the fabrics more closely.

After they had gone, she sat down, her hands pressed against her cheeks. She had not realized how much she was coming to value her independence until she had received this reminder of the time when she had been completely dependent upon the baronet. Now, she had honourable employment. When that ended, if she gave satisfaction, there would be a reference to enable her to find more work. But the arrival of Sir Jackson had put all of that at risk. He had promised not to give her away, and if she was honest, she had always found him to be a man of his word. He had also told her that he did not expect her to pay the price of his silence with a place in her bed. But she was having to pay in other ways; first by acknowledging his 'cousinship', and now by accepting this extravagant gift. It seemed as if she could not escape from being beholden to him. She would simply have to seek him out and explain to him, politely but firmly, that she could not possibly accept it because it was far too expensive. It would be an explanation for her refusal that would be acceptable and comprehensible to all. That decided, she smoothed down her hair, and opened the door of her chamber, only to find Sir Jackson standing on the threshold.

'Come in here,' she ordered him, quite forgetting about the proprieties in her need to make herself plain. 'Come in here at once.' He raised his brows, but, wordlessly, did as he was bid. When he was inside the room, she closed the door firmly – only the most pernickety person would have said that she slammed it – and demanded, 'What on earth do you mean by giving me such a gift?'

He walked over to the bed and took some of the red broad-cloth between his fingers. 'What's the matter with it?' he asked her. 'If you don't like it, I can have it changed.'

'Whether I like it or not is not relevant,' she replied. 'It is wholly inappropriate.'

'It's Christmas,' he replied. 'It's customary to give gifts to one's . . . ah . . . nearest and dearest.'

The colour flamed in her face. 'That was uncalled for, Jackson,' she said, in a voice that was not quite steady.

'Strangely enough, I was not trying to embarrass you, either by what I said just now, or by giving you a present,' he replied, letting go of the cloth and walking towards her. 'The fiction has been established that we are cousins, and cousins exchange gifts. You know that as well as I do – you wouldn't have given me those handkerchiefs otherwise.'

'Yes, but handkerchiefs, compared to . . . to this! What kind of extravagant gesture is this supposed to be? The great nobleman taking pity on the poor working girl?'

'No, dammit,' he answered, exasperatedly. He ran his hand

through his hair. 'This cousin idea was a bloody stupid one,' he concluded eventually.

'I hate to point this out,' said Fay untruthfully, 'but it was your idea in the first place. If you recall, I told you at the very beginning that it was a bad idea.'

'Yes, but I don't think that our reasons for believing it to be so are the same.' She looked puzzled, and he went on in angry tones, 'What kind of cousin would I be to let you live in such straitened circumstances? Good God, if you were *really* my cousin, I'd be looking after you properly, not allowing you to earn your bread in this menial way. Bolts of cloth which I can purchase without even noticing the cost would be a miserable sop to my conscience, don't you think?' They stared at each other for a moment, and Fay felt strangely breathless. Then, before she could think of anything to say in response, he said abruptly, 'Oh, do what you please with it, burn it,or throw it away, or give it to the poor, I don't care. But it was kindly meant.' So saying, he opened the door, stalked out of the room, and closed it behind him with what could not truthfully be called anything other than a slam.

Fay stood staring at the door for a long time after he had gone. She recalled how he had always been generous to her; more generous than she had sometimes been able to accept. She had often told herself that his attitude was one of condescension, and that for her to give a courteous refusal was one way in which she could preserve her dignity. For the first time, she began to perceive that perhaps it might be rather that he was kind, and she was ungracious. She recalled him saying just a short time ago that they seemed to have developed an ability to hurt one another. There was certainly no doubt that when he left the room, he had really looked hurt. She walked back to the bed and fingered the cloth, still undecided as to what to do. As she stood in indecision, there was a tap on the door and Mrs Stratford came in.

'I hope you do not mind my intruding,' she said diffidently, 'but Sir Jackson came downstairs just now, looking a little disturbed. I do hope that his gift was to your liking, Miss Prescott.'

Fay hardly knew how to answer her. 'I . . . that is. . . .' she began.

Mrs Stratford shook her head ruefully. 'I warned him that it might be too extravagant,' she said, 'but he insisted, and he asked me to help him choose.'

Fay looked at her, an arrested expression on her face. 'You helped with the choosing of the fabric?' she asked.

'Oh yes,' replied Mrs Stratford in a relieved tone. 'Is that why you did not want to accept it, because you thought that he might have behaved improperly? I can assure you that there is no impropriety whatsoever in accepting such a gift from a kinsman.'

'But as you said yourself, it is such an extravagant gift,' murmured Fay. 'And I only gave him handkerchiefs.'

Mrs Stratford patted her on the shoulder. 'You gave him what you could afford,' she said reassuringly, 'and I am sure that you put love into every stitch.' *Love into every stitch?* thought Fay incredulously, as she allowed herself to be led downstairs. *Impossible!* But even whilst the word came into her mind, she felt a twinge of uneasiness, as if somewhere the fates were laughing at her.

They went back into the drawing-room, where the tea tray had been brought in, and where a merry hubbub of conversation was going on. Sir Jackson was standing talking to Peter Frith, and when he saw Fay come in, he looked at her unsmilingly. The vicar unmistakably beckoned her over, and since she could not ignore him without being rude, she did as she was bid.

'Miss Prescott,' he said, 'I have taken the liberty of purchasing for you a small gift, but I want to assure you that it is nothing improper, just a book, and to ask, in Sir Jackson's presence, if I may give it to you.'

'My cousin is able to answer for herself,' said the baronet in an even tone. 'She is at liberty to accept or to refuse any gift, if she is so minded.' Then he glanced at her, smiled ruefully, and added, 'Even gifts from me.' As she looked at him, Fay felt a sudden strange feeling of release, as if, by his words, he were freeing her to make her own choice.

She took a deep breath and, smiling at them both, she said, 'It is Christmas Day, the season of good will. I am not inclined to refuse or reject any of the gifts that have been so kindly bestowed upon me.'

Jackson smiled back at her and inclined his head slightly, whilst Mr Frith beamed and handed her the book. 'It is a copy of The Revd Mr Wetenhall Wilkes's book, *A Letter of Genteel and Moral Advice to a Young Lady*, he explained. Sir Jackson suddenly felt the need to cough. The vicar coloured a little and went on, 'Not that Miss Prescott needs any advice on how to conduct herself, I am sure, but I thought that it might be helpful in lessons with Miss Rachel and Miss Horsa, you know, when one of you reads aloud to the rest.' He looked at Fay anxiously. 'Agnes helped me to pick it,' he concluded.

'It is a splendid choice,' said Fay warmly. 'I shall find it very useful, I am sure.'

'I wonder whether it says anything about which Christmas gifts a lady should accept, and which she should refuse,' mused the baronet.

With that problem dealt with, Fay found herself able to turn her mind to other matters. When she saw Rachel talking to Roger Napier, she remembered seeing her going to the Fairburns' that morning.

She did not need to refer to The Revd Wetenhall Wilkes's book to discover what her duty might be. That very proper cleric might easily insist that Mrs Stratford should be informed immediately, but Fay had no intention of indulging in that kind of treachery. Clearly, she needed to speak to Rachel privately and raise the matter with her, before Agnes Frith said anything to

Mrs Stratford; just as clearly, there was going to be no opportunity of doing that until the company had broken up for the evening.

There was no doubt that all those present were bent on enjoying themselves. Several of the ladies were musical, and naturally each one of these had to take her turn at the pianoforte. Chloe had clearly been well taught, as had Lucilla, but the real surprise of the evening was Mrs Fleetwood's performance. Fay had already decided that she was a woman who was full of self-consequence, never satisfied unless holding the attention of all the men in the room. But when she sat down to play a piece by Mozart, her face became serious and her manner unaffected and natural, and her performance was undoubtedly superior.

Fay had never had the opportunity to learn to play, although she enjoyed music very much. Her mother had played, but after her death, her piano had remained untouched, apart from the careful dusting that it received regularly, for there had been no one available to pass their musical skills on to Fay. As she listened to Mrs Fleetwood's performance, she felt a stab of envy. This was not lessened by the sea of rapt faces that she saw around her, or by the way in which Sir Jackson stood, still clapping after she had finished playing, in order to hand her back to her seat.

The highlight of the evening, however, proved to be a performance given by Magnus, Sir Jackson, and Hengist. This was introduced with great aplomb by Horsa.

'And now, at enormous expense, and following upon their great success in the schoolroom, the Fenland Players bring you "Julius Caesar, without the boring bits"; with Mr Magnus Proudfoot as Brutus, Sir Jackson Hooper as Mark Antony, Mr Hengist Proudfoot as Julius Caesar, and all of them playing all the other parts.'

Magnus played Brutus with a flashing eye, and Sir Jackson threw himself into the role of Antony with considerable gusto. Hengist carried off the part of Julius Caesar with commendable dignity, until confronted by Sir Jackson as Calpurnia with a shawl over his head. After this, he was very inclined to get the giggles, and could not keep a straight face, even during his own assassination. Sir Jackson gave the speech 'Pardon me thou bleeding piece of earth' with great dignity, and would possibly have brought a tear or two to many an eye, had he not contrived to poke Hengist from time to time, causing the corpse to wriggle most unauthentically.

After the death of Julius Caesar, Hengist was required to play a number of different roles, but owing to some confusion over the ghost scene at Philippi, Sir Jackson found himself obliged to have conversations with two other characters, both of which were played by himself.

At the end of the performance, the entire audience was helpless with mirth, and the rendition was greeted with enthusiastic applause. Fay, wiping the tears of laughter from her eyes, found her gaze locked with that of Sir Jackson, whose eyes were also alight with merriment, and in that instant, she felt more at one with him than she had ever done whilst living under his protection. Breaking that contact with a fast beating heart, she looked round to see that Agnes Frith was smiling and applauding politely, but she did not look as though her heart was in it. Peter Frith, too, looked less than delighted, and Fay remembered what they had both said with regard to drama. Clearly their strict views also applied to private family performances. It was as well that neither of them knew about her past connections with the theatre.

After this, the assembled company split up, some to play cards, others to indulge in childish games such as spillikins, and yet others to just talk. Fay found herself sitting next to the vicar's sister, and she could not resist saying, 'Did you enjoy the drama this evening?'

Agnes pursed her lips. 'I do not really approve of drama, as you know,' she replied censoriously. 'It encourages such unbridled emotions. When I looked around at everyone's faces, and heard the uncontrolled noise and laughter, I knew that I was justified in my opinion.'

'But surely, innocent enjoyment amongst friends cannot be harmful,' murmured Fay, rather regretting now that she had even raised the topic.

'Do not let us confuse innocence with ignorance,' replied Miss Frith. 'Through such activities as theatrical performances, the ignorant or the unwary can all too easily be drawn into evil.' Suddenly, Fay felt all her pleasure in the evening begin to evaporate.

She stared at Miss Frith, unable to think of what to say next, when a voice behind her declared pleasantly but firmly, 'Miss Frith, you must permit me to say "balderdash" with all the courtesy at my command.'

'Sir Jackson!' exclaimed Miss Frith, colouring a little. 'I beg your pardon. I would not for the world have you think that I intended any personal criticism of your performance. But I must say what I feel to be true.'

Sir Jackson drew up a chair and sat down opposite them. 'And so must I,' he replied genially. 'Theatre and drama can give rise to the noblest sentiments and highest aspirations. We have had a little fun at Shakespeare's expense this evening, I admit, but the works of Shakespeare contain some of the finest expressions ever to be heard on human lips. What a call to every member of the legal profession is Portia's speech, "The quality of mercy is not strained", And how could anyone behave dishonourably who could say the words, "First above all to thine own self be true"?'

'I agree that there is good to be found in some plays,' Agnes admitted, a little grudgingly. 'But others are simply an encouragement to licence, whilst the behaviour of those who work in the theatre is quite deplorable.'

'There is good and bad material,' conceded Sir Jackson, 'but the secret is to encourage the good, not to let the bad destroy it.

And the people who are involved with the theatre are not all immoral, you know. Some of them are there because they have no choice.'

Fay stared at him, but it was Agnes who spoke. 'There is always a choice,' she said self-righteously. Fay got up and walked away. She could not trust herself to speak.

The Friths did not leave until quite late, and soon afterwards it was time to retire. The ladies went up first, and Sir Jackson came into the hall to hand Fay her candle.

'Goodnight, sweet cousin,' he murmured. The flickering light of the candle seemed to bring out the beauty of the chiselled planes of his face. 'To spend Christmas with you has been an unexpected pleasure.'

Rendered suddenly brave, she answered, 'It is not the first Christmas that we have spent together.'

'Let us hope that it will not be the last,' he replied enigmatically, before bending to kiss her cheek. As she turned to go up, Fay's eyes met those of Mrs Fleetwood, and the widow looked less than pleased.

Despite this exchange, Fay had not forgotten her determination to speak to Rachel. At the top of the stairs, she managed to whisper to her, 'Come to my room. I want to talk to you.' When the two of them were in Fay's room, and the door was shut, Fay turned to Rachel and said, 'I think you have something to explain.'

'To explain?' Rachel asked, wrinkling her brow.

'Your visit to Fir Tree Farm this morning,' Fay replied calmly.

Rachel turned a little pale, but she said, 'What makes you think that I went to Fir Tree Farm?'

'Rachel, I saw you,' Fay replied. 'So did Miss Frith, as a matter of fact.'

Rachel immediately looked scornful. 'That busybody!' she exclaimed.

'She may be a busybody, but she is as entitled to look out of her bedroom window as anyone. Why did you go, Rachel?'

'I had presents to take – for Matty and Jenny, you know,' Rachel answered, looking up at Fay, then looking down at her hands and fiddling with the fringe of her shawl.

'Of course, you could not give them to them at church,' Fay remarked conversationally. Then, in a more earnest tone, she went on, 'Oh Rachel, can you not be honest with me?'

'Honest with you?' asked Rachel, her chin high.

'About Joe.'

There was a long silence before Rachel said, 'There's nothing to be honest about.'

'Then it won't matter if I tell Mrs Stratford what I saw this morning,' said Fay, hating herself for it, but feeling certain that it was the only way to serve Rachel's best interests.

Rachel turned white. 'You couldn't! You wouldn't be so treacherous!'

Fay raised her brows. 'But you have just said that there is nothing to betray.' With that, the defiance seemed to go out of Rachel, and she sat down heavily on the bed, from whence the bolts of cloth had been removed to be placed on Fay's trunk in the corner of the room. 'By the way, before you accuse me of treachery, allow me to point out that it was I who deflected Agnes's curiosity with regard to your errand by saying that you had gone with a present for Matty,' Fay added gently.

Rachel looked at her beseechingly. 'If I tell you, will you promise that you will help us?' she pleaded.

Fay sighed. 'I can only promise to act in what I believe to be your best interests,' she replied.

Rachel smiled at her uncertainly. 'Then you will be sure to help us, because being with Joe must be in my best interests,' she replied. She patted the bed next to her, and Fay went to sit beside her. 'I know that you have been told that Mama died twelve years ago. I was only six at the time, and Magnus was five.' She paused for a moment, looked down at her hands, then looked up at Fay.

'I don't want you to think that I am being critical of my elders, but you have seen Papa, and you know what he's like. He has very little interest in the practical business of life; whether he ever had any, I don't know. Perhaps he always had that tendency, and simply turned inwards even more when Mama died. But we never saw anything of him, and Aunt Stratford has always been much as you see her: willing to descend on us from time to time, but absent for the majority of the year. When Mama died, Aunt herself was quite ill, I think. We were left very much in the care of the housekeeper, who had the idea of asking Mrs Fairburn to help take care of us. So we spent as much time at Fir Tree Farm as we did here.'

'I see,' said Fay slowly. She remembered that Mrs Fairburn had told her much the same story.

'That's why Matty and I are so close, and why it seems so strange that they are not included in parties here. It's as if we are saying that they were good enough when we needed help, but not when we want to entertain our friends. Joe. . . .' – she coloured at his name – 'Joe was twelve when we first began to go to the farm, and he always seemed very grown-up to me. He had to help his father of course, but his mother insisted that he learn his letters, and mind his manners, and she was very careful that we behaved properly too. Mrs Fairburn was a doctor's daughter, and went to school herself.' Fay nodded. From observing the farmer's widow's very proper behaviour and excellent manners, she had expected this or something very like it.

'Joe and I spent a lot of time together when we were children, but one day, there came a time when we realized that we didn't think of one another as brother and sister any more.' She was silent for a while.

Eventually Fay said, very gently, 'My dear, I quite understand that having been thrown together, you could not help but fancy yourselves in love. But your experience of the world is not very large, is it? Don't you think it's possible that if you went to

134

London next year as your aunt wishes, you might find that the memory of Joe would fade?'

Rachel shook her head. 'You talk as if we were children, but we aren't children now,' she said confidently. 'My aunt was married at my age, and Joe is twenty-four. We're old enough to know our own minds. And besides, I know why my aunt is talking about London; it is for the same reason that she had brought all these visitors: it is to distract my mind from Joe, but it hasn't succeeded. Both Mr Napier and Mr Bragg are very handsome, and Sir Jackson has been flirting with me from time to time, and it has been very enjoyable indeed, but I still prefer Joe to any of them. And it is the same for him. He is regarded as quite a catch among the farming community, you know, but although plenty of girls have thrown their caps at him, he has never looked at any of them once.'

Fay thought about her own early reactions to Joe, and conceded that Rachel was probably right in stating that he was sought after by the local maidens. She did not voice this opinion, however, but simply went on to say, 'But think, Rachel, what it would mean for you if you *did* marry Joe. No London season; no parties; no chance to dress up like a princess for your court appearance. Those things may seem easy to give up now, but might you not regret letting those chances go by? And what would you have in their place? A life of hard work as a farmer's wife.'

'I would have Joe,' Rachel said with simple dignity. 'No doubt some of those who were dining with us today, would say that he wasn't a gentleman, but he has always been one to me. And for the rest, Joe has said exactly the same thing – not wanting to take advantage of me, you know. But really, I cannot think of anything better than being Joe's wife, looking after the farm, cooking, caring for our . . . our children. And besides, not everyone has a London season. *You* didn't, did you?'

'No, I didn't,' admitted Fay. 'But that was not because I didn't want one. Circumstances weren't right for me. But for you, Rachel, it's different.'

'Yes, perhaps,' agreed Rachel. 'But that doesn't change my mind. And besides. . . .' She unclasped a chain that she was wearing around her neck, and which Fay remembered glimpsing earlier. There was a locket on the end of it, which had been tucked into the neckline of her gown. 'Joe gave me this today. Look inside.' Fay did as she was bid, and saw two tiny pictures there, one of a man and one of a woman. 'It belonged to Joe's grandmother, and he gave it to me today. It's his love token. I'm going to marry him, Fay, and there's nothing that you, or Aunt Stratford, or anyone, can do about it.'

# *Chapter Eleven*

After Rachel had gone, Fay thought long and hard about what to do. It was true that Rachel was only young, but there had been a great deal of maturity in the way in which she had spoken about herself and Joe. Nor did she seem to be painting a rosy picture of herself as a farmer's wife. How could she, when she had spent so much time at the farm, and seen how difficult Mrs Fairburn's life could be? If Joe stood firm, and insisted that the girl should have her season in London, then Rachel might be persuaded, but Fay could not feel absolutely certain even about this.

Meanwhile, at the back of her mind, there lurked the fear of what would happen if Mrs Stratford discovered that she was failing so lamentably in her duty. True, the reading sessions were going well, and both Horsa and Rachel were profiting from learning some of her needlework skills, but Fay knew that this was just a sop to offer to her conscience. Mrs Stratford would be fully justified in dismissing her at the very least, for not keeping her informed about how things stood between Rachel and Joe. Then what would she do?

It was a question that she had not resolved when she awoke the following morning, but today was the day when many more festivities were to take place, and she was determined that nothing should spoil them for her. She had to admit that she was enjoying herself so much that she wanted to forget about her dilemma over Rachel for just a short time, and pretend that she really belonged in this place with these people; whereas the truth was that she belonged nowhere with nobody.

Shaking off these rather depressing thoughts, she dressed and went downstairs to have breakfast, and then help in the preparations for the evening. There was to be a party for the entertainment of the servants, the tenants and the estate workers, and it would be before that party that the servants would be given their gifts or 'Christmas boxes'. There would be a sumptuous feast prepared for all the dependants, which they would enjoy whilst the family and their guests dined separately. Afterwards, the two parties would come together for dancing and entertainment, which would proceed on very informal lines, with everyone being allowed to choose their own dancing partner, however high or low they might be.

As Fay helped to decorate the ballroom, she could not help noticing an air of suppressed excitement about Rachel, and it was not difficult to guess the reason why. The Fairburns, being tenants of the Proudfoots, would be present, and that would mean that Rachel would have the opportunity of dancing with Joe. She would undoubtedly take that opportunity, despite the presence of Mrs Stratford. Fay could only hope that amongst all the other jollifications, this would not be noticed.

She was just studying the effect of some holly in a vase when she heard footsteps behind her and, turning, saw the vicar approaching. He looked pleased to see her, but also appeared to be a little bit on edge.

'Good morning, Miss Prescott,' he said courteously. 'I must say, this is looking very festive. Is it all your work?'

'By no means,' Fay declared. 'Rachel and Horsa have both been working with me, and they have only just left. Are you and Miss Frith attending the festivities tonight?'

'Mrs Stratford has been good enough to invite us so yes, we

expect to be here. We will be dining with you beforehand. I take it that this kind of event is new to you.'

Fay nodded. 'My father was something of a recluse. We did not receive many invitations, and those that we did receive, he refused. Furthermore, the local landowner was not of a benevolent disposition, and he didn't entertain very much, even when he was there.'

'Then you will enjoy this evening all the more,' said Frith. 'May I ask if Sir Jackson Hooper is within? Might I speak with him?'

Curbing the impulse to ask what he wanted to speak to the baronet about, and to insist that if it was to ask for permission to dance with her, then he should apply to her personally and not to some distant male relative, she said, 'Yes, I believe that he has returned from his morning ride. I heard some of the gentlemen talking in the passage a little while ago. You might find him in the billiard-room, perhaps.'

'Thank you. I shall look forward to the pleasure of seeing you later.'

'Of course,' replied Fay. She turned to get on with her work, and did not watch him leave.

As Fay had predicted, Sir Jackson was to be found in the billiard-room, where he had just finished beating Magnus by a narrow margin. He could indeed have beaten him much more handsomely, but he had not wanted to humiliate the boy. Except in the matter of his play-writing, Magnus was not a confident lad, and in Sir Jackson's opinion he needed encouragement, something that was sadly lacking, certainly as far as the boy's father was concerned. Magnus had only just left school and very much wanted to go to university, but he could not see how it could be managed.

'Papa takes no interest in the estate, or the younger ones, or in anything except for his studies,' he explained to Sir Jackson, as they were playing. 'I cannot help feeling that it must be my duty to stay at home and deal with those matters. Indeed, he has said that he wants me to learn to administer the estate so that I can take the whole responsibility off his shoulders as soon as possible. What do you think, sir?' The baronet had never before been in a position where striplings were asking him for advice, and for a moment or two he was nonplussed.

'What do I think?' he returned. 'I think you sound blue-devilled at the whole idea. Clearly neither of you is naturally drawn to that kind of work,' he went on, choosing his words with care. 'Many would agree that it was your duty to learn from him; equally, many would say that you are too young to be shouldering the responsibility of the estate. *That*, I should have said, is rather your father's duty.'

'Yes, perhaps, but what if he won't? I can scarcely call him to account, can I?'

'Have you tried enlisting Mrs Stratford's support?' suggested Sir Jackson, taking careful aim, and just avoiding pocketing the next ball by the merest whisker. Really, he was enjoying the challenge of this far more than just sweeping the board, as he normally did.

'She isn't usually here very much; I suppose that now she is, it would be sensible to ask her. Father's more likely to listen to her than to someone of my age, isn't he?'

'I should think undoubtedly,' agreed the baronet, willing Magnus to pocket his next shot, and wincing inwardly when the lad failed to do so by much the same margin as he had just done, only this time by mistake. 'Has your father ever considered employing someone to administer the estate for him?'

'I don't know,' replied Magnus. Then, in a more cheerful tone, he went on, 'Of course, being here has one advantage, and that is that I can strengthen my relationship with Fay.' This time, Sir Jackson missed his shot entirely unintentionally.

'You have, of course, obtained her permission to use her Christian name,' he said evenly.

'Oh yes,' replied the young man eagerly. 'I should never dare to presume, otherwise.'

Sir Jackson looked at him keenly, his eyes narrowed a little. 'You have aspirations in that direction?' he asked Magnus. 'You will appreciate that as her kinsman, I have a right to ask.'

'Yes of course,' agreed Magnus, colouring a little. 'And yes, I have to admit that I am somewhat . . . taken with her. She is so pretty and sweet and dainty; almost like a fairy, you know?'

'Yes, I know,' agreed the baronet, chalking his cue with fastidious care.

'And she has been so kind about my play – as have you also, sir, of course; perhaps that kind of friendly interest runs in your family? – and offered to help me with some of the words.'

'Does my cousin know of your aspirations?' Sir Jackson asked.

Magnus shook his head. 'No, and I cannot think of telling her; not until I can support her, at any rate. Do you think that I stand a chance?'

Sir Jackson smiled, not unkindly. 'She is a few years your senior,' he said gently. 'Do you think that she would be prepared to wait for you?'

Magnus looked a little crestfallen for a few moments, but he soon brightened, and said, 'Five years between us is not so very much. If it were the other way round, no one would think anything of it, would they? And when you meet someone as wonderful as she is, then you cannot let trifling considerations stand in your way, can you?'

'No,' agreed Sir Jackson, savagely potting three balls in a row. 'My game, I think.' It was at this point that Peter Frith came in and begged the favour of a private word with Sir Jackson.

'By all means,' replied Hooper. 'Do you want to talk over a game of billiards?'

'No, thank you, I do not play,' replied the vicar rather severely.

'You could go into the library,' suggested Magnus. 'You won't be disturbed there.'

141

'No, and that means that you'll be able to stay here and practise your shots, doesn't it?' grinned the baronet.

Magnus grinned back. 'I should say I will! Will you give me another game later, sir?'

'With the greatest of pleasure,' replied the baronet, holding open the door for Peter Frith. 'After you, sir.'

When they were in the library with the door shut, Jackson took one look at Peter Frith and said, 'You have had a cold walk, sir. Can I offer you a little brandy?'

'Just a very little, if you please,' replied the vicar. It was hard to tell whether he was more cold or agitated, for he walked up and down, now warming his hands by the fire, now rubbing them together. He took the brandy that the baronet offered to him, and said, 'No doubt, sir, you will be wondering why I have sought you out in this way.'

'I try never to waste my time in idle speculation,' replied Hooper. 'Please be seated and tell me in what way I may serve you.'

'I had rather stand, if you don't mind,' replied the clergyman.

'Well, I wouldn't,' said Hooper frankly. 'Do you mind if *I* sit down?'

Frith made a gesture to signify his assent, tossed off the rest of his brandy, and said, 'I was not sure what to do for the best, but as you are Miss Prescott's relative, I thought that you might be the right person for me to approach.' Oh, my God, Jackson thought to himself, but outwardly he gave no sign of agitation, and merely continued to look at his visitor with an expression of polite interest. 'You see, I have become very . . . that is, I . . . in short, I do not know to whom I ought to speak in order to obtain permission to pay my addresses to her.'

Feeling that he needed some extra fortification, Sir Jackson got up and poured himself more brandy, after offering it to Frith, who refused it. 'Has Miss Prescott any idea of your intentions?' he asked.

The young clergyman flushed. 'I think that she cannot be unaware of my regard, but naturally, I have said nothing to her without speaking to you first.'

'Naturally,' agreed the baronet smoothly, turning upon the other man a smile which did not quite reach his eyes. 'Miss Prescott has no immediate family,' he went on truthfully. 'She is, of course, of age and may give you her own answer. But I suppose that I must be the nearest thing to a male relative that she has.'

'You see, sir, it is not just with regard to obtaining permission that I wanted to apply to you,' Frith went on confidingly, 'it is concerning the advisability of such a match.'

Hooper had resumed his seat. He was about to take a sip of brandy; now, he looked at the vicar over the top of his glass and said, 'Really?'

Frith looked more agitated than ever. Suddenly, he sat down opposite the baronet, his hands clasped between his knees. 'I have certain anxieties concerning ... concerning her inclinations,' he said at last.

'Her inclinations?'

'You must have noticed her interest in plays and the theatre,' explained Mr Frith. 'She does not seem to think anything wrong with either!'

'She is not alone in that belief,' replied Sir Jackson. He was now sitting very much at ease with his legs crossed, swinging his quizzing glass gently to and fro on its ribbon. 'I also enjoy plays and the theatre.'

'But − forgive me − your situation is not the same as hers. A clergyman's wife must be above reproach.'

'Like Caesar's?' interpolated the baronet, looking at him quizzically.

'I beg your pardon?'

'It doesn't matter. Rest assured, Mr Frith that my cousin has nothing with which she needs to reproach herself. I give you my word.'

The vicar looked relieved. 'You have eased my mind considerably,' he said, smiling. 'I can now ask for her hand with a clear conscience.'

'One moment,' said Sir Jackson, raising his hand. 'You may have satisfied yourself that Fay is good enough for you to marry, but I, as her relative, need to satisfy myself that *you* are good enough for *her*.'

Mr Frith looked at him disbelievingly, then sat up very straight and said, 'You forget, Sir Jackson, that I am a clergyman!'

'I forget nothing,' replied the other. 'You might be the Archangel Gabriel for all I care. What I want to know is this: what do you feel for my cousin?'

'I think I have made it plain that I esteem her very highly,' Frith responded, his tone a little indignant, his colour somewhat higher than usual.

'I dare say; but esteem is not good enough, I'm afraid. Do you love her, sir?'

'Love her?' echoed the vicar.

Sir Jackson got up from his place and walked over to the window. 'I could not possibly consent to her marriage under any other circumstances,' he said expressionlessly.

'But . . . but you said that your consent is not necessary.'

Hooper turned back from the window with a glint in his eye that might have been anger. 'Do as you please, then. Ask her to marry you. I have no right to interfere. But understand this: if she marries you, and it comes to my ears that you do not cherish her as she deserves, then you will have me to reckon with.' So saying, he stalked out of the room, leaving the young clergyman with no very clear idea as to whether he had received the baronet's blessing or not.

Sir Jackson left the library intending to go straight to his room, but as he was approaching the stairs, Fay entered the hall from another direction.

'My God, it's the siren of the fens,' he exclaimed, and made her an elaborate bow.

She looked completely nonplussed. 'Siren?'

'Oh yes, indeed,' he replied, drawing closer to her and taking hold of her chin with his right hand. 'Tell me, my sweet, how many men do you have in thrall here? Or is it impossible for you to count?'

She brushed his hand away. 'Jackson, what on earth are you talking about?' she asked him. For answer, he simply stared at her for a few moments, then went up to his room, taking the stairs two at a time.

It often amused Fay that she, with no one to help her dress, was frequently the first downstairs of an evening, whereas ladies such as Mrs Fleetwood and Mrs Napier, with abigails to help them, were usually the last to make an appearance. When no one else appeared for some time, however, she was a little puzzled until she remembered that members of the family, and others who wished to be there, would be giving Christmas gifts to the assembled company of dependants in the ballroom.

When she had first heard about this custom, she had been uncertain as to whether she would give and receive presents above stairs on Christmas Day, or whether her position would dictate that she should receive a Christmas box along with Summers the butler, Mrs Graves the housekeeper, and the Fairburns. She had raised this delicate matter with Mrs Stratford, who had assured her that she was to be included in the exchange of presents 'above stairs'.

The memory of this made her smile rather ironically as she waited alone in the drawing-room. In some respects, the money which the servants received would have been more useful to her than some of the little knick-knacks that she had been given. Then she thought back over the Christmases that she had spent in the past. When she was ten, her father had declared that since he never knew what to buy for her, it would be best if they did not exchange gifts at Christmas, or on birthdays either. Remembering that, she knew that she would not want to exchange even the simplest and most inexpensive of her presents for a purse of money, however useful it might be.

Last year, when she had been living with Sir Jackson, had been the first time that she could remember being given anything at all. As she sat alone, her mind went back twelve months to the moment when returning from church on Christmas morning – for she always attended, going to a quiet, unfashionable church where there would be no risk of her being recognized – she found Sir Jackson sitting at his ease waiting for her, a glass of Madeira in his hand, and a pile of daintily wrapped parcels on the table in front of him.

'Happy Christmas, Fairy Fay,' he said, raising his glass to her.

She looked at him aghast. 'But . . . who are these for?' she asked him.

'For you of course, my sweet,' he replied. 'Now, come and open them!' She stood staring at him for a moment or two, before bursting into tears. He laughed indulgently, before getting up to wipe her tears away with one of his fine lawn handkerchiefs. Then, when he saw that the tears wouldn't stop as easily as that, he pulled her into his arms, holding her close until she was able to say,

'Jackson, there are more presents here than I have received in the whole of my life put together!'

'So?'

'But . . . but I haven't got you anything at all.'

He laughed again. 'That doesn't matter,' he said.

'But it does,' she protested. 'My father—'

He interrupted her again. 'I've said that it doesn't,' he insisted. 'Now come and open your presents.' Then he bent and kissed her on the lips, and for an instant, something seemed to flicker to life inside her. As his mistress, she had accepted all his attentions, and had attempted to respond to him, but she could never forget that she had gone with him because she had had nowhere else to go, and not because she loved him. Now, for the first time, she felt that there might be something more.

She opened the gifts that he gave her while he looked on. That day was one of the happiest that they spent together, but straight after Christmas had come the news that he was to be married. With that news, anything else that she might have felt for him was frozen to death before it had even properly begun.

'Where are you, Fairy Fay?' A voice came from what seemed to be a very long way away, and looking up, Fay saw Sir Jackson standing in front of her, looking much as he had when they were together. This evening, he was in black, with a waistcoat of red shot silk with jet buttons, and his hair looked very smooth and glossy.

'I was remembering last Christmas,' she replied, forgetting to be cautious, because he had taken her by surprise.

He smiled. 'You were so surprised to receive anything, and so upset because you hadn't got me a present,' he said. They were silent for a few moments then he said quietly, 'Why did you leave most of them when you left me?' She said nothing, turning her face away. The next moment, Mr Napier and his son Roger came in, and there was no further opportunity for private conversation between them.

The seating arrangement at the table was much as it had been on Christmas Day, for Peter Frith and his sister were dining with them again. Fay noticed that the vicar appeared to be more stilted in his conversation than on the previous evening. The night before they had talked quite easily on a number of topics, but this time he appeared to be searching for something to say. Whenever she sought his opinion upon any matter, he seemed to make his contribution very much at random.

After the meal was over, Mr Proudfoot and Mrs Stratford led the assembled company very formally to the ballroom, where their advent was greeted with a round of applause. Mr

Proudfoot, though uninterested in the business of the estate, was a generous man, and this was appreciated by his dependants, who had been very well fed, and were ready to enjoy themselves thoroughly.

For the first dance, as tradition demanded, Mr Proudfoot partnered the housekeeper, and Mrs Stratford the butler, but after that, protocol vanished completely. Rachel danced the first dance with Joe, but as he was the most significant of all the tenants, this was to be expected. Fay was asked to dance by Peter Frith and, as predicted by Sir Jackson, he played his part correctly, if not with very much style.

'You enjoy dancing, Miss Prescott,' he observed, after the dance had begun.

'Yes, I do,' she acknowledged. 'It has never come in my way very much, so it has all the advantage of novelty.'

'I imagine that a governess or companion gets little opportunity for dancing,' he said.

'Yes, I expect that that is usually the case,' she agreed shortly. 'Do you enjoy dancing, Mr Frith?'

'I have no objection to dancing, so long as it remains rational and restrained,' he replied. 'But occasions such as this one, sadly, tend all too frequently to become a romp, if one is not very careful.'

Fay looked around at all the happy faces in the room. 'Some of these people have very few holidays away from their work during the year,' she said. 'It is surely not surprising that they should want to make the most of them.'

'Then perhaps holidays, like responsibility, should not be given until it is certain that the recipient will not abuse the gift,' he commented. 'But this subject is too serious for such an occasion as this.' The movement of the dance parted them, and Fay smiled in agreement, glad to be relieved of the necessity of giving an answer to an argument which she found offensive.

When they came together again, she said, 'I suppose you must have attended many of these occasions.'

'Yes indeed, but I do not think that I have ever looked forward to one with such pleasurable anticipation as I have this time,' he replied, with a glance so full of meaning that Fay blushed. After the dance was over, she went to stand with Mrs Stratford.

'Are you enjoying the evening, Fay?' that lady asked her.

'Very much indeed, ma'am,' Fay replied.

'I have to confess that I am enjoying myself more than I anticipated,' said Mrs Stratford. Then she dropped her voice and went on, speaking behind her fan, 'What do you think of Rachel? Have you noticed how much she is enjoying Roger Napier's company?' Fay glanced over at Rachel, looking very becoming in a deep pink gown, which complemented her colouring admirably. She was indeed talking animatedly with the young man in question, but Fay had noticed that the close friendship which had developed between Rachel and Chloe had been extended to include Roger, who seemed to be happy to play the part of an elder brother for both of them.

She did not give voice to these thoughts, but instead, she felt bound to say, 'She danced with Joe Fairburn for the first, ma'am. I am not convinced that that romance will be as easy to scotch as you may have supposed.'

'Oh, pooh,' declared Mrs Stratford. 'More company of the kind that she has been enjoying over the past few days will soon put that young country bumpkin out of her mind.' Fay thought about the conversation that she had had with Rachel, and decided that the matter simply would not be as easily resolved as Mrs Stratford supposed.

She did not say so, being reluctant to betray Rachel's confidence, but she did venture to say, 'Have you seen Joe Fairburn this evening, ma'am?' She pointed to where the young farmer was performing a country dance with Mrs Napier. His dark-blue coat and breeches were spotless, as was his linen, and his white stockings did nothing to hide the muscles in his well-shaped calves. He looked handsome and healthy, and would not have appeared out of place at any but the most fashionable assemblies. Mrs Stratford became strangely still.

'Good gracious, is *that* Joe Fairburn?' she exclaimed. 'I had thought he must be a local squire! I had not realized that he was so handsome and gentlemanly.'

Fay looked at her in puzzlement. 'But surely, ma'am, you have seen him before? At church, or when he has come to the house to bring his sisters?'

'No, I have never seen him,' replied Mrs Stratford. Seeing the look of astonishment on Fay's face she went on defensively, 'You forget that I come here but seldom, although come to think of it, I might have caught sight of the back of his head at church. But it was so busy, you know, and we came away very quickly.'

'But you cannot possibly mean . . .' began Fay, but before she could finish her sentence, Mrs Stratford said quickly, 'Oh look, I think Miss Frith wants to speak to me. Excuse me.' Moments later, Mrs Stratford was to be seen in earnest conversation with the vicar's sister. Fay stared at her retreating figure. For the very first time, it had become clear to her that Mrs Stratford had decided against Joe without speaking with him, or even seeing him with her own eyes, and the idea horrified her.

Someone touched Fay on the shoulder, almost causing her to jump, and turning round, she saw Sir Jackson standing behind her. Without thinking, and because she was still disturbed by what Mrs Stratford had disclosed, she said, 'Mrs Stratford has never seen Joe Fairburn.' He looked down at her and raised one eyebrow slightly.

'She is surely not unique in that,' he replied. 'You might travel the length and breadth of this country and meet thousands of people who have never seen Joe Fairburn. In fact, I am not at all sure that I have seen him myself.'

'Yes, you have,' replied Fay. 'You have even met him. Don't you remember, he brought the mistletoe to decorate the house?'

'Oh yes,' answered the baronet. 'I remember now.'

'You've probably met him at church too,' went on Fay.

'I dare say, although if you recall, we left church quite promptly. But why should Mrs Stratford's meeting him or not meeting him be of such significance?'

Fay looked away. 'Oh, I . . . I don't know,' she stammered. 'I . . .'

'Dance with me, Fay,' he interrupted her. 'For old times' sake.' She looked at him, hesitated, then allowed him to lead her on to the floor. As a dancer, he was far superior to Peter Frith, and probably to most other men on the floor that evening. As an experience, it was not entirely unfamiliar, since Fay had danced with him before, although not frequently. Tonight, however, as he took her hand, she felt a shiver of excitement run up her arm. She had always known that he was very attractive to women, but had thought herself impervious to his charm. Now, as she looked up into his face, she realized that this was far from being true.

For a few moments they danced together in silence, and then the baronet said, 'Our steps always did fit together, did they not?' It was true. From the very first, they had always been remarkably well attuned on the dance floor.

'Do you remember that night we went to Vauxhall Gardens and I almost lost you?' he asked her. Truth to tell, she had been thinking of that very occasion herself. They had intended to meet some of Sir Jackson's friends there, but they had not been at the rendezvous, and the baronet had gone to see if he could find them. Fay had waited patiently where he had left her, but before he could return, she had become aware that she was being stared at. Looking round, she realized that a rather disreputable-looking man was approaching her from the other side of the dance floor.

'Deserted?' he asked her. 'How very ungallant of him!'

'By no means,' Fay answered standing up. 'He will be returning shortly.'

'Is that what he told you?' replied the man, and Fay felt his hand stray around her waist.

'You go too far, sir,' she protested, trying to push him away. Then, to her great relief, she heard a familiar voice.

'By your leave, sir, this lady is with me.' Fay's assailant turned and, taking Sir Jackson's measure, immediately murmured an apology and withdrew.

'Yes, I remember,' Fay replied. So vivid had the memory been that she looked round almost in surprise to discover that she was in the ballroom at Old Drove House.

They danced in silence again, then the baronet said to her, 'Now tell me, is this young man whom Mrs Stratford had not seen on the dance floor at present?'

Fay looked around when the movements of the dance permitted. 'Yes, he is dancing with Mrs Fleetwood,' she replied.

'Ah yes. A very handsome young fellow. Now I think about it, I do recall seeing him before, only not so smartly dressed. But why this sudden interest in him? Is he another of your suitors?'

'What do you mean?' asked Fay. 'I have no suitors.' Then, thinking about Mr Frith's words and his speaking glance, she coloured.

'Be very careful, Fay,' he warned her. 'They say that there's safety in numbers, but some men are frightened by crowds.'

'So are some women,' she flashed, as the dance ended, and she then put as much distance between them as she could. When she next saw him, he was whispering in Mrs Fleetwood's ear in a way that appeared to amuse that lady enormously.

There was not a single dance that evening when Fay lacked for a partner. Among those with whom she danced was Joe Fairburn. He played his part with more vigour and enthusiasm than Peter Frith and less grace than Sir Jackson, but he still made an acceptable partner.

Fay was glad of the chance to speak to him, saying, 'Rachel showed me the locket that you gave her for Christmas.' He smiled uncertainly. 'She also told me its significance,' she went on. 'Is it fair, Joe, to give it to her when you have not approached her guardians for permission to address her?'

He coloured. 'No, ma'am, it isn't,' he replied frankly. 'But what would the answer have been if I *had* asked? It's not a ring, Miss Prescott.'

'Perhaps not,' she agreed,' but you will never win Rachel's family over by deceit, you know.'

'It's not deceit,' he replied simply. 'The locket is a token that Rachel is my true love, and so she is. If she changes her mind, then I'll have to live with that as well as I may, but that locket will continue to be hers, for there'll never be anyone else for me.'

Thinking back over the evening as she lay in bed that night, it seemed to Fay that it had been one mass of warmth, laughter and swirling colour. There were, however, certain images that stood out in her mind, as if superimposed over the rest.

One was of Joe saying that Rachel was his true love, and would always be, no matter what happened. The recollection of his words made Fay's heart ache a little. True, she had felt attracted to Joe, at first, but that was long since past. But she did long for someone to be her true love, and to cleave to her come what may.

The second image was of Peter Frith bringing her a glass of lemonade and of his earnest face as he said to her, 'Miss Prescott, might I call and see you in the morning? I have something of a particular nature that I wish to say to you.' The young clergyman's attentions had become more marked recently, and Fay felt sure that he would ask for her hand, but would he ever be her true love, in the way that Joe said he was Rachel's?

The third image, which seemed to blot out the others, no matter how she fought against it, was of Mrs Fleetwood laughing up at Sir Jackson, as he looked down into her face.

# Chapter Twelve

The following morning, the house was enshrouded with mist. So heavy and impenetrable was it that the gentlemen did not even go for their morning ride.

'I do not recommend anyone's straying beyond the confines of the garden, except perhaps to walk into the village,' Mr Proudfoot said, in one of his rare communicable moments. 'It has been known for people to become lost in the fens, never to be found again. It is what made this area so difficult for the Vikings to conquer, you know.'

Some of the party did indeed venture out into the gardens, but it was so cold and dank that no one stayed there for very long. Some of the gentlemen went to the billiard-room, and one or two wandered down to the stables. Most of the company gathered in the drawing-room, some of the ladies with their sewing, and a certain languor attended the proceedings.

Eventually, Magnus said, 'I know! Why don't we perform a play?'

'A play?' questioned Roger Napier.

'Yes!' replied Magnus. 'You remember what famous fun it was when Jackson and Hengist and I—'

'*Sir* Jackson, if you don't mind,' corrected Mrs Stratford.

The baronet waved his hand. 'You do well to uphold my dignity, ma'am, but I did give him permission to use my

Christian name,' he said. 'Go on, Magnus.'

'Well, you remember when we performed *Julius Caesar*, and what famous fun we had? Why could we not find a play for more of us, and practise it properly, and then perform it for everyone else? What do you say?'

Predictably, the response was mixed. For the most part, the young people were in favour, although Roger declared himself to be too shy to perform in public, and Lucilla confessed to a certain reluctance.

'I have no objection, although I should never dare perform,' said Mrs Napier, smiling. 'So long as the piece to be performed is perfectly proper, and so long as the performances are not in any way public, but simply for our own private entertainment.' At once, an intense discussion began on the subject of what to perform.

'It is a great pity that my play is not complete,' said Magnus regretfully, 'otherwise, I could offer that for our use.' All of the assembled company knew that Magnus's play, *The Roman General* was entirely in Latin verse, but since there was no possibility of its being ready, they were able to bemoan this unfortunate circumstance with perfect ease.

Fay looked at Magnus's eager face, and reflected that just a very short time ago, he had been wary of saying anything about his writing in front of his aunt. She suspected that his new confidence sprang from his relationship with Sir Jackson, whom he clearly regarded with something akin to hero worship. This was not very surprising in view of the fact that Magnus's father was almost an absent figure. What was surprising was the way in which the baronet seemed to accept this in such good part. Fay recalled that he had said to her only a few days ago that he fancied he would have made a good father. The thought had caused her pain then; it did so now. To distract herself from this feeling, she looked up to discover that people were now making suggestions as to the play that might be performed.

'How about a work by Shakespeare?' ventured Rachel. 'Nothing could be more proper than Shakespeare.' There were a few moments' silence whilst all those who knew their Shakespeare well called to mind passages which would not fit this bill at all.

'We could do *Titus Andronicus*, suggested Hengist, with relish.

'No we could not, you blood-thirsty young whelp,' retorted Sir Jackson. Then he went on, 'I suggest that it might be a good idea for some of you to go and look in the library to see what plays can be found there. It will be of no use to choose to perform something for which we do not have the words.' This sensible suggestion sent most of the young people out of the room in order to look for scripts, and, no doubt, argue vociferously about the merits of those found. The remaining adults breathed a sigh of relief.

'Is there any chance that they will not be able to find anything, do you suppose?' asked Mrs Napier hopefully.

'I don't know, but the search might at least keep them absorbed for as long as the weather remains misty,' replied Sir Jackson. There was a short silence.

'Supposing one could pick any role to play – any role at all – I wonder which one everyone would choose,' mused Mrs Fleetwood eventually. 'Mrs Napier – you choose first.'

'Me?' exclaimed Mrs Napier, a little startled. 'Good gracious, I shouldn't know where to begin. I can't say I know any play well enough to choose. No, really, I can't think of anything at all.'

'Well for my part, I think I should like to be Lady Lurewell in Farquhar's play *The Constant Couples*,' declared Mrs Fleetwood, striking an attitude with half an eye to Sir Jackson. 'I think that I could bring a new quality to the role. Do not you?'

Sir Jackson smiled, but did not say anything.

'I think that I should like to play something comical,' said Mr Napier. 'Perhaps one of those humorous servants in something by Congreve or Sheridan. Then I could say my piece and be off to enjoy a glass of wine whilst I watched the rest.' Everyone laughed.

'What of you, Sir Jackson?' asked Mrs Fleetwood, determined to bring the baronet's attention back to herself. 'Would you play Colonel Standard to my Lady Lurewell, perhaps?'

'Sadly, I have to admit that I have never really cared for that particular play,' confessed Sir Jackson. 'I think that instead, I would like to play Antony in Shakespeare's *Antony and Cleopatra*.'

'What a strange choice,' declared Mrs Fleetwood, her laugh rather brittle. 'A rather obscure work, surely? I don't think I know anything from that play. Does anybody?'

Fay, who had been sewing unobtrusively in a corner said quietly, almost without thinking, '*If it be love indeed, tell me how much.*'

The baronet turned his head at the sound of her voice, paused, then wandered over to her chair and leaning over her with one hand on the back of it, replied, '*There's beggary in the love that can be reckon'd.*'

She looked up from her sewing then, and supplied the next line. '*I'll set a bourn how far to be belov'd.*'

'*Then must thou needs find out new heaven, new earth,*' he answered, completing the quotation. There was a moment's silence, before the rest of the company gave a spontaneous round of applause, in which Mrs Fleetwood joined, in a rather perfunctory manner. She did not look entirely pleased.

'Bravo!' exclaimed Mr Napier. 'Why, Miss Prescott, you could take a part in this play too! You should be with the young people, choosing the script.'

'Oh no, no,' answered Fay, blushing. 'I know some of the works of Shakespeare very well, but I am no actress, I assure you.'

'Fay will be the wardrobe mistress, will you not, Cousin?' said Hooper, smiling. Thinking for one horrible moment that he intended to give her away, Fay looked up at him, her eyes wide with shock.

157

Before she could say anything, or the baronet could elaborate on what he had suggested, Mrs Stratford said enthusiastically, 'Of course! No one who had seen your exquisite stitchery could possibly allow you to do anything else!'

'That was what I meant,' Sir Jackson said, but in the general exclamations that followed Mrs Stratford's comment, he could not be sure that Fay had heard him.

Not long after this, there was a welcome diversion when Mr Frith and his sister arrived.

'I wonder you could find your way here at all,' exclaimed Mrs Stratford. 'Unless the mist is less heavy in the village?'

Mr Frith shook his head. 'By no means,' he replied. 'Nor has it lifted since first thing this morning. I don't think that there will be any change for the rest of the day. You have a very welcoming fire there, ma'am.' Mrs Stratford invited them to draw near to the warmth, and rang for refreshment. Fay, remembering Mr Frith's request for a private interview, looked up at him and surprised him smiling at her a little ruefully, as if acknowledging that given the circumstances, there would be no possibility of any private talk today. Soon after their arrival, Hengist and Horsa came in.

'Have they chosen a play, yet?' Sir Jackson asked them.

'A play!' exclaimed Miss Frith incredulously.

'We thought that we might try to perform a play – just for ourselves, you know,' replied Horsa politely. 'Would you like to take part in it, Miss Frith? Mr Frith?' Her tone was faultlessly polite, but remembering how she had been present when Mr Frith had declared his distaste for dramatic performances, Fay wondered whether the young girl was issuing her invitation out of mischief.

Agnes's face took on an expression of extreme disapproval, and she said, 'Upon no account!' very decisively.

Mr Frith looked very grave and said, 'I think not,' then added after a moment's thought, ' Thank you for asking us.'

'Oh, well, I think that probably there might not be a play anyway, because they are all arguing so much about which one to do,' said Horsa.

Miss Frith smiled thinly. 'Of course, when drama becomes involved, these nasty little disputes are all too likely to occur,' she remarked.

'Nonsense,' replied Sir Jackson amiably. 'They're only children after all, and somewhat irritable at being shut inside. They would be just as liable to argue about who left the door open.'

After the brief silence that followed this remark, Hengist said to the baronet, 'Horsa and I were wondering, sir, since you aren't busy—'

'Oh dear,' murmured Sir Jackson.

'—whether you might like to come outside and help us to train Horsa's new puppy,' finished Hengist.

'You have been inside all morning, and some fresh air would probably do you good,' added Horsa.

'Today? In the mist? On no account,' Sir Jackson replied. 'I should probably die of an inflammation of the lungs.'

'Now come on, Hooper,' urged Lord Bragg. 'Surely an hour spent chasing an untrained puppy around a damp, misty garden would be exactly to your liking.'

'Another day,' promised the baronet.

Hengist and Horsa both looked as if they might try to persuade him further, but they were forestalled by their aunt. 'Run along now, children,' said Mrs Stratford.

'But may we go outside with him?' asked Hengist.

'Very well, but be sure not to let him escape,' answered their aunt. Fay glanced unenthusiastically out of the window, but knowing her duty, she put down her sewing and prepared to go with them.

'Just because they are silly enough to go out in this weather does not mean that you need to go as well, Cousin,' said Sir Jackson, seeing what she was doing and correctly guessing why she was doing it. He turned to Mrs Stratford. 'What do you say, ma'am?'

'Oh no indeed,' agreed Mrs Stratford. 'Pray sit down again, Fay. The children are not venturing beyond the confines of the garden, and can very well go alone.' Fay did not need very much persuading, and she soon returned to her sewing. Mr Frith made an excuse to come and admire her work, but as he was too polite to attempt any kind of private conversation with others sitting around, their talk remained very much concerned with everyday matters.

The Friths did not stay for longer than was courteous, and they were on the point of leaving when Hengist came running in anxiously.

'Oh please, I'm really sorry, I don't know how it happened, but the puppy has escaped!'

'Where is Horsa?' Rachel asked immediately. Hengist gulped.

'She has gone to look for him.'

'Where have they gone?' his aunt asked, her hand going to her throat.

'Into the fens,' he replied. There was a brief silence, during which Rachel slipped out of the room.

'Hengist, I told you to keep hold of him!' Mrs Stratford exclaimed. 'How could you be so disobedient?'

'Later, when we've found them, will be time enough for recriminations, ma'am,' said Sir Jackson, getting to his feet. 'Show me which way she went, will you, my boy?'

'Yes, of course, sir,' replied Hengist, immediately looking relieved.

'In the meantime, will someone have my hat and coat fetched down, and my horse saddled?'

'I'll ask for yours when I go for my own,' said Lord Bragg, as he walked to the door.

Fay stood up. 'Wait,' she said. 'Send for Magnus. He must go with you. He knows this part of the world; take the grooms, too.'

'That's a good thought,' replied Hooper. 'Frith, will you join us? You, also, are familiar with this terrain.'

'By all means,' replied the vicar. 'Agnes, will you stay here?'

'Of course,' replied his sister. 'I will not rest easy until she has been found safely, in any case.'

Sir Jackson left the room with Hengist at his side, but came back a short time later, looking grim. 'Hengist was right,' he said. 'She has walked out into the fens, and there is no sign of her. I think we will need every able-bodied man to join in the search.'

The remaining menfolk willingly left to put on suitable outdoor clothing. As they were assembling in the hall, Mr Proudfoot joined them, clearly ready for the expedition. 'If my daughter is out in the mist, then I shall join the search party,' he said positively. 'My studies have given me as good an understanding of the area as any, I think.'

'What can we do?' Fay asked.

'Make sure that the lanterns are lit at the edge of the gardens,' suggested Sir Jackson. 'It will help guide us back, and Horsa may perhaps see them. And have some warm food and clothing ready for her when she gets back.' It took some little time to assemble those who were to be members of the search party, and they had only just done so when Rachel came hurrying in, in her outdoor clothes.

'Oh Rachel, where on earth have *you* been?' cried Mrs Stratford. 'Isn't one lost female enough?' Rachel beckoned behind her, and Joe Fairburn appeared in the doorway.

'Rachel came to fetch me,' he said. 'I reckon I know these parts better than anyone here, even including yourself, sir,' he declared, nodding to Mr Proudfoot. 'I'll find her for you.'

It was agreed that Mr Proudfoot should lead one group of searchers, and Joe Fairburn another. If Horsa was found, then two shots would be fired into the air to tell the others. All those searching were divided into pairs. No man was to go on his own, and one man out of each pair should be familiar with the terrain.

'Are we better off on foot, or on horseback, do you think?' Sir Jackson asked Joe, who was to be his hunting partner.

'I'd always go on foot,' replied Joe. 'I reckon there's signs and trails that you can miss on horseback, especially in this mist. On the other hand, we might be glad of a horse to carry her back.' He looked away a little, as he spoke.

The baronet grinned. 'Confess it, Joe, you don't think that I can walk far enough, do you?'

The young farmer smiled slowly. 'I'll admit that thought had crossed my mind,' he said.

'Don't worry about me,' said Hooper, clapping him on the shoulder. 'I'm fit enough, and I've got a good pair of boots on. And as for the return journey, one of us can carry her back, if need be. Why that rope?' he asked, indicating the coil which the farmer was carrying slung over one shoulder, and about his waist.

Joe's face took on a serious expression. 'Yonder is the sixteen foot,' he said. 'It might be as well to be prepared.'

'The sixteen foot?' questioned Sir Jackson, half guessing what the answer might be.

'The dyke,' answered Joe. 'Come, sir, let's go.'

'Very well,' agreed the baronet. 'But call me Jackson. This business is far too serious for us to be standing on ceremony.' They walked together in silence for a while, the sound of their feet scrunching through the frosty grass seeming unnaturally loud in the foggy air.

'I can see why it was considered necessary for people who know this area to lead the way,' remarked Sir Jackson after a while. 'There is a complete lack of landmarks in any direction.'

'Even in good weather, it's difficult to find your path,' agreed Joe. 'I've heard people say that this would be a good place to keep convicts. They'd only have to be lost in the fens for a day, I reckon, and they'd be glad to be caught.'

The baronet gave a crack of laughter. 'I can well believe it,' he said. 'Tell me, Joe, do you like living here?'

The young farmer thought for a few minutes. 'Reckon I do,' he replied eventually. 'It's hard to say. You can't judge what you've never seen. The land's good here. Wherever I went, I'd want to grow crops. Livestock's a bit outside my experience, apart from the few beasts we keep for our own needs.'

'What do you know about Coke of Holkham?' asked Sir Jackson.

'I've read a bit about his work, and I'd like to try some of his ideas,' answered Joe.

'They're certainly very successful,' agreed the baronet. 'I'm told that he's doubled the income from his land.'

Joe grinned. 'Reckon I'll wait till the place is my own, then,' he remarked. 'Have any of them been carried out on your estate?' This gave rise to a discussion on agriculture which would have very much surprised those of Sir Jackson's London acquaintance who believed that he was almost exclusively a man-about-town.

Eventually they reached a point where Joe said, 'Careful now, sir. The sixteen foot's only a little way ahead now, and the banks are steep.'

'Now how the devil do you know that?' asked the baronet. Joe grinned. Sure enough, after only a few more steps, they reached a place where the ground dropped away immediately in front of them. Below them lay what would normally be water, but what was now ice. The cut extended to the right and the left as far as the eye could see, which in the present conditions was hardly any distance at all.

The baronet looked down at the ice that lay below them, like a green sheet of clouded glass. 'How thick is the ice, and how deep the water beneath?' he asked.

'Deep enough,' replied Joe. 'Let's hope the ice is thick enough.'

After another short silence, Jackson said, 'If she came this way, she would be bound to meet the water, wouldn't she?'

'There's no other way to go,' agreed Joe.

By silent mutual consent, they walked along by the side of the dyke, looking down at the ice, but looking to the left as well although, as the baronet said, 'It's the dyke I'm most worried about. If she should have fallen down the bank, and the ice should have broken. . . .'

'It doesn't bear thinking about, sir.' They fell silent, looking and listening intently for anything that might betray the presence of Horsa or the puppy. They had not walked very much further when they heard a faint cry. Glancing at one another, they hurried forward.

'Look!' exclaimed Sir Jackson. At the bottom of the bank, with her foot turned out at an awkward angle, was Horsa; on the ice, at about the middle of the cut, was the puppy. 'Horsa! Don't move, but tell us if you are all right!' called the baronet.

'I . . . I think so,' replied Horsa. 'But I think I've hurt my ankle.' She looked and sounded thoroughly chilled and miserable.

'Don't worry, we'll soon get you out of there,' he replied. He turned to see Joe unwinding the rope, and carefully tying one end around his middle.

'Now you see what the rope's for,' he said.

The baronet nodded, but said, 'Joe, I'm lighter than you. If you take the strain, can you lower me down on the rope to get her?'

Joe looked thoughtful. 'Normally I'd say yes straight away. But the ground is slippery, and there's nothing to tie the rope to that's nearby. I'd be glad of another man, but it can't be helped.'

Hooper took out his pistol. 'I'll fire this to say they're found,' he said. 'Someone may come to help us. Horsa, don't be alarmed; I'm just going to fire my pistol to tell the others that we've found you.'

'As if I would be afraid of a pistol,' she replied scornfully, in so much her usual voice that the two men grinned, despite the seriousness of the situation.

'She'll do,' said the baronet. He fired his pistol, and the sound echoed hollowly in the dank air. Moments later, they heard the sound of footsteps, and to their great astonishment, Rachel and Fay appeared out of the mist.

'What the devil are you two doing here?' Sir Jackson exclaimed, his brows drawn together.

Fay opened her mouth to protest at his tone, but Rachel spoke before she could do so. 'We've come to help,' she said. 'And before you say that I shouldn't be here, please remember that Horsa is my sister.'

'I know she's your sister,' protested the baronet, 'but the danger. . . .'

Rachel squared her shoulders. 'Sir Jackson, do not forget that I was brought up in this area, too. If marooned in the fens, I would probably be in less danger than you.'

Joe took a step forward. 'Forgive me, sir, but surely this discussion can be continued later. In the meantime, we have the help that we need to fetch her up.'

Hooper grinned. 'You put us all right, Joe. Let's do it, then. I trust you are both wearing a good pair of gloves, ladies, for you'll need them.' He then tied the other end of the rope around his waist, and Joe coiled the rest of it up so that he could pay it out slowly as needed. Rachel and Fay both stood behind Joe where he told them, at a reasonable distance from the dyke, ready to take the strain.

The descent went well, with no mishaps, and before long, Sir Jackson was at the edge of the ice, where Horsa was crouching. As soon as he arrived, she flung herself against him, putting her arms around his neck.

'Good girl,' he said, returning her embrace. 'How is your ankle? Does it still hurt?'

She nodded, biting her lip. 'I don't think I can stand,' she said.

'I'll carry you,' he said reassuringly. 'Keep your arms around my neck and hold on tight, and we'll soon have you out of here.' He called out to Joe, 'Pull away!'

The three of them at the top of the bank felt the difference immediately. For one thing, there was extra weight on the end of the rope; for another, because he was holding Horsa, Jackson was not able to give very much assistance by climbing himself, as he had done on the way down. Joe's muscles bulged as he pulled on the rope, and Rachel and Fay heaved with all their strength, but with the additional weight, they were pulled forward a little, Joe's feet slid and Rachel slipped and fell.

Fay held on grimly, leaning back hard. By great good fortune, a rock in front of where she was standing had just broken through the soil. Determinedly, she wedged her feet against it, in order to keep herself from slipping. All that she could think of was Jackson, dangling on the end of that rope with Horsa in his arms.

Meanwhile, Rachel scrambled to her feet as quickly as she could and Joe, using the baronet's Christian name for the first time, called out, 'Jackson! Hold on!' After that things went smoothly, and soon Horsa was being embraced by Rachel, whilst Jackson stood at the top, breathing heavily.

He was about to untie the rope from his waist, when Horsa said tremulously, 'My puppy . . . on the ice. . . .' They all looked down to see the little bundle of fluff shivering in the middle of the dyke.

Jackson raised an eyebrow, and grinned ruefully. 'Let me down again,' he said with a sigh.

'No,' said Fay stepping forward. 'I will go.' They all stared at her. 'I'm the lightest of everyone. We don't know how thick that ice is. It is more likely to hold me than anyone else. And it will be much easier to pull me up. Besides, I have played with the puppy as much as anybody. He may remember me.'

Sir Jackson hesitated.

'It makes sense,' urged Joe.

The baronet looked at her. 'I don't want you to do this,' he said. He untied the rope from around his own body and wrapped it around hers, tying it carefully about her. When he had done so, he held her lightly by the waist for a moment, and gently kissed her on the brow. 'Be careful,' he said, looking down into her eyes. She was so moved by this tiny incident, that it took all her powers of concentration to listen to what Joe was saying to her.

'Don't try to walk on the ice. Lie flat, and crawl, so that your weight is spread across a larger area. If you hear it crack, call out and we'll pull you straight up, puppy or no puppy.'

It was a strange sensation, being lowered down the bank, and trying to gain hand holds and foot holds. At last, she stood at the bottom on a small lip of ground at the edge of the ice, and before her, she saw the puppy.

'Lie down,' called the voice of Sir Jackson. Obediently she lay down on the ice, and began to creep towards the puppy. Part way to the little creature, she suddenly realized how quiet it was, and how intently she was listening. The group at the top of the bank had fallen completely silent, as they watched the diminutive figure creeping across the ice. Fay herself was also listening hard for the slightest hint of the smallest sound that might indicate the cracking of the ice.

At last, after what had seemed like an eternity, she reached the puppy and stretched out to take hold of him. She had wondered whether he might growl or snap at her in his panic, but, as if realizing that she was his only hope, he allowed her to take hold of him and, as she drew him near to herself, he wriggled up and licked her face. The warm, wet patch on her face left by his tongue soon chilled in the cold air, and at once she realized how very cold she was, lying on the ice. Suddenly, she began to shiver violently, and then she heard an ominous cracking sound.

At about the same time as she screamed to the group on the bank, she heard a desperate male voice, which she recognized as being that of Sir Jackson, call out 'Pull her up, for God's sake!' For a split second, it occurred to her that she might die there on the ice. Suddenly, she found herself thinking, I'm glad he held me and kissed me once again. Then, almost immediately, she felt herself being drawn steadily across the ice to the side of the dyke. When at last she scrambled to her feet on the same lip of ground from which she had started her journey, she looked round and saw that the ice had indeed cracked, just where she and the puppy had been. They had been pulled to safety just in time.

'If we pull you up, can you manage to use your hands and feet to keep you steady, or shall I come down?' The baronet asked her.

She looked up at him. 'I think I can manage,' she replied. 'Don't pull too fast.' She was a little afraid that the puppy might wriggle too much, but again, as if he had learned his lesson, he allowed her to hold him in her left arm, so that she could climb with her right hand and her feet.

'Are you all right?' Sir Jackson asked her intently, as he unfastened the rope from around her waist. She was shaking a little, and briefly, he allowed his hand to remain on her waist.

'I am now,' she replied, smiling a little uncertainly. 'But please, no one make me do that again!'

'Good girl,' said Jackson, his eyes glowing with admiration.

'Come, let's get back to the house as fast as we can,' said Joe. 'It's not getting any warmer out here.' He and Jackson took it in turns to carry Horsa, whilst Rachel and Fay similarly took turns to carry the puppy. As Fay was walking behind Sir Jackson at one stage, she looked at his straight back, broad shoulders and long dark hair, coming loose from its confining ribbon.

Suddenly, she realized why she had fainted at the sight of him; why she had been so afraid to accept gifts from him; why she had felt so afraid when he had disappeared over the bank to rescue Horsa, and why she had been so glad to see his face just now at the top of the bank. She might not have been in love with him when she had been his mistress, but she was in love with him now. If she had perished out on the ice, the one thought that she would have clung to as the water had closed over her face would have been the memory of the feel of his hands on her waist, his lips on her brow.

When they arrived back at the house, they were surrounded by well-wishers, mostly other members of the search party, who made haste to get them into the warm. Horsa was carried upstairs to a warm bed and the doctor, who had quickly been summoned, pronounced her to be unharmed by her experience. The ankle injury, he said reassuringly, was just a severe sprain.

'Keep her off it for a few days, and it will soon be mended,' he declared, then shared a glass of punch with the rest of the household, before leaving to make his next call.

Mrs Fleetwood was there amongst those who were waiting with congratulations for the returning rescuers, but her praise was chiefly directed towards Sir Jackson. Her fine eyes glowed with admiration at his courage, and the baronet seemed to Fay to be basking in the handsome widow's approval in a quite unnecessary way. Fay was very conscious of her own dishevelment, and although Mrs Fleetwood exclaimed 'Miss Prescott, how ... surprising of you!' the look in her eyes spoke of contempt, rather than admiration.

The whole exploit was described by Rachel, who left out no one's heroism, least of all Joe's. Joe, who had been brought into the drawing-room, also shared in the punch.

Mr Proudfoot expressed his gratitude to all of the rescuers, marvelling at the courage of Fay as she crossed the ice, and of Sir Jackson, who had lifted Horsa from danger. 'And you, young man, steadied the rope,' he said to Joe. 'Your father was my tenant before you, wasn't he?'

'Yes, sir, he was,' Joe replied. 'And his father before that.'

Mr Proudfoot looked at him carefully, eyeing his blond locks with interest. 'So the farm has always been tended by Fairburns.'

'No, sir. My grandfather married into the tenancy, and his wife was an Erikson.'

'Erikson!' exclaimed Mr Proudfoot. 'There wouldn't be any Viking blood in you, would there?'

'I should think there must be, Papa,' said Rachel, with a twinkle in her eye. Fay smiled. It looked as though the young lady might have found a way of getting what she wanted after all. Turning round, she saw Peter Frith standing nearby and looking at her hopefully, and her heart sank as she remembered that he had expressed a desire to speak privately with her.

'My dear Miss Prescott, my admiration of your courage knows no bounds,' he declared.

Fay shook her head. 'I only did what needed to be done,' she replied. 'Plenty of others would have done the same.'

'I'm not so sure of that,' he answered. 'But I can see that you had rather not speak of this further. As you know, I wanted to talk to you privately today, but now is clearly not the moment. Might I hope that tomorrow, you will grant me the favour of an interview?'

Fay, with a sinking heart, said 'Yes, of course.'

After the Friths had gone, and all the excitement had died down, Sir Jackson took the opportunity of seeking out Mr Proudfoot. The gentleman was in his study, poring over a map of the area.

'What is it that interests you particularly, sir?' asked Sir Jackson.

'I am just wondering how the Eriksons came to settle here,' he said. 'Fascinating, that young man coming from Viking stock. Fancy, his being one of my own tenants, and my not realizing it!'

'The Vikings were people of enterprise, and Joe Fairburn has inherited some of that,' said the baronet diplomatically. 'Had he not brought a rope with him, we might well have found ourselves in grave difficulties.'

'Indeed!' exclaimed Mr Proudfoot. 'Perhaps we ought to reward the young fellow. What do you say?'

'No doubt something will occur to you,' murmured Sir Jackson. 'But in the meantime, is not a young man of his ability wasted on a small farm? Could you not find more scope for his talents elsewhere?' The baronet came away soon afterwards, leaving Mr Proudfoot looking very thoughtful.

# Chapter Thirteen

Mercifully, no one appeared to suffer any ill effects as a result of the day's adventures. Even Horsa was agitating to get up the next day. The doctor paid her a short visit and declared her to be well on the road to recovery, and after that she was not really satisfied until she had been carried into the schoolroom so that she could join in with the morning's reading session. Matty and Jenny were brought over by their elder brother, who seemed to have made a special effort with his appearance, having dressed in his Sunday best, with his clothes neatly pressed and his boots shiny. After the girls had been safely delivered, he went to seek out Mr Proudfoot. Sir Jackson met him in the hall.

'Dare I guess your errand?' he asked. Joe smiled a little uncertainly.

'I suppose you might,' he replied. 'Do you think me presumptuous?' The baronet eyed his diffident demeanour.

'I think that's one thing I would never call you,' he said. 'Does Rachel know about this?'

Joe shook his head. 'I didn't want to get her hopes up,' he said. 'But it's time this was talked about openly, now. Seeing Horsa on the ice yesterday made me realize how precious Rachel is to me – how I would have felt had it been she down there. I don't want any more sneaking about in corners, even if the answer *is* to be no.'

'I think you might find him more open to your suggestion than you expect,' said Sir Jackson. 'In the meantime, if you want me to stand your friend, Joe, you have only to ask.'

'Thank you, sir,' replied the other.

The baronet held his hand out. 'My name is Jackson,' he reminded him.

A few minutes later, a maid came to the schoolroom, where the assembled company was listening to Matty reading some poetry by Spenser, and asked if Miss Rachel might step downstairs to her father's study. Looking somewhat mystified – for this kind of summons was almost unprecedented – Rachel hurried downstairs, and within half an hour, the news was all around the house that Miss Rachel was engaged to be married to Mr Fairburn.

'And that isn't all,' she told the schoolroom party when she came back upstairs, her face aglow. 'Papa has asked him to manage the whole of his estate!'

'Well, thank the Lord for that!' exclaimed Magnus. 'Perhaps now, I'll be able to go to Cambridge! I can't tell you how much I've hated riding round and saying what needed to be done, when I knew that the people I was telling had a much better idea than I did myself!'

At that moment, Sir Jackson came strolling in. 'Do I gather that congratulations are in order?' he asked.

No sooner did she see him, than Rachel flew across the room and flung herself into his arms. 'Thank you!' she exclaimed, reaching up and kissing him on the cheek. 'Papa told me that you had spoken warmly of Joe. I shall have to spend the rest of my life thanking you, I think!'

The baronet laughed, and returned her embrace in an avuncular style. 'Pray do not waste your time in such a manner,' he declared, his smile taking any sting out of his words. 'I merely encouraged your father to observe Joe's best qualities.'

Rachel smiled up at him and, as she did so, Fay felt a stab of jealousy. It was not that she suspected either of them of feeling other than excessive gratitude in the one case, and disinterested benevolence in the other, but she suddenly realized that she felt a deep longing for Sir Jackson to take her in his arms, and that there was nothing else that would provide an acceptable substitute for his embrace.

A few moments later, Rachel hurried over to where Horsa was reclining on a day bed, which had been brought to the schoolroom especially for her use while she was temporarily incapacitated. 'It's thanks to you as well, little sister,' she said, bending down to embrace her. 'If it hadn't been for your falling down the bank, and Joe saving your life, Papa might not have given his consent.'

'Yes he would, as soon as he realized that Joe had Viking blood in him,' replied Horsa. 'Anyway, it wasn't just Joe who rescued me, it was Sir Jackson and Miss Prescott as well.'

'Yes, but the rescue gave Joe the courage to put his fate to the test,' Rachel answered.

Horsa was quiet for a moment, then said, 'I hope I'm not going to be expected to roll down into the dyke every time a member of my family wants to get married.' Needless to say, this caused great amusement, Hengist even going so far as to say that he had by far roll into a dyke himself than ever get married, so Horsa could save herself the trouble. This exchange effectively marked the end of the reading session. Rachel went downstairs with Matty and Jenny to say goodbye to them and, more importantly to Joe, who was just finishing his interview with Mr Proudfoot. Chloe and Lucilla went away deep in discussion and, at Horsa's request, Magnus carried her downstairs to watch her two brothers play billiards.

Fay remained in the schoolroom, fully expecting Mrs Stratford to come in search of her, breathing fire. She was convinced in her own mind that the task that the older lady had given her had always been an impossible one. Rachel and Joe were clearly made for each other, and their destiny had been set long before she had ever arrived upon the scene. To what degree Mrs Stratford would blame her for not keeping them apart, however, she had no way of knowing.

But when Mrs Stratford did arrive, she was much more inclined to look for sympathy than to blame Fay for what had happened. 'All my plans brought to nothing!' she wailed. 'I might have seen what was coming. My fool of a brother! I *knew* that unless something was done, there would be disaster, and you see that I have been proved right. Of course, he gave his consent immediately, without even consulting me! Just to know that the young man is of Viking descent is enough to satisfy him, apparently. It is past all bearing! It makes me think that I would have done well to tell all our male guests to come bearing battle-axes, and sporting helmets with horns on them! Then perhaps he might have singled one of *them* out for special favour!'

Fay tried, but failed, to imagine any of the visitors in such garb, and before the very thought gave her a fit of the giggles, she led Mrs Stratford to a chair and said soothingly, 'Come now, ma'am. As you have said, the matter has been decided; so why not look and see what advantages there are to be had from the situation?'

'Advantages!' exclaimed Mrs Stratford scornfully. 'I should like to know what advantage can possibly be salvaged from such an unmitigated disaster!' But she consented to sit down, and listened nonetheless.

'First of all, he is presentable,' said Fay. Mrs Stratford snorted. 'Now ma'am, you thought so yourself, I know you did, for you were surprised when you saw him in the ballroom that night,' Fay went on firmly. The older lady shrugged, and nodded reluctantly. 'Secondly, he is in a position to be able to buy his own property, or so I am told, and now that he is to manage this estate for your brother, that will also improve his standing, will it not?'

'Perhaps,' was the grudging answer.

'And then, there is Sir Jackson's friendship,' went on Fay, hoping that she was not blushing too much at the baronet's name. 'His support will surely help them.'

'If Sir Jackson does not disown him,' replied the other woman gloomily.

Fay straightened immediately. 'Jackson is a man of his word,' she declared. 'If he has offered Joe his friendship, then he means it.' As soon as she had stopped speaking, she became very self-conscious at her heated championship of the baronet, until she remembered that it would not be thought strange for her to speak up in her kinsman's defence.

Mrs Stratford thought for a time, but then burst out with, 'But her London season! All my plans wasted!'

'No, they need not be,' urged Fay. 'Plenty of girls enjoy their first season when they are already engaged. In fact, it might be more enjoyable for you, because you will have none of the trouble of finding a husband for her. Just think: all of the fun and none of the anxiety.' By the time Mrs Stratford left the school-room, only the most inveterate optimist would have said that she was completely reconciled to the match. Fay felt though that she had given her plenty to think about, and sown a seed or two, which might bear fruit later, if carefully tended.

It was only after she had gone that Fay began to think about what her own fate might be. She had been hired to be a companion to Rachel, with the understanding that she would encourage her to think of men other than Joe. This plan had failed, and although Fay had made herself useful in other ways, notably by reading with Horsa, and teaching her to sew − for which work the majority of the household believed she had actually been employed − this was not what she had really been engaged to do. It would not be at all surprising, therefore, if she were told very soon that her services would no longer be required.

What would she do then? It seemed likely that Mrs Stratford might be prepared to give her a good reference, but for what work would she be eligible? Certainly nothing in London, for there was always the danger there that she might meet someone who had known her when she was Sir Jackson's mistress. True, she had gone about very little at the time, but there were some who might remember, and she could not risk the scandal that disclosure would bring. Her only hope would be to find employment with someone else who lived a secluded life, or perhaps with someone who intended to live in the colonies. She would have to be very careful.

She thought of Sir Jackson, and the look that she had seen in his eye at times, which seemed to indicate that he might want to pick up the threads of their old relationship. Now that she had acknowledged to herself that she was in love with him, the temptation to succumb would be very strong, but she knew that for the sake of her own sanity, she must resist. Sooner or later, Sir Jackson would be bound to marry, for the sake of his name, and then his wife would insist on his sending her packing, just as he had been about to do before she had taken the intiative and left him first.

The thought of going from him to another man would be quite unthinkable, but she knew at first hand the difficulties of obtaining honourable employment; and these would be increased a hundredfold if she became the baronet's mistress again. Furthermore, the pain of leaving him, now that she knew that she loved him, would be far worse than before, although as she looked back, she recalled how lost she had felt when she had left his protection. At the time, she had thought that this was simply anxiety at being adrift once more in an indifferent world. Now, she wondered whether deep down she had loved him even then.

There was no doubt that the only sensible course would be to look for employment well away from London. Her mind was still grappling with this problem as she tidied her books away when there was a tap on the schoolroom door, and Peter Frith appeared, looking rather ill-at-ease.

'Good morning, Miss Prescott,' he said. 'I trust that you are not suffering any ill effects from your ordeal yesterday.'

'None at all, thank you, sir,' she replied, with a curtsy. 'Not even from being dragged backwards across a frozen dyke on the end of the rope!'

'You showed remarkable courage,' he declared.

Fay shook her head. 'It was Horsa who was remarkable,' she replied. 'Heaven knows how long she was huddled there, but she kept calm, and had the presence of mind to keep on talking to the puppy so that it wouldn't be afraid. By the way, they have decided to call the puppy Moses! Is that not appropriate?'

'Indeed,' agreed Mr Frith with a smile. 'Miss Prescott, I am glad to find you alone, for there is something of a particular nature that I wish to say to you.'

'Very well,' replied Fay, not giving any outward sign of the apprehension that she was feeling. 'Shall we sit down?'

Mr Frith did as he was invited, but almost immediately, he got to his feet again. 'I must tell you, before I speak, that I am only daring to do so because I have been given permission.'

'Permission? By whom?' asked Fay, wrinkling her brow.

'By Sir Jackson of course,' replied Mr Frith. 'When I decided to . . . to speak to you on this matter, I knew that I must not do so without obtaining consent from your nearest male relative. Sir Jackson assured me that he was the nearest male relative that you had.'

'Did he indeed?' said Fay, in a tone which must have aroused Mr Frith's curiosity, had he been capable of thinking of anything except for the task in hand.

'I felt I needed to consult him . . . or someone . . . because . . . . in short, Miss Prescott, I am desirous of obtaining permission to address you.'

'To address me?' Fay had been almost certain that this was why he had wanted to see her, but she could not help exclaiming out loud. It was, after all, the first offer of marriage that she had ever received.

'Why yes, Miss Prescott,' he went on, pulling at his neckband, which seemed suddenly to have become rather tight. 'You cannot be unaware of the esteem in which I hold you – have held you from the first time I met you when I brought you back from March that day. I have thought and prayed very earnestly abut this, and I have consulted my sister Agnes. She is in agreement with me that your background fits you perfectly to be the wife of a clergyman.'

Biting her lip to prevent herself from saying *which part of my background*, Fay said instead, 'And what of your sister? What would she do in those circumstances?'

'Why, she would remain with us, of course,' replied Frith, as if surprised that she should even ask such a question. 'I am sure that you will get on extremely well together. Can we consider it as settled, then?'

Fay looked puzzled, as if she was not really taking in what he was saying. 'I beg your pardon?' she uttered. Then, pulling herself together, she went on. 'Oh no, pray, Mr Frith. I am deeply flattered that you have chosen to address me, but I'm afraid that I cannot answer you straight away. Will you be so kind as to give me some time in order to think about it? It has come as something of a surprise to me.'

Frith beamed, his smile betraying the relief that he felt at actually having got his proposal out after thinking about it for several days. 'By all means,' he replied heartily. 'Naturally, a young lady must think carefully about an offer of marriage; no doubt you will be seeking the advice of your kinsman as well.'

'No doubt,' agreed Fay, speaking between her teeth. 'Before you go, Mr Frith, there is one question that I would be grateful if you would answer for me.'

'If I can.'

'When you asked my cousin for permission to address me, did

he actually give his consent?'

'To be strictly truthful, he said at first that you could answer as you pleased,' replied Mr Frith. 'But. . . .'

'But?'

'But later, he did give his consent.'

'I see,' answered Fay colourlessly. 'Perhaps you will leave me, now, to think about what you have said?'

'Why yes, of course. And may I return tomorrow, to ascertain your feelings on the matter?'

'Tomorrow?' She looked at him blankly for a moment, before saying quickly, 'Certainly. When I have discussed the matter with my cousin.' She stood up. 'Thank you for coming, Mr Frith.'

'Oh. Yes, indeed! Good day!' The vicar left, a little puzzled by some of the things that Fay had said, but with a heart not unhopeful of a happy outcome.

Fay herself went downstairs in a very different mood. After what she had heard, she felt ready for battle. For Jackson to claim her as his cousin, for what he maintained were altruistic reasons was one thing; for him to assume the authority that went with the position of a senior male relative was quite another. As luck would have it, the baronet was the first person that she saw when she got downstairs.

'Come with me,' she said imperiously. 'Now!' Sir Jackson looked down from his 6'1" at her 5'2" and grinned. 'And you can stop smiling, because by the time I have finished with you, you will have nothing to smile about,' she concluded, and turned to go back up the stairs to the schoolroom, judging that that was the place where she would be most sure of privacy.

When they were inside with the door closed, he remarked, 'Perhaps you should be a governess after all.'

'Why do you say that?' she asked him suspiciously.

'You seem very authoritative. It's a side of you that I have never seen before.'

'Perhaps it is high time that you *did* see it,' she declared. 'Tell me, Jackson, exactly what gave you the idea that you could give Peter Frith, or anyone else for that matter, permission to address me?'

'Fay, my dear!'

'And don't you "my dear" me!' she stormed, stepping closer to him and poking him in the midriff. 'My hand is to dispose of as I see fit, and neither you, nor anyone else, has any say in the matter at all.'

'As a matter of fact—' he began, but again she interrupted him.

'I don't know whether when you claimed to be my relative, you hoped to gain some kind of . . . of power over me, but—'

At this point, he seized hold of her hands and held her still. 'Now wait a minute. What is all this rubbish?' he demanded. '*Power* over you? Why the devil should I want that?'

When she discovered that she could not shake herself free, she simply stared up at him and said, 'I don't know – maybe for revenge.' There was a silence.

'Revenge?' he asked incredulously.

'For leaving you.'

He released her then. 'So that's what you think of me, is it? You could actually live with me all that time, and suppose that I'm capable of that?'

She coloured. 'I don't know what I thought,' she admitted. 'But I know that you had no right to give Peter Frith permission to address me.'

'For your information, my sweet, I did not give him permission. I told him exactly what you have just told me – that your hand is yours to dispose of, and no one else's.' He walked to the door, then turned, his hand on the handle. 'Oh and by the way, I also told him that you deserved to be loved and cherished – but maybe I was mistaken.' He left the room, closing the door behind him.

It took Fay some time to catch her breath after he had gone.

She felt as if she had been running for some time. Up to a point that was true, she acknowledged ruefully. In a sense, she had been running away from the truth. She had already admitted to herself that she was in love with the baronet; now it had become clear to her that she had loved him ever since she had decided that she could not bear to see him marry another woman whilst she bore his child.

She sat down and thought seriously about Peter Frith's proposal. In many ways, marriage to the vicar would be the perfect way to re-establish herself, and Frith had been right, in that her early background had in some senses prepared her to be a clergyman's wife. She would have a role in the community, a home, a family, and she would be near to the Proudfoots, of whom she had become very fond. She would be included in the Christmas and harvest festivities, which she knew she would very much enjoy. In addition, and most importantly, she would belong somewhere, and she was tired of being rootless.

The question that she had to ask herself, before she could accept Peter's proposal, was could she marry another man whilst she was still in love with Jackson? She tried to tell herself fiercely that romantic dreams would not put bread in her mouth, and that she must provide for her future in a practical, sensible way. But how could she be a wife to Peter, when every time she closed her eyes, it was Jackson's face she saw?

And what of Peter himself? In all honesty, could she really marry him without telling him of her past? True, she might never meet anyone who knew about her past life, but could she herself live with such dishonesty? And was he enamoured enough of her to be able to accept not just her theatrical antecedents, but her intimate past? She did not want to answer any of these questions, but as the next day drew nearer, she knew that she could not avoid them.

She had one further encounter with Sir Jackson before the vicar came for his answer. Instead of taking a morning ride the following day, he came up to the schoolroom to find her. She stood in front of the window looking at him half defiantly, half regretfully, very conscious that she had wrongly accused him of assuming authority over her the previous day.

'Are you going to accept Peter Frith?' the baronet asked her without preamble. She opened her mouth to speak, but before she could say anything, he raised his hand. 'You will say, quite rightly, that it's none of my business. I have two things to say to you. The first is that it is up to you what you tell Frith. He won't hear anything about our past association from me. But the second thing that I want to say is this: when I asked you to come with me that first time, why did you do so?'

She looked at him in silence for a moment, then answered in a thread of a voice, 'Because I had nowhere else to go.'

He took a step or two closer to her, took hold of her by the shoulders and said, in a voice almost as quiet as her own, 'Make sure you don't marry Frith for the same reason − he deserves better.'

'And you don't?'

For answer, he bent and kissed her lightly on the lips. 'Remember what I said,' he murmured. He bent towards her, and for a moment it seemed as if he was going to kiss her again and she held her breath.

Then the door opened softly, and the voice of Mrs Fleetwood said, 'I do beg your pardon. I hope I am not intruding?' To her great annoyance, Fay could feel herself blushing, and she walked quickly to the window.

'I was just giving my cousin some worldly advice,' said Jackson. 'Have you come to find me, Deborah? Shall we take a stroll in the gallery, perhaps?'

Fay did not look round until the door had closed behind them. How much had Mrs Fleetwood heard, she wondered? She tried to think back over the conversation that she had just had with Sir Jackson, and eventually came to the conclusion that only the most suspicious person could have made anything of what had been said. Unfortunately, however, it seemed likely that Mrs Fleetwood could easily be that sort of person especially if, as Fay suspected, she had her sights set on the baronet. She could have wished that the widow had not come in at that moment, but it was no use repining now.

To revive her spirits, she tried to whip up her anger by telling herself that the baronet was guilty of a kind of hypocrisy; he was instructing her not to go to Frith out of desperation, when, in other circumstances, he had given her no choice himself. But suddenly, deep down inside, she was quite sure that despite what he had said, he would never have left her to fend for herself alone in London.

She began to think about what he had said to her before Mrs Fleetwood had interrupted them. He had not told her anything that she had not told herself already. To hear it confirmed, however, showed her beyond a shadow of a doubt that she could not in all honesty marry Peter; not because she had been another man's mistress, or because she had been in the theatre, but because he deserved to be someone's first choice. Sir Jackson's caress had shown her that Peter could never be that for her. Even the memory of the baronet's feather-light kiss had the power to send a shiver down her spine.

When the vicar arrived later that day, he could see her answer written in the expression on her face; his own face fell as she explained to him as kindly as she could that she was unable to accept his proposal. 'I cannot love you, Mr Frith,' she said sadly. 'Not in the right way. I am so sorry.'

'But will you not take a little more time to consider?' he urged her. 'Perhaps you could come to love me in time. Many marriages begin with just liking, or even with esteem; love will surely follow, with good will on both sides.'

'Yes,' agreed Fay. 'But not if one of the two is . . . is still in love with . . . with someone from the past.'

Instantly the light died out of his eyes. 'I beg your pardon,' he said. 'I had not realized; Sir Jackson did not tell me of this. But perhaps he does not know?'

Fay flushed. 'No, he does not,' she replied.

'Should you change your mind,' he went on.

'I will not.'

'Then I must bid you good day, and ask you to accept my best wishes for your future happiness,' he said before leaving. She watched him go with sorrow, but without regret. Sir Jackson was right. He deserved better.

# Chapter Fourteen

That evening after dinner, Roger Napier said, 'By the way, did anyone know that there is a troop of strolling players visiting March at the moment?' Fay dropped her embroidery, together with some of her cottons, and bent to pick them up.

'No, really?' exclaimed Magnus eagerly. 'What are they performing?'

'Have a look,' replied Roger. 'I picked up a playbill while I was in March. They're performing at The Griffin. I thought that since we didn't get round to choosing a play to do ourselves, we might go to see them instead.' So saying, he drew the playbill out of his pocket and handed it to Magnus.

Whilst he had been speaking, Sir Jackson had wandered over to help Fay pick up her embroidery things. When the job was done, he contrived to place himself between her and the other occupants of the room, ostensibly admiring her work.

' "The Llewellyn players present *King Lear* by William Shakespeare",' read Magnus, ' "with tasteful adjustments, thus omitting the scenes distressing to all, and adding the happy ending which so many deserve". *King Lear* with a happy ending! Good Lord!'

'I saw *King Lear* once,' said Lord Bragg. 'Depressing piece! I'm all for a happy ending. Is there a farce as well?'

'Yes,' replied Magnus. ' "*Love or Money*, an entertaining piece, in which true love triumphs over avarice".'

'A fairy-tale, then!' laughed Mrs Fleetwood. 'In my opinion avarice triumphs every time. What do you think, Miss Prescott?' This was so unexpected that Fay looked up, startled, and almost dropped her embroidery all over again.

'I think that my cousin was concentrating on her embroidery,' said Sir Jackson.

This gave Fay a few precious moments in which to regain her composure, and she merely remarked tranquilly, 'I generally prefer a serious play to a farce, I must confess.'

'Well, I think that we should all certainly go,' said Mrs Fleetwood. 'The children too. Miss Prescott! I appeal to you! You are a lover of drama, are you not? We have all heard about your play-reading sessions. What a valuable opportunity it would be for them to go! Perhaps they may come to be as well-informed as you are yourself.'

'Such a decision is not for me to make,' replied Fay, who was rapidly beginning to feel that she has stumbled into a nightmare. 'Mr Proudfoot and Mrs Stratford will decide.'

Here, at least, it appeared that things were turning in Fay's favour, for Mrs Stratford said, 'The drama may be perfectly proper, but the company will probably be rather too mixed for the children. And I would certainly not favour *King Lear* as a first choice to which to take them, happy ending or no. But I see no reason why any of the adults who wish to go should not do so.'

Fay was suddenly conscious of an overwhelming feeling of relief. If the children were not to go, then she would have the perfect excuse for staying at home. The relief that she felt came to an abrupt end, however, when she looked up and encountered the knowing expression on Mrs Fleetwood's face. All at once, she was quite certain that Mrs Fleetwood had somehow found out about her past, and that she had correctly interpreted the conversation that she had overheard Fay having with Sir Jackson. Her suggestion about going to see the travelling theatre company had, therefore, not just been an innocent enthusiasm of the moment, but on the contrary had been born out of quite deliberate malice. She was not entirely surprised therefore when Mrs Fleetwood came to the schoolroom the following day after the reading session was over.

'Another lesson successfully completed,' murmured Mrs Fleetwood, as she picked up first one book then another and laid them down again. 'Quite a contrast to your previous existence, I should imagine.'

Fay paused briefly in her tidying, then carried on, saying, 'I'm not sure I understand you, ma'am.'

'On the contrary, I am quite sure that you understand me very well,' replied Mrs Fleetwood. 'Do your employers know about your previous . . . activities, I wonder?'

Fay turned to face her then. 'I repeat, I do not understand you,' she said firmly. 'I think I must ask you to explain yourself.'

The widow sat down by the fire, in the chair which Rachel had only recently vacated. 'Come, my dear. We are both women of the world, are we not? You perhaps more so than myself.' When Fay remained silent, Mrs Fleetwood went on. 'It really is no use your playing coy like this. You ought to know that Tony Nantwich is my cousin – my *real* cousin, not some kind of fictitious cousin – and he mentioned your name to me when you were in Hooper's keeping. It took me a little while to put two and two together, but when I overheard the two of you talking the other day, I knew that my suspicions were justified.'

Fay lifted her eyebrows. 'You overheard us talking?' she murmured. 'Oh, I suppose you mean that before you came in here the other day, you listened at the door. How . . . er . . . enterprising of you.'

Mrs Fleetwood's smile disappeared at the contempt in Fay's voice. 'There is no need for you to be so self-righteous,' she declared. 'After all, you are only an actress and a trollop.' Fay turned a little pale and she drew herself up very straight, but before she could say anything, Mrs Fleetwood spoke again, standing up as she did so. 'I have not yet decided what use to make of my information,' she said conversationally. 'It may be that I shall not need to use it at all. But understand this: if I feel that you are coming between me and anything – or anyone – that I want, then I shall know how to act. I hope I make myself clear.' So saying, she turned and walked out, without waiting for an answer.

So Mrs Fleetwood knew her story. The only consolation was that it had not been from Sir Jackson that she had learned it. The previous night, when Fay had been tossing and turning, and thinking about the way in which the widow had goaded her concerning the theatre company, she had wondered in her darkest moments whether the baronet had told her about their relationship. Now, thankfully, it was clear that he was innocent of this betrayal.

Just as clearly, however, Mrs Fleetwood believed that he was showing an interest in her, and she was obviously determined to protect her interests, even to the point of going to any lengths to make sure that no other woman got him. If she only knew that Fay had already decided that she could not belong to Sir Jackson again!

Suddenly, Fay found herself longing for the departure of the London guests. The leaving of Sir Jackson would be painful; all the more so because over these past days she had discovered a side of him that had revealed a witty, good-humoured, patient man, whom she could like as well as love. But to see the back of Mrs Fleetwood and her threats would bring blessed relief.

That afternoon brought what promised to be a pleasant diversion. Mrs Fairburn had invited those who wanted to visit Fir Tree Farm and meet her niece and admire the new baby. Rachel of course was to be present, and Horsa wanted to go, too. Mrs Stratford, conscious of the need to make what she could of this new relationship, went with them. Mrs Fleetwood had declined

189

the invitation with contempt at first ('a visit to a farmer's widow and a lawyer's wife – oh my!' was her reaction) but when she discovered that Sir Jackson had offered to escort them, she changed her mind.

Once the widow had decided to be of the party, Fay's immediate instinct was to decline the invitation in order to safeguard her future position, but Rachel and Horsa were quite insistent that she should go. In truth, she was quite glad to get out of the house for a while. Perhaps it had something to do with Mrs Fleetwood's threats, or perhaps it was more because of the fog that had enveloped them on previous days, but the atmosphere inside the house felt strangely oppressive.

On their arrival at the farm, they received a very warm welcome from Mrs Fairburn, who was clearly delighted with her new great-nephew and wanted nothing better than to show him off. Her niece was a quiet, well-spoken, dignified young woman, who was very happy to tell the visitors about the new arrival who was, needless to say, the best-behaved baby in the entire world.

Mrs Fleetwood coldly rejected the suggestion that she might like to hold the baby, and Mrs Stratford, who had had no children of her own, much preferred to see them being held by someone else.

'Miss Prescott,' said the baby's mother. 'I am sure that you would like to nurse him.' Fay sat down and, half eagerly, half fearfully, allowed Mrs Fairburn's niece to put the baby into her arms. For a minute or two, the world was shut out, and she could only think of the tiny perfect being that she was holding. She was conscious of neither the arrested expression on Sir Jackson's face, nor of the calculating way in which Mrs Fleetwood looked at the man she wanted and at the woman whom she believed stood in her way. Then, suddenly, as she looked down at the baby, Fay began to remember what she had lost, and she found that tears were pouring uncontrollably down her face; tears which she could not brush away for she did not even have a hand free to do so.

Around her she heard voices exclaiming things like 'Miss Prescott!' 'Fay!' 'The poor young lady! What can be the matter?' Then, mercifully, someone took the baby from her, and at once she got up and ran from the room and out of the front door. All she wanted was solitude, and she found it in the same barn in which Rachel had met Joe. She sat down on a hay bale, her face in her hands. Behind her closed eyes moved pictures from her recent past.

When she had left Sir Jackson's protection, she had not really known where to go. All she had known was that she must get away from him of her own free will, before his forthcoming marriage forced her to leave.

She took very little with her. She had a cloak bag in which she had placed some of her favourite clothes, but of necessity, she had left most of her things behind. She took with her some of the presents that he had given her for Christmas, and a small amount of money, saved from her allowance. It was not a great deal, but it was enough to provide for herself for a short time until she could find employment.

As a beginning, she took a hackney to The Bull and Mouth, intending to catch a stage-coach which was going to some provincial town. Her instinct told her that although work of a kind could be found in London, she would be more likely to find something respectable outside the capital. She had no idea in her mind of where to go, but she had a feeling that somehow, guidance would be given.

On her arrival at The Bull and Mouth, an incident took place which encouraged Fay considerably. A coach was just arriving, and amongst those who got down was a fresh-faced girl, bright-eyed, excited, and obviously from the country. Fay looked at her for a moment, seeing herself from what seemed a lifetime ago. Then for some reason, she felt the hairs prickle on the back of her neck and, turning, she saw Mrs Bellham standing a short distance away. Without hesitation, she walked up to the girl and said politely, 'Pardon me, but have you come to London looking for work?'

The girl looked relieved at having someone speak to her. 'That I have, ma'am,' she replied in a country burr. 'I have an address to go to on this little piece of paper, but I don't know where it is, or who to ask.'

'Well, take my advice and go inside and ask the landlord,' said Fay. 'And whatever you do, don't go with that lady over there. She may look respectable, but she's a bawd, and is only looking for girls to work in her brothel. I nearly got caught by her myself when I was first in London.'

The girl looked horrified. 'Thank the Lord I met you!' she exclaimed. 'The rector warned me of such wickedness, but I never believed him. I'll do just as you say, miss.' Fay smiled as she watched the girl go inside. At least she had saved one girl from Bellham's clutches. It was little enough, but it gave her confidence.

On impulse, she approached one of the other passengers. 'Where has this coach come from?' she asked him.

'From Cambridge, miss,' was his reply. Cambridge! She smiled ironically. Strange how fate seemed to be leading her back there again.

Inside the inn, she enquired when the next stage would be leaving for Cambridge, and found that it would not be until the following morning. She paid for a room, and asked for a tray to be brought to her there with a bowl of soup – for in her present condition, she found that she could not face meat at all – and retired for the evening.

Once all that had been done, she found herself free to think about her situation. Of the life, and the man that she had left behind, she did not allow herself to think at all. They were in the past. For now, she was homeless, friendless and with child, but she was not penniless, and she had proved to herself that she was not without personal resources and, moreover, that she could even help someone else as well. Although outwardly, her situation was more desperate than before, somehow, she could not feel pessimistic about the future. Something would turn up, she felt certain. She could not have explained why she was so sure of this, but she was.

The following morning, when she took her place in the stage, events proved how right she had been. The last passenger of the four to get in was a young woman who arrived all of a bustle, and only just managed to take her place before the stage began to move out of the inn yard. She sat back with a sigh, then looked across at Fay, and sat upright again with a jolt.

'It *is*! It's Fay Prescott! Why, I hardly knew you, so fashionable as you look!' Fay coloured. She was indeed wearing clothes which Sir Jackson had purchased for her, and they were in the latest style. Had she wanted to put on any others, she could not have done so, because the clothes she had had with her when she had moved in with him had been so worn that the baronet had insisted that they be destroyed. 'You do remember me, don't you?' went on the other woman. 'Angela – from the Llewellyns!'

'Of course I remember you,' smiled Fay. 'But you have changed as well.' It was true. Angela had always had a good eye for colour, which was revealed in her dress, but the clothes that she wore now were not just stylish, but carried an unmistakable air of respectability.

Angela laughed, her eyes twinkling. 'In more ways than one,' she agreed. 'I'm married now, and living in Cambridge.'

'In Cambridge!' exclaimed Fay. 'I recall when we were there—'

Angela interrupted eagerly. 'Yes, that was when I met him. Perhaps you remember it?' Fay nodded 'He followed me to London and proposed to me there, the day after we left Islington. The beauty of it is that he knows all about me, so I have nothing to conceal. I've just been back to London for a few days to visit my sister, but I'm on my way home again, now. And what of you?' Fay opened her mouth to speak, found herself unable to think of anything to say that could possibly be said in front of two complete strangers, shut it again, and just looked at Angela helplessly.

Angela's expression changed, and she said quickly, 'Never mind. Tell me later. Where are you going? Do say that you will be with me for most of the journey, then we can have a nice long chat.'

'I am also going to Cambridge,' replied Fay. 'But once there, my plans are . . . are uncertain.'

'Well, until they *are* certain, why not stay with us? Maurice won't mind. He likes visitors.'

Fay smiled gratefully and said, 'Thank you. I would like that.' But she resolved that at the earliest moment, she would tell Angela her exact circumstances, and give her the chance to withdraw her offer if she wished.

It was to prove unnecessary. At the first staging post, where there was a short break for coffee, Angela took Fay on one side and said to her in a serious, direct way which was quite unlike her usual airy manner, 'Correct me if I am wrong: you had nowhere to go, a man took you in, he bought you those clothes, then threw you out when he found that you were with child. Is that your story?'

Fay turned white. 'Almost,' she faltered.

'I knew it!' declared Angela. 'Well, you're still invited, and as Maurice is a doctor he can easily attend you. Of course, I insist that he must be told the truth, but for everyone else, I think that you had best be a widow. Do you have a ring?' Fay wore her mother's ring on the third finger of her right hand, so it was only necessary to transfer it to the left for the deed to be done. 'Well, *Mrs* Prescott, shall we have coffee?' said Angela. 'And during the journey, you can tell me your sad history, and if you can't think of anything, I'll make it up for you.'

Before they rejoined the others, Fay caught hold of Angela and hugged her tightly. 'I'll never forget your kindness to me; never!' she whispered, in a voice that was not quite steady.

Angela smiled. 'Do you remember that obnoxious man who was hanging around the stage door in Royston, and you made up some tale to keep him away from me?' she said. 'And do you recall the time when you sat up half the night mending that costume that I ripped on a nail? And what about the numerous occasions when you helped me into my costume and virtually threw me on to the stage in time? I'm just glad to have the chance to repay your many kindnesses, my dear.'

They were on the point of getting back into the stage when Fay stopped and whispered urgently, 'If I am a widow, why am I not in black?'

'It was against his express wishes,' replied Angela, after a moment's thought. 'Dress in black and you don't get a penny in the will.'

'I've scarcely got a penny anyhow,' Fay replied candidly, and they both laughed.

Angela's husband Maurice proved to be as kind as his wife had predicted. To him alone, as Angela had wished, did Fay disclose the real story of her pregnancy, only keeping back the name of her child's father. Maurice was as little inclined to judge her as his wife.

The two of them insisted that Fay should stay with them until her baby was born at the very least, and when Fay protested that this was too much, Angela said, 'There is plenty that you can do to help me, if you like. We have only just moved into this house, and there is so much that I want to do in it. I want to renew all the curtains, for example, but I haven't the skill to do it myself, and I would also like new seats embroidered for the dining-room chairs. If you can do some of those things for me, then you will have more than paid for your keep, and you will have made me happy, too.'

Under these circumstances, Fay agreed to stay and, as her

pregnancy became more advanced, she was glad to have something to do which meant that she could sit down, for she tired easily, especially since the weather was very warm.

Fay's baby was born on a hot, wet night in early August, a tiny boy who only lived for an hour, despite all Maurice's efforts. Angela, seeing how matters were going, sent for the priest immediately, so that the baby should be baptized.

'What do you want to call him?' the priest asked.

'Jack,' Fay whispered, with what seemed to be the last of her strength.

'She must mean John,' said the priest to Angela.

At that point, they were all astonished to hear a strong, clear voice from the bed say, 'No, no. His name is to be Jack, not John. Jack.' So baby Jack was baptized: when he died twenty minutes later, Fay was holding him in her arms.

'Fay! Fay! What is it? What's wrong?' An urgent voice called her back to the present, and she became aware that someone was putting her cloak around her shoulders. She took her hands away from her face, and there, standing in front of her, was the father of her child.

'What's wrong?' she echoed his words, as she got to her feet. 'You stand there and ask me what's wrong? He died, that's what's wrong. My baby died!'

Jackson stared at her, his face ashen. 'Your baby! You had a baby? But whose. . . ?'

'Yours, of course!' she shouted, beyond discretion, and almost beyond reason. 'Of course it was yours. Who else's could it be? There *was* no one else. There never has been anyone else!'

He continued to stare at her. 'Did you know that you were with child when you left me?' he asked her.

'Yes, I knew,' she answered proudly, her head up.

'You didn't tell me,' he said.

'No, I didn't tell you. And why not? Because I didn't think you would be interested.'

'*Didn't think I would be interested!*' he exclaimed incredulously.

'You were engaged to be married,' she replied defensively. 'Besides, I heard you say that you didn't know how to get rid of me, so I saved you the trouble.'

'I said no such thing,' he retorted swiftly.

'Jackson, I *heard* you!'

'Fay, I swear by God that I never said that of you. I don't know what you heard or misheard, but of that at least I am innocent.' He paused for a moment, then went on. 'When did you have the baby? Where?'

'It doesn't matter,' she said bitterly. 'He died, didn't he? One less encumbrance to worry about.'

He took hold of her shoulders and shook her hard. 'You are talking about my son,' he said and, incredibly, his voice sounded less than completely steady. 'I know you are ready to think the very worst of me, but I assure you that I would never think or speak of any child of mine in such a way.' She closed her eyes as if in pain, and instantly he let go of her. They were silent for some time, then at last he said, 'Fay, you should have told me. I should have been there.'

'What could you have done?' she asked him wearily, turning away from him.

He ran his hands through his hair. 'I don't know,' he said helplessly. 'I don't know what I could have done: perhaps nothing very useful. But I could at least have held you . . . in the night. . . .'

Suddenly, Fay was transported back again to the days after baby Jack had died. Angela had been so kind, and had put her arms around her, had held her hand and been a real friend to her. But it had been at night that she had felt so alone. It had been then that she had remembered her life with Jackson, and how it had felt to be held close by him in the dark watches of the night. In her desolation, she had forgotten that he had wished for her absence, and simply longed for him to be there to comfort her.

The memories of that time were so vivid that she found herself sobbing great tearing sobs for all that she had lost. But this time Jackson was there, pulling her into his arms, and for a time she wept on his shoulder. Then, as her crying subsided, she looked up at him; a current of feeling darted between them, and his mouth covered hers in a long kiss of searing passion.

He had often kissed her before, but never like this, and she had never responded to him as she did now. Only on one occasion whilst she was living with him had she felt a spark of desire for him, and that had been on Christmas Day over a year ago when he had given her his gifts. But now, it was as if they were each possessed of a hunger that only the other could assuage.

When finally he released her after what seemed like an eternity, she stumbled as if her knees would not support her, and he caught hold of her again. Once more, this time briefly, their lips met and clung.

'Fay, there is so much that I want to say to you, but this is not the right time or place. . . .'

Fay stepped back out of the circle of his arms. 'No, you are right. We will be missed,' she said anxiously.

'That wasn't quite what I meant: but let that pass,' said Jackson. He pulled the ribbon out of his already dishevelled hair. 'We will talk later. You go first. I need to tidy myself a trifle.' Fay left the barn, and walked back towards the farmhouse. She had not quite reached it when Mrs Fleetwood emerged, dressed in her outdoor clothing, and with Fay's bonnet in her hand.

'Ah, Miss Prescott,' she purred, with a smile which did not reach her eyes. 'Are you ready to return to the house, now? I have said your goodbyes for you, as you are clearly not well. Come, let us walk together.'

Still drained by the scene that had just taken place, Fay put on her bonnet and allowed herself to be steered by Mrs Fleetwood. When they had left the farmhouse behind, the widow said tranquilly, 'I think I warned you not to trespass upon my territory:

Jackson is mine. You may have had a little fling with him, but you cannot seriously imagine that he would want you now, can you? Oh, I can well imagine that he enjoyed misbehaving with you in that dirty barn, but he would never want to take matters any further with you. You're soiled goods, my dear, and for him you do not even have the merit of novelty. Your time is over and done. He wants someone with an unblemished reputation as his wife.'

Fay turned pale, and faltered a little in her step.

'Yes, his wife, my dear. Didn't you suspect?' went on Mrs Fleetwood, the mock sympathy in her voice at variance with the look of triumph on her face. 'It was no accident that we both came here this Christmas, although for our own reasons, we might have pretended that it was. So since you don't have any chance with him, I suggest that you leave immediately. Naturally, I will be glad to provide you with a reference. . . .'

At this, Fay stopped and turned to face her, her eyes flashing. 'Pray don't trouble yourself, madam,' she said spiritedly. 'I want nothing from you at all. And you are right in thinking that I did not suspect that you were to marry Jackson. I had thought that he had better taste.' At her words, every vestige of a smile disappeared from Mrs Fleetwood's face, and her mouth became a thin line.

'You will regret speaking to me like that, Miss Prescott, I assure you,' she hissed. Old Drove House was now within sight, and Fay picked up her skirts and ran, not stopping until she had reached the safety of her room. Only it wasn't safe any more, she told herself. Mrs Fleetwood had the power to have her turned out. What could her parting words mean, other than that she would use that power mercilessly?

She sent a message downstairs, saying that she was not feeling well enough to dine with the company that evening. That done, she sat down to think. She loved Jackson, and for one heady moment in the barn that day, she had thought that her feelings were returned. Of course, it was quite possible that he still desired her, but clearly he did not want her for his wife. That position was going to be occupied by Mrs Fleetwood. Jackson himself had said that it was the wrong time for them, and Mrs Fleetwood had echoed those very words.

Fay did not underestimate her rival's vindictiveness. The handsome widow was quite capable of revealing her knowledge of what had happened in the past to everyone, if it would mean the removal of her rival. And Jackson would not lift a finger to prevent it, because Mrs Fleetwood had now replaced her in his affections. Whichever way Fay looked at the matter, she could not feel anything other than very pessimistic. Whatever happened, it seemed that she must leave Old Drove House without delay.

# *Chapter Fifteen*

The following morning, Fay awoke after a rather disturbed night at much her usual time. She had just finished getting dressed when there was a knock at the door. Fay opened it to find one of the chambermaids standing outside.

'Please, miss, Mrs Stratford asked me to give you this note,' she said.

'Thank you,' said Fay, closing the door and opening the note with a sinking heart. It was every bit as bad as she feared. Without any preamble, it said,

> *You will kindly have the goodness not to present yourself at the break-fast-table. I have no wish to see my family polluted any further by a woman of your stamp. The maid will bring you something in your room, which you may eat whilst you are packing. When you are ready to leave, the maid will conduct you downstairs. Kindly do not attempt to speak to Rachel, Magnus, Hengist or Horsa.*
>
> *E. Stratford*

So Mrs Fleetwood had decided to tell. Fay was not really surprised. She had always looked as if she would relish spreading such a juicy piece of gossip. Undoubtedly, she must be very sure of her hold upon the baronet to get rid of her rival in such a way.

There was another knock at the door, and Fay opened it to find a maid with a tray, with tea and bread and butter on it. At least she wasn't to be sent forth starving, which she had half expected, despite what Mrs Stratford had said in her letter.

'Mrs Stratford said, would you say what is in the schoolroom that's yours, and I'm to get it for you.' The maid spoke politely, but seemed a little puzzled. Clearly, the news had not gone all around the house as yet.

'Wait,' Fay said, before the girl could leave. 'Can you tell me where Sir Jackson is, if you please?' She could not have explained quite why she had asked for him, except that in her mind there was still a small hope that perhaps, for old times' sake, he might help her in some way.

'Oh, Sir Jackson left this morning, quite early,' said the maid. 'Will that be all, miss?'

Fay sighed. 'Yes, that's all,' she said. So Jackson had left her to face the music alone. He might even have gone at Mrs Fleetwood's behest. So be it. It would not be the first time that she had been cast upon her own resources. It did not take her long to pack the essentials into her bag; the rest of her things she put into the trunk which she had acquired whilst staying with Angela. Amongst these things were the bolts of cloth which Sir Jackson had given her, and some of her other Christmas presents. She could feel tears coming into her eyes at the memory of how happy she had been and of how it had all been spoiled, but she refused to give in to them now. For the present, she must be strong, and she would walk out of the house with her head held high. There would be time and opportunity enough for tears later.

The maid came when she rang.

'I have put everything that I cannot carry into my trunk,' she said. 'I'm not sure what is to be done with that.'

'Very good, miss,' replied the maid. Fay picked up her bag and followed the girl downstairs. She was expecting to be ejected forthwith, but to her surprise, she was conducted into the small bookroom, which was to the left-hand side of the front door. Present in the room were Mrs Stratford, Mrs Fleetwood and Peter Frith, together with his sister Agnes.

'I trust you are ready to go,' said Mrs Stratford coldly.

'I am ready,' replied Fay, somehow managing to keep her voice steady. 'I did not think to find myself sent on my way by a delegation, however.'

'Such insolence!' exclaimed Mrs Fleetwood.

Mrs Stratford held up her hand. 'The sooner you are out of this house the better,' she said. 'I have been grossly imposed upon, and it is only thanks to Mrs Fleetwood that I have learned the truth.' At the edge of her line of vision, Fay was conscious of Mrs Fleetwood looking serious, but with an unmistakable gleam of triumph in her eye. 'I believed you to be a woman of good character, but thanks to her, I find that you are a . . . a person of ill repute and an actress! Well, miss? Can you deny it?'

Fay thought about saying that she had been a wardrobe mistress, and not an actress, but decided that it would make no difference. 'I do not deny anything,' she replied, her colour high, but her voice firm, 'Even though I might dispute some of what you say. I had reasons for doing what I did—'

'I don't want to hear your *reasons*,' snapped Mrs Stratford. 'I just want to see the back of you. The sooner you are gone, the less likelihood there will be of your corrupting any more members of this family.'

'What do you mean?' Fay asked, her face losing some of its colour.

'Do not suppose that I do not lay the fiasco of Rachel's engagement at your door,' replied the other woman. 'You were determined to undermine me from the very first.'

'That is quite untrue,' declared Fay. 'Rachel had committed herself to Joe long before I had ever arrived here, but no doubt your informant told you all about that.' She looked steadily at Agnes.

'I at least know my duty,' put in the vicar's sister. Two spots of colour had appeared on her cheeks.

'Thank goodness *someone* does,' said Mrs Stratford. 'Your task, Miss Prescott, was to detach her from such a disastrous entanglement, but you did nothing but encourage it from start to finish. Well, do not think that I have finished with you yet. I shall spread the news of your perfidy far and wide, and not a soul will want to employ you. Now, get you gone. Mr Frith and his sister will drive you to March. Don't trouble to thank me. I only want to be rid of you as quickly as possible. Be thankful I don't make you walk.' After Fay had gone, Mrs Stratford took a letter down from the mantelpiece and stood looking at it, turning it over in her hands.

'What is that you have there?' Mrs Fleetwood asked her curiously.

'It is a note for her from Sir Jackson,' the other woman said anxiously. 'He asked me to give it to her, but I forgot to do so just now because I was so angry. Maybe I should go after her with it.'

Mrs Fleetwood shook her head. 'By no means,' she said. 'She does not deserve such attention. Doubtless it only gives her her dismissal.'

'Perhaps I should destroy it, then,' said Mrs Stratford thoughtfully.

'Don't do that,' said Mrs Fleetwood quickly. 'Give it to me. I will keep it safely and return it to him.'

Mrs Stratford thought for a moment, then said, 'No. Since we have withheld it from her, it is better that it should be destroyed.' So saying, she dropped it into the fire. Looking up, she surprised a look of chagrin on Mrs Fleetwood's face, which the widow quickly turned into a smile.

'No doubt you know best,' she murmured, glancing regretfully at the flames which licked around Sir Jackson's note.

'I wonder why he said that she was his cousin,' mused Mrs Stratford.

'Oh, many men are capable of these strange quixotic gallant gestures,' replied Mrs Fleetwood carelessly. 'You can let me deal with him when he returns. Why don't you forget about the whole wretched business, and concentrate instead upon how you might extricate Rachel from the clutches of that vulgar young farmer?'

'You think it could be done?' asked Mrs Stratford eagerly.

'Not a doubt of it,' replied the other. 'Let's have a cup of tea while we consider the matter.'

Meanwhile, the Friths had accompanied Fay outside and down the steps.

'I have brought the gig,' the vicar said coldly. 'I will escort you to March, but I will take no pleasure in it.'

Fay turned and looked at him. 'From which part of the scriptures did you learn to be so censorious?' she asked him.

'I beg your pardon?' he exclaimed angrily.

'And furthermore, what is your sister's reason for being here? Does she simply want to gloat over my downfall? Or do you feel that you need her chaperonage for fear that I corrupt you between here and March?'

He flushed, but Agnes took a step towards her. 'Miss Prescott. . . .' she began, but her brother gestured to her to keep silent.

'To think I actually asked you to marry me!' he declared. 'What a fool I was! I thank heaven I had such a lucky escape!'

Fay laughed humourlessly. 'Escape! You! May I remind you, Mr Frith, that *I* was the one who refused *you*? And I did so because I thought you deserved better!'

Frith stared at her. 'I—' he began.

'You know nothing about me,' she interrupted, her voice shaking only slightly. 'Nothing about the straits to which I was reduced, which made me take the actions that I did. You know nothing of the fear, the desperation, the anguish and the pain

205

that I have felt, but that doesn't matter to you, does it? All that matters to you is the supreme assurance that you are right. Well, I have no desire to sit next to you and your sister all the way to March: I had much rather walk. Perhaps, when it is convenient, you will make sure that the rest of my belongings are sent on to The Griffin.'

'I have no idea when it will be convenient,' he replied, looking a little pale after her tirade, and sounding somewhat sulky. 'Miss Prescott—'

'Then I shall have to wait for them, shan't I?' she replied, before turning on her heel and setting off in the direction of March.

It was five miles. She had walked such a distance before, but never carrying a heavy bag. Although her spirited speech to Peter Frith carried her along for some short distance, it was not long before she began to tire, but at least the physical effort took her mind off Sir Jackson's desertion. She would have to think about that quite soon, she knew; for now, she needed to concentrate on putting one foot in front of the other.

After she had walked for what seemed a long time, during which March did not seem to get any closer, and after she had had to take a number of rests, she heard the sound of some kind of conveyance coming up behind her. She sent up a silent prayer that it should be anyone other than Peter Frith – for nothing would persuade her to beg a ride from him – but when the gig drew up beside her, she saw Joe Fairburn up on the box, and sitting beside him was Rachel.

Rachel jumped down unassisted almost before the gig had drawn to a halt, and ran round behind the cart and hugged her. 'We couldn't possibly let you go like this,' she declared.

'Rachel, you don't know,' said Fay, alarmed to find her voice breaking. 'Your aunt has dismissed me, and rightly. I was . . . have been. . . .'

'I know,' replied Rachel reassuringly. 'And it doesn't matter.

We're going to help you.'

'You know?' murmured Fay. 'But you can't! You—'

'I'll explain as we go. Now take Joe's hand and get up into the gig.' Fay looked up at Joe, who was extending his strong right arm to help her up, and for a moment, she hesitated.

'When we were pulling on that rope by the dyke and Rachel fell, we might have all gone, but you held on,' he said. 'A man doesn't forget a thing like that.' Fay put her hand in his, and allowed him to help her up into the gig.

'How did you find out about me?' Fay asked, after the gig had started to move.

Rachel smiled. 'Well, I guessed from the beginning that you could not have been hired to be Horsa's governess. Once I knew that, it was easy to see that my aunt must have employed you to keep an eye on me.'

'Was I so very bad at teaching?' Fay asked ruefully.

'By no means,' answered Rachel. 'Horsa has minded you better than any other teacher I can remember, and we have both gained skills in needlework that we did not have before. But your way of teaching and your attitude to lessons is unlike that of any governess I have ever come across or heard about.'

'That explains that; what of the rest?' Fay asked.

Rachel thought for a moment. 'It occurred to me that your reaction to Sir Jackson's arrival was somewhat excessive, even given that he was a relative that you had not expected to see. My aunt was satisfied with the explanation that you had come into the warmth rather too swiftly, but I had been with you before when we had come into the house on a cold day, and had never seen you even slightly affected in that way. It made me wonder whether there was something more in your relationship than you were telling everyone, especially since you said nothing about his being your cousin when Horsa and I came to your bedroom. If he was indeed your relative, it was odd that you should not have said anything about him at that point. Then, of course, once I was suspicious, all kinds of little things in your attitudes to one another confirmed my suspicions.'

'You may not realize that he and I were . . . were . . . very close,' said Fay bravely, her face pale.

Rachel was silent for a moment, then she said, 'I did not know that for certain until today,' she admitted.

'And today?'

'Horsa was listening at the door,' Rachel replied rather self-consciously. 'One of the maids let slip that you were leaving, and were not to see us. Well of course, we knew then that you were being sent away in disgrace, and we wanted to know why, and help if we could.' She paused. 'When Aunt talked about your connection with the theatre *and* your immoral behaviour, I became convinced that my suspicions must be correct.' She paused again. 'I have said nothing to Horsa about them. It was enough for her to believe that your theatrical connections had brought about your dismissal.'

Fay gripped hold of her hand, and felt the tears come to her eyes. Rachel's kindness had broken her self-control as Mrs Stratford's unkind rejection could never have done.

'You do not . . . fear corruption by association with me,' she murmured.

'Corruption? When you were practically falling over yourself to make sure that Joe and I could not meet clandestinely?'

Fay smiled wanly. 'I know how a young lady should behave, even if I have fallen short of the expected standard myself,' she replied. Very soon afterwards, they arrived in March, and Joe steered skilfully through the busy streets until they reached the courtyard of The Griffin.

'A room for this lady, if you please,' Joe said to the landlord, after he had given the gig into the care of the ostler, and helped Fay in with her things.

'With the players here?' the landlord asked looking a little harassed. 'There might be a bit of difficulty.'

'Then solve it,' replied Joe, with a hint of steel in his normally pleasant, easy-going voice that made both of his female companions stare. A room was soon found for Fay, and Joe carried her bag upstairs, making it look like a featherweight as he did so. 'I'll fetch your trunk over first thing tomorrow,' he promised. 'No need for you to wait on the vicar's convenience. It'll take some doing to get me back inside that church, I can tell you.'

Fay clasped his hand. 'Joe, don't let my misfortunes spoil your relationships with people in the village,' she urged him.

'I've no patience with a man of God who lacks Christian charity,' he replied bluntly. With a nod, he went downstairs, tactfully leaving the two ladies alone to make their farewells.

'What will you do now?' Rachel asked her.

Fay smiled. 'You seem to have noticed so much that I am sure you recall the occasion when Mrs Fleetwood tried to persuade everyone to come to March and see the players perform? If you recall, Magnus read out the name of the troop that is performing here.'

Rachel clapped her hands. 'Is this the company that you belonged to before?' she asked excitedly.

'Yes, but I was never an actress,' Fay insisted. 'I was only ever the wardrobe mistress. I will see if they have any need of me, and if not, I will go back to my friend in Cambridge. Perhaps she will be able to provide me with a reference for a position with someone who is going to America, or Australia.' She tried to appear optimistic, but only succeeded in sounding somewhat forlorn.

'Oh, Fay!' exclaimed Rachel. 'So far away!'

Fay turned away from her abruptly. 'I *must* put myself beyond the reach of the scandal surrounding my past,' she said in a harsh voice.

'And what of Sir Jackson?' ventured Rachel.

'He ran away from the scandal when it really seemed to threaten him, didn't he?' was the reply. 'I shall hear nothing of him again.'

'Are you sure he has run away?' Rachel asked. 'It doesn't seem like him.'

'How else would you explain his absence?' Fay asked baldly.

Rachel had no answer to this, but she did say, after a moment's silence, 'Why do you think that he said you were his cous—'

Fay cut her off impatiently. 'Oh, I don't know. To amuse himself, I suppose. He is very fond of being amused; he does not really care for anyone – I know that now – to my cost.' There was a long silence.

Eventually, Rachel said, 'Fay, I must go.'

Fay turned round and said brightly, 'Of course; you mustn't keep Joe waiting.'

Rachel hugged her. 'I'll miss you,' she said, her voice breaking in a sob.

'I'll miss you, too,' replied Fay, similarly moved. 'I'll write to you as soon as I am settled somewhere.' After Rachel had gone, Fay sat for a while wondering whether this would be the pattern of her life: to find people whom she felt she could care about, only to lose them when the story of her past became known. Before she could become too depressed at this thought, she stood up, left her room and went in search of the Llewellyns.

It was nearly four days later when Sir Jackson returned to Old Drove House. By this time, almost all the guests had gone. The baronet's hasty departure had acted as a signal for the others, who soon made their farewells in order to return to town, or to go to their own estates. Even Mr Proudfoot had left, going with the Napiers to their house in Lincolnshire in order to explore a village near there which Mr Napier had told him was probably Viking in origin.

The question of Fay's departure and the need to engage another duenna and governess had left him completely unmoved, as did most problems of the present day. His last words to his sister were 'You deal with it all, my dear. You are so much more capable than I.'

The only guests who had not yet left were Mrs Fleetwood (with, of course, her daughter) who had stubbornly remained, despite one or two broad hints from Rachel. The widow was quite determined to stay in order to welcome the baronet, who, she felt certain, was sure to return.

Rachel had never cared for Mrs Fleetwood, and after her part in the scene in which Fay had been dismissed, she had begun to regard the older woman with intense dislike. Whilst Mrs Fleetwood had plenty of ammunition in the shape of derogatory remarks about Joe, Rachel was not above reminding the widow about her age, and subtly drawing attention to real or imaginary wrinkles or grey hairs. Consequently, warfare had been declared between them: if Mrs Fleetwood was determined to see Sir Jackson, Rachel was equally determined to make sure that he was told about how Fay had been ejected from the house.

As luck would have it, however, he arrived during the late morning when the only inhabitants of the drawing-room were Mrs Stratford and Mrs Fleetwood. Over the past days, Mrs Fleetwood had attempted to implant the idea that Sir Jackson had been more sinned against than sinning, and that Fay had been the real villain of the piece, but Mrs Stratford had refused to discuss the matter. In fact, she was very much regretting the hastiness with which she had acted with regard to Fay. The only evidence against her had come from Mrs Fleetwood, a woman whom, if Mrs Stratford was honest, she did not really like. Furthermore, all the young people had been very fond of their governess-companion, and without saying anything, or behaving in a way that was openly defiant, they had made their opinions very clear. Never having had children herself, Mrs Stratford was unsure of how to deal with this situation.

When the baronet entered the room, both women sat for a moment as if transfixed. Predictably, Mrs Fleetwood was the first to recover.

'Jackson, my dear,' she exclaimed, rising gracefully, and walking towards him in order to take his arm. 'How delightful.' He glanced down at her, but although he inclined his head politely and crooked his arm, he neither spoke, nor smiled.

By now, Mrs Stratford had had time to make a recovery, and at this point, she rose to her feet. 'It is not delightful at all; it is an affront,' she declared, two spots of bright colour appearing on her cheeks.

The baronet stared at her for a moment. 'I seem to be all at sea,' he said eventually. 'Perhaps someone would have the goodness to explain.'

'I? Explain?' replied Mrs Stratford incredulously. 'It is you who needs to provide an explanation for your astounding effrontery and appalling behaviour.'

'Ah,' murmured the baronet, taking out his snuff-box and making use of it. 'I think I begin to see light. And Miss Prescott?'

'You need have no worries about Miss Prescott,' cooed Mrs Fleetwood, patting his arm with her free hand. 'She has left quite willingly, so you need have no further anxiety about her.'

'Indeed?' he replied, an arrested expression on his face.

'Of course, I have explained to Mrs Stratford that you were more sinned against than sinning,' she went on. He looked at her with his brows raised, and there was something in his expression which made her colour a little. 'Naturally, you were a trifle indiscreet to have brought her here,' she went on, 'but fortunately, she has had the sense to see where she is not wanted.'

'Who told you that I had brought her here?' he asked her, fastidiously disengaging his arm from her clutches, and carefully brushing down his sleeve in a way that brought patches of unbecoming colour into her cheeks.

Before she could answer, the door opened and Rachel came in. 'Better late than never, I suppose,' she said tartly, staring at him.

Hooper looked at each of the three women in turn, an expression of bewilderment on his face. 'Upon my soul, I would be glad if someone would enlighten me,' he declared. 'From one of you I gather that my arrival is late, from another that it is apparently well-timed, and from a third, I understand that I am not welcome at all. As for Miss Prescott, I have been told that she has left of her own volition, which I must say I find hard to believe, when I left a note saying that I would return for her.'

'You do right not to believe it,' said Rachel. 'She was driven out of here four days ago.'

'Driven out?' he exclaimed, his brows drawing together in a bar. 'By whom?'

'By me,' answered Mrs Stratford, determined not to be outfaced by him. 'It is thanks to Mrs Fleetwood, here, that I have been enlightened as to the doubtful character of the . . . the person whom you insinuated into this household. A woman of ill repute—'

Sir Jackson held his hand. 'Stop,' he said. 'I cannot allow this to continue. Firstly, I did not insinuate anyone into this house. The employment of the lady whom you have known as Miss Prescott was decided upon with no help from me. But secondly, and more importantly, you will speak no slander concerning the lady whose name it is my right and my duty to protect.' Silence fell upon the room. Upon Rachel's face there appeared a tiny, mischievous smile, whereas Mrs Fleetwood's expression gradually took on a look of dawning horror.

It was Mrs Stratford who spoke first. 'Your right, and your duty?' she asked, in a small voice.

The baronet permitted himself a small smile then. 'Certainly,' he replied. 'It is always a man's responsibility to protect his wife's name.'

This time, it was Mrs Fleetwood who spoke first. 'I don't believe it,' she exclaimed, looking a little pale. 'It's a fabrication.'

For answer, Sir Jackson took a folded paper from within his coat, and turned to Rachel. 'Perhaps you would inspect this document on everyone's behalf,' he suggested, handing it to her.

She unfolded the paper, looked down at it for a long moment, then folded it up again, looked up and returned it to the baronet. 'It is a marriage licence,' she said evenly. Mrs Fleetwood stared at him for a long moment, before leaving the room with a flounce and an infuriated sound.

'I am afraid that you have allowed yourself to be manipulated by a selfish, jealous woman,' remarked the baronet to Mrs Stratford, after the door had closed.

Mrs Stratford sank down into the nearest chair. 'Miss Prescott is your wife!' she exclaimed. 'But why was no one aware of this? Why was no one told?'

'Because we were estranged, ma'am,' replied Sir Jackson, with a great air of frankness. 'Fay and I were married some months ago, but because I knew that some of my family would be unsympathetic to my choice of bride – Fay not having any money of her own, although having other gifts which are, of course, past price – we kept our marriage secret. But such secrecy puts a strain even on the closest of relationships and, due to misunderstandings for which I take full responsibility, Fay ran away from me. I had no notion of where she might be, and had run out of places to look, when, by chance, I heard you speak of a new member of the household here, Miss Prescott by name. I confess that I did something towards engineering your invitation to me to spend Christmas here, hoping desperately that the Miss Prescott in your employ might indeed be my wife.

'Once I had found her, I knew that I wanted our marriage to succeed, and it seemed to me that she felt the same. When I left four days ago, it was to ensure that this time my family would be ready to receive Fay as my wife, with none of the secrecy of which I now feel so ashamed. Indeed, I left her a note to that effect, as I believe I may have mentioned to you earlier.' Mrs Stratford looked at him, then looked away quickly, flushing. After a brief silence, he added softly, 'Am I right in thinking that she did not receive the letter?'

Mrs Stratford nodded. 'Mrs Fleetwood thought. . . .' she began. She looked guiltily towards the fire.

'You have no need to say any more, ma'am,' he said, following her gaze. 'As for myself, I will not dwell on the impropriety of withholding someone's correspondence from them, or of destroying it. As long as I can find her safe and sound, I shall be quite content. Is anyone aware of her destination?'

'I am,' said Rachel. 'But I remain to be convinced of Sir Jackson's sincerity.'

'Rachel!' exclaimed Mrs Stratford in shocked tones. 'Kindly remember to whom you are speaking!'

'I don't forget,' Rachel replied, looking straight at him. He held her gaze squarely. Eventually, she said, 'Joe and I took her to The Griffin in March. I don't know whether she will still be there, or not.'

Jackson took hold of her hand and kissed it. 'Bless you for that,' he said. 'And now, if you will excuse me, I will go to find my wife.'

'Sir Jackson. . . .' began Mrs Stratford impulsively.

'Yes, ma'am?'

'You may bring her back here, if you so desire.' The baronet raised his brows.

'That will be as my lady wishes,' he replied. Rachel followed him out into the hall. He turned to her and said, 'Thank you for not giving me away.'

She looked straight at him once more. 'Sir Jackson, there was nothing written on that paper,' she said in a low voice.

'But there will be,' he replied seriously. 'If she will have me.'

# Chapter Sixteen

On his arrival at The Griffin he discovered that the Llewellyn theatre company had finished performing in March, and had travelled on to Ely two days before.

'To Ely, you say?' remarked the baronet, just before taking a sip of the glass of hot punch which he had ordered.

'Yes, sir,' replied the landlord, in answer to his question. 'It was a lot of work to have them, but they brought in a good deal of business. Was you wishful to go and see them, sir?'

'Perhaps. But first of all, I would like some information from you.' The baronet took some coins from his pocket.

'I'll help if I can,' replied the landlord.

'When the company left, did they take with them another person, a young lady who has been living in these parts?'

The landlord's eyes brightened. 'They did indeed,' he replied. 'A slight, pretty young thing, she was. She was helping with the costumes, I believe.'

'Thank you,' said Sir Jackson, finishing off his punch. 'You don't happen to know to which inn in Ely they went?'

The landlord shook his head. 'I'm sorry, sir,' he said.

'Never mind,' answered the baronet. 'I'll find it.' He left the inn and mounted his horse. It was still only midday. With any luck, he would be in Ely later that afternoon.

Fay's arrival had come at just the right time for the Llewellyn theatrical company, and they had greeted her advent with profound relief. Their wardrobe mistress was prostrate with toothache, and there was no one to help the performers in and out of their costumes, and effect the minor repairs which so often proved necessary.

The news that they were to travel on to Ely and then to Cambridge was very welcome. In return for her help with the costumes until Maisie was restored to full health, Mr Llewellyn was very happy to allow her to travel with them, until she was within reach of Angela's house.

Upon one thing she was absolutely determined: she was not going to take advantage of Angela's kindness. She would only remain with them for so long as it would take for her to find other employment.

She had welcomed the chance to be very busy straight away, as it meant that she would not be able to think too deeply about what had happened. The reaction of Mrs Stratford had been perfectly understandable. As far as that lady was concerned, a woman who had worked in the theatre and been a man's mistress – and, moreover, the mistress of a man who was a guest in the house in which she resided – was by any normal standards beyond the pale. The fact that she had lied about her background only strengthened the case against her.

Of Jackson's desertion, she could not bear to think. The kiss that they had exchanged in the barn had meant so much to her, but clearly it had meant nothing to him. Probably, he had only been trying to comfort her, and things had gone further than he had intended. Rather than have her fling herself at him in such an embarrassing way again, he had obviously decided to retreat, leaving Mrs Fleetwood to get rid of her for him in her own way. She would not have expected him to be either so cowardly or so cruel.

Another actress, named Nan, had taken Angela's place but otherwise, the composition of the company was much the same.

They were to spend five days in Ely, two preparing, followed by three performances. After that, they were to go on to Cambridge. Maisie soon felt better after her tooth had been pulled, but she was glad of Fay's help, especially since Fay went out of her way to assure her that she was not trying to take her job.

'There's really far too much for one person to do,' Maisie confessed, as they bustled around backstage during the first performance at Ely. 'Especially with the quality coming around and getting in our way.' Fay agreed, thinking of the time when she had first seen Sir Jackson in similar circumstances.

'Fay, my hem has come down again. Pin it up for me, will you?' Nan asked during the interval.

Fay hurried across with her pin tin in her hand. 'It's that cheap thread we bought,' she said to Maisie, in passing. 'It doesn't hold properly.' She knelt at Nan's feet, and began to pin up the offending hem. She had just finished her task, when out of the corner of her eye, she caught sight of a pair of shiny black boots. They were no different from many another pair of boots that she had seen at such an angle. She could not have explained, therefore, why she was suddenly transported back to the moment when she had met Sir Jackson for the first time and, as on that occasion, she dropped her pins on to the floor.

'Allow me,' said the owner of the boots, and he went down on one knee to help her. She looked into his face with a fast beating heart, and encountered the gaze of Sir Jackson Hooper. At once, she sprang to her feet, the pins forgotten. Carefully, he placed the few that he had just found in the box, then looked up at her from his half-kneeling position. 'This was how it started, wasn't it, with both of us looking for your pins?' he said. He grinned ruefully. 'I'd have shown a trifle more wisdom, had I remained kneeling at your feet.'

She took a step or two backwards, not taking in his words. 'I don't understand,' she whispered. 'You left me without a word.

Why have you followed me here?'

He stood up then. 'Had my note not been purloined at Mrs Fleetwood's instigation, then you would have known exactly why I left, and why I have come back.'

'But you are going to marry Mrs Fleetwood,' she said.

'I think I can guess who told you that,' he replied; 'she has no authority to speak on my behalf.'

'Then aren't . . . aren't you. . . ?' Suddenly, she swayed, and Jackson only just prevented her from falling. He picked her up in his arms, and turned to those in the room who, despite the need for haste in preparation for the next half, had all stopped what they were doing to watch the real live drama that was unfolding before them.

'Where can we go to be private?' he asked them.

When Fay came to, she could not remember at first what had transpired, nor could she think where she might be. She turned her head and realized that she was lying on the *chaise-longue* in the little parlour which had been set on one side for the use of Mr and Mrs Llewellyn. Sir Jackson was sitting in a chair on the other side of the fire.

'Ah, you're awake; that's good,' he said, getting to his feet. 'I'll pour you some brandy; or I'll ring for tea, if you prefer?'

'Tea, please,' she replied.

'Don't sit up until you are ready,' he warned her, as he rang the bell. His tone was cheerful, but he knew that he must be very careful in what he said to her, and also in how he said it. One wrong move could mean that he would lose her forever.

When the maid came with the tea, Fay found that the baronet had ordered a plate of little cakes as well.

'I don't think you always remember to eat as well as you should,' he remarked. His tone was friendly, and not at all critical, and Fay discovered that as she ate and drank, the tea and cakes did her good. Sir Jackson had ordered a glass of brandy for himself, and he sipped from it while she was drinking her tea.

At last, she set her cup down, and said, 'Will you now explain to me what is happening, and why you are here?'

'Very well,' said Sir Jackson, sitting down in the chair which he had just recently vacated. 'I have just come from Old Drove House via The Griffin in March. I went to the house and discovered that you had been dismissed. I stayed only to rout Mrs Fleetwood, convince Mrs Stratford that she had done you an injustice, and obtain directions from Rachel.'

'How did you demonstrate to Mrs Stratford that she had done me an injustice?' Fay asked, mystified.

He was silent for a moment, after which he got up, but only to walk over to the *chaise-longue*, kneel on one knee and take hold of her hands. Then, in a diffident manner that was quite unlike his usual way of speaking, he said, 'I will tell you, but may I say something else first?' She nodded. 'My dealings with you have been fraught with mistakes – *my* mistakes – right from the beginning, and I don't want to get this bit wrong. I want to be completely honest with you. I could say to you that had I realized what you were really like when I first met you, I would never have made you my mistress, but that would be a lie. Although I think I sensed almost from the beginning that you were good and virtuous, I wanted you so very much that I managed to convince myself that no one involved with the theatre could possibly be like that. I made myself believe what I wanted to believe, and I gave you no choice in the matter at all.'

'You saved me from Mrs Bellham,' Fay reminded him.

He laughed derisively, and got to his feet. 'Yes, perhaps, but where was the credit in that? I only did it so that I could have you for myself.'

She got up then. 'I don't believe it,' she said. 'If you saw any girl whom you knew in the clutches of that woman, you would do something – wouldn't you?'

He looked at her. 'Yes, perhaps,' he agreed. 'But I wouldn't make them all suffer a similar fate at my hands. And the fact of the matter is, I had you at my mercy and I used the power that I had to make you do something you didn't want to do.'

'You did offer to take me back to The Bull and Mouth,' Fay pointed out.

'What kind of offer was that?' he demanded. 'A night's lodging, and the chance to meet another Mrs Bellham!' He turned away from her and looked down into the fire. She looked at him and thought of his kindness to Magnus, of his courage in rescuing Horsa, and his graciousness to Joe.

'You would never have left me like that,' she replied. 'You would have done something more to help me.'

He turned his head to look at her. 'Perhaps,' he said again. 'But you didn't know that. That's why I want you to have a choice now.' He took the paper that he had shown Rachel from the inside of his coat, and stood looking down at it for a long moment. Then he handed it to her.

Fay opened it. 'It is a . . . a marriage licence,' she murmured.

'I told you that I had left you a note, but unfortunately it was destroyed before you could read it. Looking back, I suppose that I was foolish to leave you behind without saying anything about where I was going, but I had no idea that Deborah Fleetwood would be so vindictive, and anyway, I wanted to show you this as proof of the seriousness of my intentions.'

'I don't understand,' said Fay. 'There is nothing written on it.'

'I told Mrs Stratford that we were married, but had become estranged,' he said. 'She is full of remorse, and wants me to bring you back there. But I don't want to make the same mistake as before: I want you to have a choice. If you wish, I can provide you with an income, so that you can live somewhere under an assumed name, as a widow, perhaps. Or, I have acquaintances who are to sail for America in a few weeks' time. I could pay for you to go with them, and provide a reference so that you might make a new start there.'

Fay looked up at him, the paper still in her hand. 'Is that what you want me to do?' she asked him forlornly.

'No, of course it isn't,' he declared. 'What I want is for us to find the nearest available cleric, and make use of that licence so that my lie to Mrs Stratford can become a reality.'

'Why, Jackson?' she asked him 'To save your reputation?'

'No,' he replied, taking hold of her free hand. 'Not to save my reputation, or yours, or anyone's, but to save my very sanity, because I can't live without you: I know I can't, because I've tried. Do you remember telling me that you thought you heard me saying I wanted to be rid of you? I've recalled the incident, and when you heard me say that, I wasn't talking about you, but about that wretched engagement of mine. I knew almost from the moment I entered into it, that it was a mistake. I didn't realize why until you disappeared, and I knew that I had lost the one thing in life that really mattered to me. Then when I spent all my time and energy trying to find out where you were, Edith became exasperated and threw me over.' He paused for a moment then said, in a voice filled with great tenderness, 'Fay, I love you. That's what I told you in that poor note. I want you to marry me, but whether you agree, or whether you throw that licence in the fire and go to America, or wherever, I am yours for ever.'

She looked down at their clasped hands and smiled, for suddenly she remembered how Joe had spoken about his feelings for Rachel. '*There'll never be anyone else for me*,' he had said, and Jackson had just said the same thing in his own way. She had longed for a love token, and when she looked into his face she saw it there, in the tenderness of his expression. 'You want me to choose,' she said softly. 'And all I ever wanted was to be able to choose. Very well: I choose you.' The licence fell unheeded to the floor as he pulled her into a close embrace; she put her arms around his neck, and their lips met. 'I love you, Jackson,' she whispered, as soon as she was able.

'It amazes me that you can possibly do so,' he replied at last, still holding her close. 'After all I've done to you.'

She took one hand from round his neck, and laid it against his lips. 'No more,' she said. 'Let that be an end of it. Tell me, instead, how you knew that I was at Old Drove House in the first place. Your arrival wasn't purely a coincidence, was it?' They sat down together on the *chaise-longue*, Jackson's arm around her.

He shook his head. 'I barely knew Mrs Stratford, but I was at an occasion where she was talking to an acquaintance about how fortunate she had been to find someone to go to some benighted part of the country to be chaperon to her niece. When your name was mentioned, I pricked up my ears. It seemed like a very slight chance that you might be she, but in the meantime, I had to spend Christmas somewhere. If I had gone to see my mother, she would only have nagged me about losing Edith, and by that time, I was clutching at straws. So although I had hoped I might see you there, I had no great expectation of doing so. You were very nearly not the only one to faint on that occasion, my darling!'

'That would have caused a stir,' said Fay demurely.

He bent to kiss her. 'How soon will you marry me?' he asked her.

'As soon as you like,' she replied.

'Then let it be tomorrow,' he said. 'I can't wait to call you my own.' They kissed again, this time lingeringly. Eventually he said, 'I have told you about how I came to find you again, but you have never told me how you came to be with the Proudfoots.'

Fay told him about her chance meeting with Angela, the care offered to her by Angela and her husband, and the discovery of Mrs Stratford's advertisement in a London paper, which had led to her employment at Old Drove House. She did not dwell on the difficulties of her pregnancy, or upon the death of her baby, but she was aware of the seriousness of his expression and his slight loss of colour, and she felt him hold her a little more tightly.

After she had finished speaking, he was silent for a long time, then eventually, he said in a tone which sounded almost humble, 'Fay, my dearest one, are you sure, really sure that you want to marry me?' For answer, she cradled his face in her hands, and this time it was she who kissed him. A little later, he said, 'When we are married, we can go back to Old Drove House if you wish, but first of all, I want us to go to Cambridge, so that I can thank those kind friends who helped you when I so manifestly failed in my duty.'

'I want you to meet them as well,' she replied. 'But only if you will stop talking nonsense.'

He looked down for a moment at his left hand clasping hers. Then he said, 'There's another reason why I want to go to Cambridge.'

She looked at him with understanding. 'You want to see where Jack is buried, don't you?'

His eyes widened. 'Jack? You named him after me?'

She nodded. 'I can't explain it,' she said. 'I didn't love you then, or at least, I didn't know that I loved you. But I knew that I had to name him after you.'

He smiled tenderly at her. 'There will be other children,' he promised her, and she coloured. 'I adore you,' he declared, and kissed her.

At that moment, there was a knock at the door. 'Beg pardon, sir,' said the waiter who came in. 'But I thought you'd want to know. The players'll all be out in a minute. It's finished.'

The baronet turned his head to look at Fay. 'No, it isn't,' he said, smiling tenderly. 'It's just beginning.'